MURDER BOARD

A BOSTON CRIME THRILLER

BRIAN SHEA

Severn River
PUBLISHING

Severn River Publishing
www.SevernRiverPublishing.com

This is a work of fiction. Names, characters, businesses, places, events and incidents are either the products of the author's imagination or used in a fictitious manner. Any resemblance to actual persons, living or dead, or actual events is purely coincidental.

ISBN: 978-1-951249-04-5 (Hardback)
ISBN: 978-1-951249-08-3 (Paperback)

ALSO BY BRIAN SHEA

The Nick Lawrence Series

Kill List

Pursuit of Justice

Burning Truth

Targeted Violence

Murder 8

The Boston Crime Thriller Series

Murder Board

Bleeding Blue

The Penitent One

Never miss a new release! Sign up to receive exclusive updates from author Brian Shea.

BrianChristopherShea.com/Boston

Sign up and receive a free copy of

Unkillable: A Nick Lawrence Short Story

To my wife.
You've stood beside me every step of this journey, never wavering and always pushing me forward in those moments of doubt. It's not easy being married to a writer. We are a constant ebb and flow of creative energy.
This book is possible because of your love and support. Forever will never be long enough for us.

PROLOGUE

Twelve minutes doesn't seem like a long time. It's the time a morning commuter waits for the next T to arrive. Or somebody idles in line at their local Dunkin' Donuts in anticipation of their morning jolt. To those people, twelve minutes is an inconvenience, but to Michael Kelly, it was an eternity.

He looked down at the glossy black handle of the phone, resting in the receiver. *A watched pot never boils,* he heard his mother's thick Irish brogue adding whimsy to the phrase. Even with his mother's words at the forefront of his mind, Kelly couldn't help but stare. His gaze focused, willing the person on the other end to call back.

His partner, David McElroy, sweated profusely. Not uncommon for the large man, but today's dermic downpour went beyond the norm. His shirt clung to his skin. His headset had drifted down, now wrapped tightly around the lumpy folds of his neck. The man was anything but the epitome of health, but his mind was as sharp as any. He wrung his hands, cracking his knuckles. Kelly was glad for his presence.

He had been teamed with McElroy since joining the Boston Police Department's Crisis Negotiation Team. McElroy's gruff exterior had pushed others away, but not Kelly. They were a bit of an odd couple. The pairing worked, each counterbalancing the other's weakness.

Their teamwork on the Shoenthal incident, a year and a half earlier, had earned them the Medal of Valor. Kelly and McElroy were returning from a training session and heard a call for a suicidal party on the interstate. Realizing they were only a mile down the road, the two took it upon themselves to assist. A disturbed Herb Shoenthal was sitting in his beat-up Corolla with a pistol in his mouth. For three straight hours, in ninety-degree heat, they'd sat twenty feet from the armed man and played a mental chess match, ultimately leading to the man's surrender. The photo with the mayor was tucked in a box some-where in Kelly's mother's attic.

The two locked worried eyes. Kelly returned his focus to the dry-erase board affixed to the wall on his right. Notes were scribbled in a variety of colors, denoting different parties and their relation to the man in the house. The most important piece of information gathered over the last ten hours of negotiation was noted in a two-column table—one category marked with an H and the other a T. Hooks and Triggers were the linchpin of any successful negotiator's ability to control a situation.

Some of these came from outside sources, usually family and friends. Most were gathered during the brutally long hours of conversation, the seemingly mindless banter taking place between negotiators and the distraught. The trig-gers, sometimes discovered at great cost, were mental landmines to be avoided at all times. Hooks were positive, a lifeline connecting the disturbed person to a piece of their life that still held meaning. Like reeling in a fish, the hook could pull a person back to a sense of reason. These returns from madness were often short-lived but gave small windows of opportunity to seek peaceful resolution.

The trigger list on the slick white surface of the dry-erase board was as long as any Kelly had ever seen in his two years on the Crisis Negotiation Team, or CNT, as it was commonly referred. Kelly so far had only one item listed under hooks. Son—Baxter.

The call originated when members of BPD's District E-13 Uniformed Patrol Division were called to the man's residence after he'd fired a gun multiple times in an otherwise quiet Jamaica Plain neighborhood. The information gathered was that the man in the house, Trevor Green, worked in IT at a local bank and had taken an overtime night shift to debug some accounting software. Green was good at his job, and after a few hours, he'd apparently remedied whatever crisis his company faced. His boss let him out early.

He arrived home at 11 p.m. to find his wife in the deep thralls of sexual embrace with his best friend. They were too engaged in their carnal activity to notice him. Trevor Green, as he'd recounted numerous times while talking with Kelly, had no choice. Green went to the kitchen and took the revolver stored in a cabinet above the fridge, out of the reach of their seven-year-old son. He returned to the bedroom and stood in the hallway, listening to his wife's pleasureful screams. In a fit of rage, he fired at the two. It had taken four of the six shots to render his wife and former best friend lifeless.

The shots woke their son, Baxter, sleeping in his bedroom down the hall. The noise also alerted several neighbors in the multi-family brownstone. When the Patrol Division arrived, Green refused to exit his third-floor apartment. With his son inside, it quickly escalated to a barricaded hostage situation. Consequently, SWAT and CNT mobilized.

Officers Kelly and McElroy had been briefed by the on-scene supervisor. Initially, there wasn't much to go on. Other tenants in the six-family building had been escorted from the premises by patrol and debriefed. There were varying accounts, but most of the residents claimed hearing between two and five shots. Green said little to the first officer who'd made contact except that he swore to kill anyone who entered.

They'd been able to locate a cellphone for Green, but it went straight to voicemail. Patrol used a cruiser's PA system to bark commands, demanding the gunman inside give himself up. Green shut all of the blinds, reducing any visibility to a zero point. Upon Kelly's arrival, patrol hadn't heard or seen any sign of movement within the domicile for forty-eight minutes. The only positive was that they hadn't heard any additional gunshots. Forty-eight minutes could mean a world of possible outcomes, and people, especially deranged people, did horrible things when left to their own mental devices. Just because there weren't gunshots didn't mean Trevor Green hadn't used another method to end his or his son's life.

SWAT took over the close perimeter and relieved members of the Patrol Division staggered around the exterior of the house. Once set in place, a three-man tactical element approached on the east alley side. After several poorly aimed attempts, a throw phone was tossed through the east bedroom window. It broke the glass, but the heavy case containing the phone was designed for just that. Nine hours had passed since that point in time. Kelly and McElroy had settled into the tight space of the Mobile Command Center. It was basically an oversized RV fitted with all the bells and whistles needed to sustain long-term operations. As far as all that was concerned, Kelly was really only grateful it was outfitted with two essential items—coffee maker and a bathroom. Impossible to maintain focus without access to both. During the Shoenthal negotiation he'd been reduced to urinating into an empty Dunkin' Donuts cup.

CNT was comprised of eight members, divided into two-man teams, who worked on a rotational basis. They worked in tandem for a multitude of reasons. First, always good to have a second set of eyes on a problem. But more important, there were times when personalities between negotiator and suspect failed completely, and calling for a relief pitcher to take the mound was sometimes the only way to continue. This had not happened in Michael Kelly's time in the hot seat, but on any given day the equation could play out, and the team would need to be seamless in their transition. The other member needed to be able to pick up exactly where the other left off.

"Mike, aren't you going to call back?" Captain O'Brien asked. He was the district commander, and although jurisdictionally in charge of the overall scene, negotiations did not fall under his scope. Therefore, the question was one of unnecessary annoyance, as Kelly didn't answer to him. Kelly's team fell under the auspices of the tactical commander, Captain Darren Lyons.

Here we go again, thought Kelly. The impatience on the part of the brass for long, drawn-out situations had potentially disastrous complications. Kelly looked down at his watch; he knew why. The horde of news reporters clamored for an exclusive and Captain O'Brien loved the spotlight. He wasn't officially the Public Affairs Officer, but everyone could see the captain had his eye on that job. Kelly was never one to get excited about seeing his name in print or face on the television. He did his job for many reasons, not one of which was being in the limelight.

Kelly looked at his notepad and shook his head absentmindedly. "Got to give him time. We push and that phone's coming back out the damn window."

The captain turned and began strategizing with one of his lieutenants. Kelly looked over to his large partner, who rolled his eyes in response.

"They'll never understand what we do without sitting in the hot seat. Don't waste your energy on them," McElroy said.

"Maybe when you make rank it'll be different."

"They ain't got room for a guy like me in their ranks." McElroy gave a laugh and patted his large belly.

Only two more years to retirement for McElroy. All of his thirty years of police experience would be lost to the ether when he left. Kelly planned to absorb as much as he could from the wise veteran. Physicality aside, the rotund man was one of the best cops he'd ever known.

The last contact they'd had with Green ended poorly. The TacOps guys were salivating at being put into action. Kelly understood their enthusiasm; he used to play for that side of the team. Captain Lyons had devised multiple tactical options, and the team had been in a hold position for nearly nine hours. Perimeter team members were rotated out every two hours to give them a little down time and to keep fresh eyes on the target. The entry team rested in a nearby BearCat, an armored personnel carrier parked a hundred feet from the dwelling, idling loudly in the early morning air. It was an intimidating vehicle painted in matte black, with bright white SWAT lettering on both sides. Sometimes the sight of it caused suspects to surrender. No such luck today.

Ring. Ring. The red light flashed in sync with each wail of the phone. The voices in the room went silent without additional cueing. McElroy slipped the headphones back on, mussing his unkempt, greasy hair, nodding his readiness. Kelly, taking the cue from his counterpart, picked up the phone on the third ring. The red light transitioned to green, indicating an established connection. The system was designed to record all conversations, but Kelly never relied on technology; he had his notepad ready to jot down any pertinent information.

"Trevor?" Kelly asked calmly.

"You think this is a game? I said on the last call you need to leave. Do it now!" Trevor Green's voice was shrill, each word accented with a raspy hiss. The long night and overwhelming stress were wreaking havoc on the man.

"Trevor, as I said before, we can't leave you and Baxter alone at this point. We need to ensure you both are safe."

"You shut your stupid mouth! You don't want me safe. You're going to shoot me dead the minute I open the door or come to a window."

Kelly rubbed his eyes. They were dry and irritated, a combination of fatigue and the recycled air sapping out moisture. Even though it was chilly outside, the heat generated by all of the electronic components, coupled with the body heat, made the command center uncomfortably warm. The air conditioning fought a losing battle.

"The government is corrupt and you and your department are just as dirty. I watch the news. I'm not stupid. I see what goes on."

"I'd be lying if I said there weren't bad apples in every bunch." Kelly looked for any angle to give him a foothold in the man's manic world. "I'm sure the media morons are wrong about what they're saying about you."

"How's that?"

"You have the news on?" Kelly knew the answer because the audio feature of the throw phone enabled him to pick up background noise in the room. He'd heard the news reports and he'd heard Green's angry reaction to their summation.

"Yeah."

"They don't know anything about you, but they're out there filling the airwaves with your story. They don't know what I know. They're completely in the dark. I want them to get it right."

"Yeah? Why's that?"

"Because it matters." Kelly looked at McElroy, who nodded back. "Because you matter, Trevor."

"I'm already dead. My life's over. My son's life is over."

"When you start talking like that, I get nervous. I need you to see beyond your current circumstance."

"There's nothing to see."

"Your son needs you."

"I killed his mother. He's never going to get past what I did. His life is over."

"You'd be surprised what kids can overcome. In the end, things may never be the same, but if you don't give it a chance, you'll never know."

"You don't care what happens to me or my son."

"Let me prove you wrong. Let me show the tactical unit surrounding the house that you're a reasonable man. One who put his son's life ahead of his current circumstance."

"Why don't you leave me and my kid alone and we'll figure this out."

"You know there's no way we can leave. You're a smart guy. You and I need to come up with another solution."

"There's only one solution."

Kelly was making little headway in redirecting the last few conversations away from this topic. "I haven't heard from Baxter since we first started talking. How about you put him on the phone so I can hear his voice? Let's start there. A show of good faith."

"I don't want you filling my son with nonsense. He's my son, and I know what's best for him!"

"Tell me what you think is best for him. Tell me how you think I can help him." Kelly had marked the boy as Green's hook but was concerned at playing this card too often.

"You can't help my son. You couldn't help my daughter. The police turned their back on me when I needed them. Now she's lost. Maybe dead for all I know. No thanks to guys like you."

"I'm sorry about your daughter." Kelly looked at the board. Listed under the triggers column: Daughter – Sabrina. "You mentioned Sabrina before. I will look into that when this is all said and done. I keep my word."

"Promises! Empty promises!"

"Trevor, let me help make this right. Let me help Baxter."

"I'm his father! I know how to make this right!"

"Talk to me, Trevor. Tell me what you're thinking. How do you plan to make this right?"

No words. Just deep, ragged breaths filled the phone line. Kelly looked at McElroy, who shrugged, then tapped his wristwatch. Kelly understood his partner's message. They hadn't seen proof of life with the boy and time was running out before the tactical side took the reins. An entry with a hostage in place was one of the most challenging scenarios any tactical team could face. It required perfect timing and flawless, coordinated execution.

Kelly had spent two years as a member of SWAT's entry team. He'd been good, actually excelled at it, but after killing a suspect during a critical incident he decided to switch gears and become a negotiator. The TacOps guys liked having him on calls because he understood the roles of both sides and struck an even balance.

Lyons walked across the narrow space and stood over Kelly, who was still waiting for Green to speak again. It was important to let them talk. Uncomfortable silence compelled many to open up. Trevor Green hadn't disconnected yet, and this was a good thing. He was now sobbing loudly. This was sometimes the moment before submission. Lyons slid a folded piece of paper across the formed plastic table.

Kelly unfolded it and read the message. *Time is almost up. 10 minutes. Making entry.* He looked up at the commander towering above him. Kelly scribbled something onto his notepad and slid it over to Lyons. *Too risky. I've got this. Let me direct him into the open.* The captain nodded, then pointed at Kelly's chest. The outcome of this now hinged on Kelly's ability to deliver. Lyons walked away and returned to his small contingent of tactical leaders.

McElroy hit the mute button on the connection. "What the hell are you doin', Mike?"

"This guy's going to do his kid. You know it and I know it. We've passed the point of no return."

"I see that." His eyes narrowed. "Why aren't you letting tactical make the entry? It's protocol. Negotiation ends. Tactical takes over."

"I know the drill, Dave. But I also know that if SWAT storms that room, the kid is as good as dead."

"So, what's your thought?"

"Direct him to the window. Put Trevor into the open so snipers can end it."

"I don't like it."

"It's my show right now, and until somebody unseats me, this is the play."

McElroy grunted and shook his head.

"I was a good dad. I really was," Green sobbed.

Kelly quietly exhaled his relief at hearing the despondent father's voice again. "I believe you. I can tell you care about Baxter. You want what's best for him, but I'm not sure your head is clear enough to make that decision right now. That's where I can help."

Green groaned loudly. "I told you before. I know what I have to do. His mother's dead. I did that! I killed her. You know I'm going to jail for the rest of my life for what I did. My kid's going to end up in the system. He's going to be in and out of foster care until he ages out. Just like I was. No way he's going to go through what I had to. Not my kid. No way."

"Listen, I'll work with Baxter and ensure whatever happens he has the best care possible. You have to give me a chance to let me help you. Haven't I proven myself a man of my word so far?"

"You didn't send those cops home. They're still out there now!"

"I never said I would do that. I don't make promises I can't keep. What I will promise you is that I will not let Baxter slip through the cracks."

"Do you know what happens to kids raised in the system?"

Kelly grew more worried. Green was locked on the dire image of his son's future. "There are good people in place to help children like Baxter."

"I can't let that happen. I can't fail my son!" Green's voice squeaked.

"I have to know Baxter's okay. I need to see him right now, Trevor!" Kelly said forcefully. "We need proof that Baxter is still alive."

He tallied the number of times Green referred to his son by name during this conversation. Zero. He was dissociating himself by dehumanizing Baxter. Kelly intentionally injected Trevor's son's name in as many times as possible when he spoke.

"There is a team of highly trained operators preparing to enter your home if you don't show us that Baxter's okay right now. This is not how you want this to end. You care too much about your son."

"Let 'em come."

"I don't want that. I need you to understand that if that happens and you force their entry then you'd be putting Baxter's life at risk. I know you love your son and would never do anything to put him in harm's way. Isn't that right, Trevor?"

Green slammed the phone against something hard, a wall or tabletop. The reverberation caused McElroy to jump slightly.

"Trevor?"

Kelly heard the distinct sound of a revolver's cylinder spinning. He'd assumed Green had reloaded since shooting his wife and her lover, but even if he hadn't, two of the chambers were still occupied. Enough to bring about a terrible end to the negotiation.

"Trevor?"

The ratcheted spinning of the cylinder stopped and was followed by a metallic click.

"What?"

"The gun in your hand concerns me."

"It's my only ticket out of here."

"I'm giving you another option. Let me help you. And your son, Baxter. Let me be your ticket."

"Nothing you can do for us." Trevor Green's voice was a mumbled whisper.

"Show us that Baxter's okay. Do that and we can slow things down again. I need you to tell me you understand. And then I need you to make your way over to the window with the gray blinds. The same one we threw the phone into. I've got someone watching that window. They need you to open the blinds slowly. Present Baxter in front of the window and have him wave so we know he's all right. After that you can close the blinds and we can continue talking."

"That's it?"

"That's it. All they need is to verify Baxter's okay and we can slow things back down. It's been too long on our end and people are getting nervous he's hurt."

There was a long pause. Kelly cracked his neck, releasing the tension in three loud pops.

"Promise."

"I promise no funny stuff. The powers that be need a proof of life to allow us to continue talking. Do you understand?"

"My son ain't going to be raised in no foster system!"

"That's something we can discuss further after I see Baxter's okay."

Kelly turned and looked over at Lyons, back on the tactical side of the RV. He gave a thumbs up and held up two fingers, indicating the middle window, second from the front.

Green mumbled something out of range for the phone to pick up any words. Kelly heard a higher-pitched voice. The sound of Baxter's voice provided minimal relief. The seven-year-old was only six months older than Kelly's daughter. The age proximity between the two had been in the back of his mind during this entire standoff.

"Stay on the phone with me. I can talk you through it again. I want you to be nice and calm."

"Are you talking to me? I was getting my son up from the couch."

"I was just saying that you can stay on the phone with me while you do this."

"Sure—whatever. I am going over to the window now. I've got him with me."

Kelly held his hand up. Lyons read the signal and communicated with the team set up in the neighbor's bedroom only thirty feet away. The sniper and spotter would be set back in the room. Unlike television's typical portrayal, no self-respecting marksman would lean his weapon out the window. Most likely the sniper team would be prone on a bed or in a seated, supported firing position.

"Trevor, put the gun down before going to the window. Do not have anything in your hand that could be deemed a threat."

"I'll do as I damn please. If you plan to shoot me, you'll have to go through my boy to get me. Better than the life he's got ahead of him now."

A muffled shuffling and then the sweet voice of Baxter Green could be heard. "Daddy, please. You're scaring me."

"Shh. Don't worry. It'll all be over soon."

"Trevor? I need you to open that curtain now. Remember, nice and slow. No sudden movements."

Kelly's calm composure was disintegrating. McElroy was shaking his head.

"Movement at the window," one of the SWAT members whispered. "No visual confirmation of target yet."

Kelly had muted the phone line to avoid Green picking up any unwanted communication.

"His son is with him. Not sure how he's going to present. I still have him on the line. Let me guide him into the open," Kelly said calmly. "We want him clear of his son before engaging."

The others in the room were watching a live feed from two cameras deployed under the cover of darkness. One camera was of the interior hallway and showed the front door. Camera two was in the kitchen window of the same apartment where the sniper team had been deployed. It zoomed in to show a clear vantage of the number-two window with gray blinds, the window where the deranged man and his young son stood.

The curtains came apart. Baxter Green was thrust upward, and the thin, pasty right arm of his father was wrapped tightly around the boy's waist with the throw phone visible in hand. Baxter's tiny frame was somehow able to mask Trevor almost completely from view. What was visible was a revolver, pressed against Baxter Green's left temple.

"Are you satisfied?" Green yelled.

Kelly did not like what he saw on the screen. He unmuted the phone. "Take the gun off your son's head. Do it now!"

Trevor lowered his son back down. He stayed behind him, the gun still pressed against Baxter's head. Tears streamed down the boy's face.

Kelly held his fist in the air, giving the tactical command for hold position.

Trevor knelt behind his son. The gun shook, but held fast against his son's temple. Silence in the command center as the two sides, tactical and negotiation, held their breath.

Trevor's head lowered, disappearing from view behind his son. The only sound came through the phone's receiver. It came in the form of pitched whimpers.

The gun slid away from Baxter's head. No clear shot. Only the head and upper torso of the child were visible, and Trevor's exposed left arm. Kelly knew the sniper was holding his trigger at the break point. The most miniscule of muscular tension would send the .308 caliber boattail hollowpoint out of the Remington 700 rifle.

This momentary lull could flare up at any moment. Kelly replayed Trevor's resolution, as twisted as it was. He knew the deranged father had no intention of releasing his son. He was working up the nerve to pull the trigger.

Trevor spun his son toward him and the two now faced each other. He'd separated enough to see Trevor's exposed face. Kelly opened his hand, finally signaling to take the shot.

"Green light," Lyons said into his radio.

Kelly heard the sweet, lyrical voice of Baxter Green come across the phone line. Baxter launched toward his father, embracing him in a hug.

The crack of the rifle sounded as Kelly watched the boy move. Both immediately disappeared from the camera's view.

"Call the shot!" Lyons commanded into the radio.

"Shots away. No visual confirmation." The spotter's voice echoed over the command center's speaker.

Kelly took two short breaths, trying to regain his composure. Combat breathing. He tried to get oxygen to his brain to maintain calm. He was going to be sick. He looked across the table at McElroy, whose face was an unhealthy shade of white.

An agonizing, high-pitched wail, animalistic and unrefined, penetrated Kelly's ear. "You killed my baby boy!"

"Breach the door," Lyons ordered. "Breach now!"

Kelly watched the monitor fill with the large frames of the tactical unit as they approached the apartment's front door. A sixty-pound ram obliterated the locking mechanism, and within seconds, seven men flooded into the apartment of Trevor Green.

"Show me your hands!" one of the team members boomed. Kelly heard the commands through the throw phone.

A series of grunts and crunching furniture could be heard. A team member called out over the comms system, "Subject secure. One down. No pulse. Medevac requested on the fly!"

There was a pause. "Target was struck in the upper chest. Conscious and breathing. He's in custody. We've got a gunshot wound to the kid's head."

McElroy pushed back in his chair and slammed his large fist into the table with a thunderous boom. He flung his headset against the nearby wall.

The room began to spin. Kelly dropped the phone and stood up from the negotiations table. He looked at the board, staring at his scribbled handwriting under the H. Son – Baxter. Kelly pushed past everyone, out the door, into the light of day.

The fresh air did little to alleviate his nausea. Officer Michael Kelly bent at the waist, bracing his hands on his knees as he vomited into the sewer gutter beneath him.

Baxter Green was dead. His promise to keep the boy safe went unfulfilled.

1

How long have I been here? Faith thought madly. *It's colder now than I remember. The party. I was at another party. Nice place. Not so nice men. Running. Now here?* Nothing added up. The thoughts and images were coming in disjointed bursts, like watching twenty different TV shows at the same time.

Her surroundings were unfamiliar. What little she could see made no sense.

A bubbling grew louder in the stillness. A trickle from the nearby building's rain gutter sang its melody as water passed down to the muddy ground below. The gurgle was somewhere off to the left, a reference point for her new surroundings.

It was dark. The only light came from a poorly maintained streetlight and the neon red emanating from an exit sign near a dumpster. The two weak sources of illumination covered the ground in a kaleidoscope of yellow and muted red as the subtle beams intertwined, dancing on the glisten of the wet earth at her feet. Faith Wilson's appreciation was quickly dashed with the crunch of approaching footsteps from somewhere in the near distance.

Her mind played a desperate game of catch-up to a set of events eluding her understanding. Faith clearly remembered this morning at the coffee shop. They treated her to a fancy coffee, a sign she was becoming valued. It wasn't often she'd received such lavish offerings, and the reward temporarily balanced her daily shame. She recalled the warmth of her frothy latte; the sensation of the memory was in total contradiction to the cold that now crept up from the hard ground. Her lips, stuck together in cottony dryness, relented as she slid her tongue along the jagged expanse of her dry, cracked mouth. The bitter taste of blood carried the hint of cinnamon. Her last taste of the morning's easy start soured in her mouth.

It had been a good day. A long time since she'd remembered what that felt like. It was the first time she'd been allowed on an outing. Shopping had been fun. And the new dress she had picked out for the party was amazing. *It's all my fault. Why did I have to go and screw it up? I should've just stayed. It wasn't like it was the first time. Stupid, stupid, stupid.*

Faith willed her body to move. Her limbs ignored the commands and a palpable fear swept over her. Her eyes shifted rapidly, wildly searching the darkened surroundings. It was like her body was encased, pinning her to the cold wet ground. Like being trapped in a nightmare, where your blanket blocks your subconscious from allowing your body to run freely. Even breathing took effort.

The crunch was closer now, gravel and dirt pressed by the approaching footsteps.

Move! Faith's mind yearned for her body to cooperate.

The only movement she mustered came in a slight shift of her head. She toggled and craned in all directions. The slow, agonizing writhing of her neck gave way to blinding pain. Her eyes watered and her lids fluttered as she teetered on the edge of unconsciousness. She willed herself to remain alert. She willed herself to fight. But, with all of her intestinal fortitude, little came in the way of action.

A drizzle of rain carried on the strangely mild breeze brought with it the salty taste of the ocean. She tried again to move only to remain teetering on her right side. Finally, she fell onto her stomach. A burger wrapper fluttered across the ground, stopping in front of her face. It smelled of pickles and mustard. A memory, like a wave receding from a sandy shore, pulled her to a time when Dad's butterfly kiss was all she needed. It'd been several years since she'd thought of him kindly. And even odder was the timing of it now.

Her father was a gregarious man, known throughout the town for his legendary ability to throw a football. Time had stopped for him some thirteen years earlier when he'd led the team to the high school state championship. Some people peaked in those moments of simple success, never to move beyond. The night of the big game was the same night he learned he was going to be a father.

Faith had heard her father's story many times before, but knew two very distinctly different versions existed, the one that he told Faith, and the one she'd heard him whisper to his closest friends. It was the latter retelling that haunted her. *That girl wrecked my chance at greatness. She stole my dream. I could've gone on, probably played in the pros, but I passed on scholarships for her. Had to take that dead-end job to make ends meet.* Faith had been eight the first time she'd heard that version. His words crushed her in ways she still didn't fully comprehend. Her mom had left shortly after her tenth birthday. She never saw her again. *Who leaves their daughter and never visits, or even calls?* She never found the answer to that question and probably never would. Faith had been abandoned to live with a father who never truly wanted her. Unwanted by either parent was a terrible feeling.

As Faith's world imploded, she found solace in food, and by the time she'd crossed over to her pre-teenage years she was already heavier than some of the linemen on her middle school football team. She spent most of her time devising ways to fix herself. Her confidence flatlined, until her twelfth birthday, when she blew out the candles but refused to take a bite of her favorite— peanut butter ice cream cake. Instead, Faith picked up the entire cake and threw it in the trash. She could still see the look on her father's face as the metallic lid slammed shut. It was a big first step in getting her life back on track.

At the time it seemed like a major obstacle. Her commitment to weight loss gave her a bit more confidence, a slight boost in her self-image. Faith remembered when she'd uploaded a picture of the new and improved Faith Wilson to her profile. She remembered the boy who took notice. He was not only cute, he was downright gorgeous. He actually posted, *Wow! You're hot!*

My God, had it really been a year since that day? She remembered the way he looked at her when they first met. He didn't pass judgment as so many others did. His smile disarmed her completely. It was the reason for her current circumstance.

Faith licked her lips again, and again tasted the hint of cinnamon. She regretted her latte had been made with non-fat milk. She resented her father for punishing her for being born.

The flash of self-pity and anger was instantly replaced by fear as a mud-tipped sneaker appeared in the corner of her peripheral vision. Even the burger wrapper seemed terrified of the person looming over her. She craned hard to see but the person was already gone. The footsteps moved rapidly clockwise around her body. Her head angled to follow but was too slow to keep pace.

I remember being at the mall. I remember the struggle. And then what? Nothing.

A tugging, and her body began to slide across the uneven ground. She couldn't feel it anywhere except her neck and head. Jagged rocks lashed at her scalp and stung the back of her head. Her head bumped along the cold, unforgiving ground. The jarring movement jostled her head violently. Each time it felt as though a knife was buried deep in the nape of her neck. Faith willed herself not to give in to the excruciating pain, but some things could not be overcome by willpower. Some things overpowered all strength of character.

"Help!" Faith yelled. The words barely carried enough power to reach her own ears. She swallowed hard and tried again. Her breathing became more labored and she found herself consciously making an effort to inhale and exhale. Each shorter than its predecessor.

The dragging stopped. *Did it work? Did someone hear? Maybe the monster in the dark heard Faith's voice and had a change of heart?* Her mind raced, searching for the answer.

No words. Something was happening. Her head now shook as if being shoved. The new position gave her twisted neck an angle from which to see her assailant. A piece of her damaged recall came to the forefront. A person she'd come to know and trust over the past year stood nearby. A person who, until today, had provided and cared for her. Eyes that had once given Faith hope now held only the promise of death.

A sudden whip of her neck sent her face down into darkness. The movement was accompanied by a pop, followed by a searing pain. Faith could no longer move her head. All efforts to free herself from her current position were lost. She drew a weak breath and swallowed dirt. Her next scream was buried in her mouth, never to be uttered. The gritty chalkiness of freshly churned earth filled her mouth. Faith spat with all her might, trying to clear her mouth. Her breath came in rapid and shallow bursts.

Then a light patter on the back of her head. It felt like rain without the cold dampness. In her horror she realized it was not water but dirt.

In her mind, Faith called out in vain, as the last bits of light gave way to the deep, pitch- black enveloping her.

2

Routine was everything. Detective Michael Kelly sought to find it wherever and whenever he could. He entered, as he did every morning, through the side entrance of One Schroeder Plaza, Boston Police's main headquarters.

He bumped into Bernie Cross on the way to the elevator. They'd worked the same patrol district together. Cross had gone the administrative route, climbing the PD's ranks quicker than most. Kelly liked Cross. The newly adorned lieutenant was more of a bureaucrat than a cop, but Cross had a way of taking care of his people. At least, that's what Kelly had heard. He'd actually never served under him. But, in a city like Boston, reputation was everything. Cross looked to be in a bit of a huff.

"Hey Bernie, where's the fire?"

Bernie slapped a stack of papers and made an effort to smile. "Trying to compile the stats for the morning briefing. I had to run down and use the admin secretary's printer. Big, fancy place and nothing works."

"Keep fighting the good fight," Kelly jested. He knew every supervisor dreaded the admin meetings. It was a part of the job he hoped never to face.

Cross scurried along as Kelly pressed the elevator button for the second floor.

He navigated the hallway to the secure door marked Homicide. His boss was already hovering around the coffee maker. Kelly liked being the first one in the office, but the pounding in his head was a not-so-subtle reminder as to why he was moving a bit more slowly this morning.

Kelly logged in and pulled the highlights of the preceding twenty-four hours of patrol-related calls for service. Each district supervisor was required to close out his or her shift with a secured email documenting any priority calls for service. He knew there hadn't been a homicide, no alert had been sent to his phone over the course of the night, but it didn't mean there wasn't a shooting or stabbing on the cusp of making its transition to his unit. He scanned the lines of entries. Then he saw it. District C-11, his old unit, were on the scene of a body. He checked his phone again. No alert. He thought he was next up on rotation, but every once in a while, cases got shuffled. Still, it was strange the alert message hadn't been sent. Typically, every time a body dropped, a group text would be sent to all members of Homicide, a way of keeping all in the loop.

If he were still working the street, his next stop would be the main desk to check in with the booking officer and look over the previous night's arrest log. It was a habit he'd picked up while in Narcotics. He'd found it was good to check if any drug arrests had been made overnight. Morning holding cells were prime time to gather new informants. The dope sickness of the night's long wait usually left people desperate for an escape so that they could hit the street and get straight. For Kelly, it had been the ultimate leverage, and dramatically increased his stable of snitches. He still kept many of his contacts from those days. Drugs and murder went hand in hand. The exchange of favors for information was a critical part of the law enforcement model. Provide protection for smaller fish in the hopes they'd ante in on bringing in a bigger collar. The gray area was where the best cops operated. Kelly spent much of his career working within its delicate balance.

Being in headquarters, he resigned himself to digitally checking the names on the arrest log. None caught his attention, so he moved on.

Michael Kelly spun in his swivel chair and grabbed a bottle of ibuprofen from the corner of his desk. He downed four of the orange pills with his coffee.

The cubicle was sparsely decorated. The only picture sat next to his phone —Kelly and his eight-year-old daughter, Embry. The photo was from a few years back. Her excitement at going to her first Red Sox game was forever captured in the 5x7 photo taken at Fenway Park's Gate B on Van Ness Street.

They'd gone many times since, each enjoyable, but nothing compared to the magic of that first game. At least for Kelly. Watching that first crack of the bat through his daughter's eyes, seeing them widen as the ball soared up into the air was a memory he hoped would never fade. She didn't care that it was a pop fly or that the Sox had lost by four that afternoon.

The lower half of the three partitions shaping his office space were covered in a powder blue fabric, most of which was invisible due to the info flyers and wanted persons sheets push- pinned in place. He never seemed to take down any of the old stuff. Kelly just pinned the new on top. The weight of the papers eventually won out over the strength of the pins, and they'd scatter to the floor. On those days, he saw it as divine intervention and would take a moment to do some upkeep.

Two columns containing five workstations lined the large office space. The clusters had their own designated sergeant. In total, thirty-eight detectives and two civilians comprised Boston Police's illustrious Homicide unit. Kelly was its newest member, a rookie by their standards. Every time he transferred units he took on rookie status all over again. He'd undergone this transformation four times thus far in his career, and he hoped this would be his last stop. His small team was comprised of Jimmy Mainelli and Cliff Anderson, led by Sergeant Dale Sutherland.

He stared at the board fastened to his cubical wall and sipped at the medium regular Dunkin' Donuts coffee. The hot liquid burned as it rolled down the back of his throat. The caffeine fought to clear away the remnants of his hangover. The corkboard was his way of managing his cases, a visual system of organizing his workload that served as a reminder to the departed souls' justice he sought. He kept index cards neatly arranged into rows and columns. Each card had a name and date written in bold block lettering. Always the same style. The name of the victim, last-comma-first, and the date the body was discovered. Blue cards denoted closed cases. Red ones were open investigations. He affectionately referred to it as the Murder Board.

No case outweighed the others. Except one. It wasn't even his case. One red card was set apart from the others. ROURKE, DANNY 3/17/2011. Kelly's patrol partner. Rourke was killed while off-duty, during a home invasion robbery. It forever changed Kelly's memory of Saint Patrick's Day.

Even with all the attention the case was given, no suspect ever developed. It hadn't been the first unsolved murder. The city's cold case files bulged at the seams with nearly a thousand bodies absent closure. But this was the first unsolved murder of a Boston police officer. It was a permanent black eye for the department in the subsequent eight years since Rourke's murder.

The investigation into the violent death of Danny Rourke was eventually recategorized as a cold case. For Kelly it was anything but. Frank Joyce had been assigned the case, among a sea of others. It wasn't officially on Kelly's case list, so he worked the file on his own time, obsessing over it. Sadly, he hadn't learned much more than the preceding detectives responsible for the initial investigation.

It made sense he was now working in Homicide, but it hadn't been his partner's murder that drove him there. After the Baxter Green shooting, Kelly needed a fresh start. He seriously considered hanging up his shield and gun. But on a whim, he took the detective test and came out on top of the candidate list. Making the grade with eleven years of service under his belt, Kelly had first dibs, and took an opening with Homicide.

Sergeant Sutherland, his direct supervisor, rapped on the flimsy metal file cabinet near the opening to Kelly's cubicle. "Hey Mikey, you're up on rotation. Got Jane Doe over on Von Hillern Street, at Sheffield Electric. I know you're familiar with the Dot."

The Dot, Boston's Dorchester neighborhood. Predominately populated by Irish Catholics when Kelly grew up there, it had now become one of the city's most diverse places to live. The area had a long-standing history of violence. One of the most infamous mobsters, James "Whitey" Bulger, was born in The Dot. Kelly had seen first-hand the influence on his community. At an early age, he chose his side.

"What do we got so far?"

"Not much. Some homeless guy stumbled across her earlier this morning. Patrol's holding the scene. Crime Scene is already on their way. M.E.'s been notified."

"Why are we always the last to know?"

"Pretty sure she'll still be dead when you get there. I know that Jimmy's out on vacation this week. Anderson's at court prepping for the Briggs trial. Leaves us a little light. If you want, I can task someone else to work with you on this one."

"Nah. Don't bother. Everybody's got their own bodies to work. I'll call in if I need a hand."

"Oh, yeah, and I just heard. Happy birthday."

Kelly rubbed his temples. The throb of his headache came back at the mention of it. "Yesterday."

"That explains why you look like a steamin' bag of monkey crap."

"You say the kindest things."

Sutherland began his hobbled walk away from Kelly's desk area. He had been injured a few years back, shattering his kneecap while chasing a perp. He lost his footing hurdling a chain link fence, landing knee-first on the concrete below. The handicap was a source of contention as he'd been battling with the brass to raise his disability rating high enough to allow him to take an early retirement. The probability of that happening looked bleak, and thus the embattled Homicide sergeant was most likely destined to work his remaining three years overseeing the body beat.

Kelly took a sip of his coffee, pulled out his leather-bound notepad, and made his first case notation. Jane Doe. Notification time: 0907hrs 3/12/2019.

He unlocked the file cabinet's bottom drawer and withdrew his department-issued Glock 22 semi-automatic pistol. Two times he'd discharged his weapon in the line of duty. Both times justified. Both times costly. He was in the very small percentile of law enforcement who deployed deadly force, and Kelly hoped a third opportunity never presented. But, with fourteen years to go on his pension clock, the odds were not in his favor. He undid his belt and looped the leather holster in place. Kelly then slipped the gun inside and snapped the retention strap closed. A beaded chain centered his badge on his chest, swinging like a pendulum as Kelly stood up from his chair. Detectives were given the option of wearing their badge on their beltline in front of their firearm or around their neck. Kelly always chose the neck. He'd learned during his time in Narcotics that it was much easier to see a badge centered over the heart. Very important as a plain clothes working in the field.

As he was about to set off for the scene, he checked back at his calendar. An E was marked in the upper corner by today's date. He pulled out his cellphone.

"Hey, it's me. I'm not going to be able to grab Embry tonight. I caught a case."

"Again?"

"You tell the family of the dead that it's an inconvenience. Do you think I like missing time with our daughter?"

"It's really hard to answer that honestly. This is the second time in the last week you've had to cancel on her. Can't you pick her up and drop her with your mom?"

"Mom's got a busted hip. Not sure how much help she's going to be." Kelly gave an aggravated sigh. "I'm not sure when I'll get a chance to break free. Case popped up a few minutes ago and I don't have a feel for it yet. I don't want to say yes to that. I think it's just best you plan on picking her up, and I'll call if I can swing it."

"Maybe we need to adjust the custody arrangement. We could just stick to weekends when you're not on call."

"Seriously? I'd end up seeing her only a couple times a month."

"Wouldn't be much different from what you are doing now."

"I'm telling you, I'll get this thing under control. You'll see. I don't see why you're making this such a big deal. When we were married, I had to adjust my schedule all the time and you never gave me any crap."

"We're not married anymore, so yes, things are different now."

"I'll call her tonight and explain. It's not like I'm out on a hot date."

"What about Thursday? Marty and I have dinner plans. I really hate getting a sitter if you're available."

"So, now I've been reduced to date night babysitter?" Kelly let the hostility linger for a moment. "I can't. It's Thursday. I've got Pop's."

"At some point, you and your childhood buddies need to grow up and part ways."

"Those guys used to be like brothers to you. Same neighborhood you grew up in. Remember?"

"I guess I've moved on."

"Sam, we're not doing this today."

Silence. Samantha Jordan had reverted to her maiden name once their marriage ended. Kelly knew his ex-wife well enough to be able to picture her face. He could envision her pursed lips holding back the onslaught of expletives she wanted to bury him in. Although a reserved person by nature, Samantha had a hot streak, and once unleashed, there was little to stop it. Like the breaking of a dam. Kelly was glad she held back. The last thing he needed this morning was a verbal lashing courtesy of his ex.

"Listen, Sam, I'll get this sorted out. Promise. I'm still adjusting to the new job. Things'll settle down. Embry's going to be all right. She knows I love her."

"Just don't go around making promises you aren't capable of keeping." Samantha ended the call.

Kelly slid his crime scene go-bag out from under his desk. He stuffed his notepad into the zippered slot on the outside of the satchel. Grabbing his coffee and stepping out into the crisp air of spring, Kelly cleared his head. The body he was about to see would need him to be at his very best.

3

The Impala shuddered and whined loudly as he put it into park. Michael Kelly wasn't a car expert by any means, but it didn't take a mechanic to tell his department-issued Chevrolet was on its last leg. Being the newest addition to the unit meant he was the last on the list for a new vehicle. Rookie crap. Most of these sedans had been phased out of service and replaced by the Caprice. There was a little peace of mind in driving a clunker; nobody would care if he wrecked it. He figured the quicker it got totaled, the better off he'd be.

Kelly stood ten feet from the bright yellow tape denoting the scene. More times than not, he was forced to adjust this barrier, extending scenes far beyond the initial layout determined by the Patrol Division's assessment. Kelly took out his notepad and jotted down his arrival time. Flipping to a blank page, Kelly started with a rough sketch of the area. Not an artist's rendering by any stretch, but it served its purpose. He'd go back later and do a more comprehensive diagram with measurements, but it was always a good idea to get a gist of the layout before stepping inside the scene. The crime scene technicians would do a digital mapping and 3D reconstruction, most of which was done with case prosecution in mind. On occasion, the mapping software enabled him to get a better perspective on bigger scenes. But Kelly found nothing beat experiencing it first-hand. No camera could capture the intangible essence of those moments when walking among the deceased.

He eyed the Crime Scene Response Unit van and saw Raymond Charles sitting on the back bumper, inhaling his morning cigarette. Kelly liked working with him. Charles never entered a scene until Homicide directed. Others weren't as considerate to protocols and jumped the scene, trying to impress their bosses. Charles had been working crime scenes longer than Kelly had been alive; he didn't need to impress anybody.

Charles noticed Kelly and raised his green thermos of coffee in mock cheers. Kelly smiled and went back to his sketch, adding a few bits of detail.

Before him stood a strip of small, rectangular warehouse buildings. Most of them were vacant and had signs on the windows for numbers to call if looking to lease. On the far right, nearest the crime scene, was Sheffield Electric, more of an extended double-wide trailer than a building. Extending out from the building was an eight-foot chain link fence. The yellow tape extended from the post closest to the building and out to a telephone pole on the other side of the dirt parking lot. Two patrolmen in thickly lined patrol parkas stood outside the tape. Kelly was glad to see they weren't on his side, playing junior detective.

The fence extended along to an open gate. Located inside was a variety of construction equipment, some of which looked as though it hadn't been serviced in quite some time. There were piles of gravel near stacks of PVC piping, tethered into a pyramid of sorts.

Rough sketch complete, Kelly approached the two patrolmen.

"Mornin', boys," Kelly said. "You guys first on scene?"

"Yup," the stocky officer said. His nameplate, affixed across his broad chest, said his last name was Russo.

"Let me get your full name and badge number for my report." With over two thousand cops working the city, Kelly often found himself asking this of more and more patrol guys, especially if they were new to the job.

"Antonio Russo, 2146."

"Gabe Lancaster, 2163," the tall, thin patrolman said. His voice had the squeaky shrillness of a prepubescent teen. The man's Adam's apple protruded outward as if he had a gobstopper lodged in his throat. The two made for a uniquely odd pair and, working the rough streets of Dorchester, were sure to catch some colorful comments from the more vocal citizenry.

"I assume you boys will be getting me a report before you go offline today?"

"Yes, sir. As soon as we get relieved, we'll write up our initial," Russo said.

"Sounds good. And don't call me sir. Makes me feel old and useless. I'm Michael Kelly. Call me either." Kelly liked to dissolve any barriers created by rank and title. He found them to be one of the great hinderances to investigation. "Give me a quick rundown on what you found when you got here."

"We got a call about a body. Called in by that sloppy piece of work over there in our squad car." Russo thumbed in the direction of their cruiser.

In the back seat sat a man. The morning's gray light bounced off the car's lightly tinted windows and Kelly was only able to make out the shape of a wild mess of long dark hair, as if he'd stuck his hand on a Van de Graaff generator.

"Name?"

"Robert Blevins. Homeless. Verified him through an old DMV photo. No warrants. Pretty long history. Mostly drunk and disorderly related. Bunch of larcenies. No violent crimes in his past."

"Did he give any reason as to why he was over this way?"

"He said he was rummaging for trash, but we found some copper wiring in his cart. My guess is he was out here stripping copper. Said he saw the girl's shoe. I guess he was surprised to find the girl was still attached to it. He called it in."

"You guys got a statement from him already?"

"Yeah. Figured we'd help out."

"I appreciate it. I'm flying solo this morning." Kelly peeked over at the man bearing more than a passing resemblance to a feral cat. "So, why's our good citizen in the back of the cruiser?"

"Pinched him on the stolen copper and trespassing." Russo folded his arms as if satisfied he'd solved a major crime.

"We're not pinching Mr. Blevins today, fellas. He's done himself a good deed. Maybe work on getting him a warm meal and cup of coffee." Kelly watched as the words deflated Russo's ego.

"Talk to Massie. His call to make. He's over there on the other side of the crime scene van."

"Paul Massie? He's the supervisor on this?" Kelly asked. He knew Massie from years ago. A small man with a Napoleonic complex. Massie was one class ahead of him in the academy and the two had butted heads on more than one occasion when out on the street. He hoped today would not be a repeat occurrence.

Kelly walked past the homeless man in Russo and Lancaster's car. Blevins seemed not to notice. He was otherwise engaged in a rather intense conversation. One is never alone if you've got friends, imaginary or otherwise.

"Hey Ray. We'll get started in a minute," Kelly called to the senior crime scene tech.

"Your show, boss." Raymond Charles sipped from his thermos.

"No Dunkin' this morning?"

"Wife cut me off. Said I spend too much damn money on the stuff. Can you believe she made a dang spreadsheet to show me how much money I waste on coffee? A spreadsheet! What's my life come to?"

Kelly shook his head and laughed. "I don't know what I'd do without it. I'll bring you one next time. It kills me to see you reduced to this."

"I think she hates me." Charles took a swig and winced. "She put some chicory crap in it. Told me she saw it on a cooking show. Supposed to be sophisticated. Personally, I think she's trying to kill me."

Sergeant Paul Massie's Ford Explorer idled quietly, the exhaust visible in the cool March air. Kelly approached and rapped lightly on the window, startling the small man inside. He likened the man's jerky movements to that of a squirrel. Massie exited, pulling on a black skull cap to protect his bald head from the cold.

"Hey Paul."

"Where's Mainelli and Anderson?" Massie asked.

"Good to see you, too. Sorry to disappoint, but it's just me today."

"Sucks to be you." Massie rubbed his hands together. For somebody who worked in the Northeast, the BPD sergeant had little tolerance for the cold. Short, thin, and bald—a veritable hat trick of genetic disaster for the street cop.

"I just talked to your guys. Apparently, they pinched the caller on some minor trespass stuff."

"What about it?"

Kelly's assumption was immediately dashed by the curt response from the sergeant. He understood it had been Massie who'd made the call on arresting Mr. Blevins. "Paul, I'm cutting him loose on those charges."

"Why's that?"

The fact that he had to explain this to Massie spoke volumes of the street boss's incompetence and irked Kelly to no end. He refrained from saying what was really on his mind. He had a long day ahead of him and the thought of engaging the man in a verbal duel was low on his priority list. Plus, the slight pulsing of his hangover weakened his energy for the fray. "It plays better if this thing ends up going to prosecution. It looks a lot cleaner if our first witness isn't in jail or awaiting his own trial. Work with me here on this one."

"Fine. Do whatever you want with the bum. It's your case. Far be it for us lowly patrol guys to piss all over it." Massie looked away. He huffed silently, but his warm breath fogged in the cold air. Kelly had pissed off the man. "Me and my guys have been on all night. I've already called for relief. When it arrives, I'll let you know before we cut loose."

"Sounds good." Kelly shook hands with Massie. A forced gesture of camaraderie. The patrol sergeant turned to his vehicle. A blast of heat poured out when the door opened. The bald squirrel retreated to his nest.

Kelly walked over to Russo and Lancaster's patrol car. He opened the back-passenger side door. The repugnant smell of the man inside caught Kelly off-guard. Robert Blevins smelled more like a Porta-John than a human being. For that reason, Kelly wanted to do his best to treat him like the latter.

"Mr. Blevins?" He controlled the need to gag.

The homeless man turned. His eyes squinted and Kelly assumed the man was working hard to determine if the voice he'd just heard was real or one of his imaginary friends. Blevins wore a heavy brown trench coat, stained and torn in multiple spots. Kelly could see three additional layers visible at the neckline. There were probably a few more, unseen and saturated with the man's stink.

It was tough being homeless. Tougher so in the cold of New England. Kelly guessed it had been several months, or longer, since the man had bathed. It was difficult to make out his ethnicity because of the grime. Blevins's cheeks and nose were swollen to cartoonish proportions, an obvious testament to the man's overindulgence in alcohol. Not the best first witness Kelly had in a case. Not the worst, either.

"Mr. Blevins?"

"Didn't hurt her. Promise. Not me. No way. Found her is all. I didn't do it." His voice was pitchy, ranging from baritone to falsetto. His words released like an untuned accordion.

"I never thought you did. Most people don't call the police after they kill someone."

Blevins was cuffed in front and held up the stainless-steel bracelets. The silver looked brighter against his filth. "They arrested me. I'm no killer. I told them. They arrested me." He started to growl.

"Mr. Blevins, I want to take those cuffs off, but you're growling."

"Guess I'm a pit bull."

"Um—yeah. Just don't bite or I'll have to send you to the pound. Fair enough?"

The strange rumbling growl subsided, and Kelly pulled a handcuff key from his pocket. He bent deeper into the cloud of stink surrounding Blevins and unlocked the cuffs. "You're not under arrest. We just had to check some things out."

"I'm free to go?" Blevins rubbed his wrists.

"Yes. The officers said you've already given a statement."

Blevins stepped out of the cruiser. Kelly gave the man a wide berth. Even in the open air of the lot, the funk still persisted, penetrating deep into Kelly's nostrils. The homeless man gave a humble bow as if departing royalty.

"Did you see or hear anything you may have left out when talking to the other officers?"

"I told 'em everything." He looked off to the side as if listening intently to someone else. "Yup. Everything."

"Mind lifting up your shoes?" Kelly was well within his power to force the man to do so, but always found it better to ask.

Blevins leaned against the cruiser's side panel near the gas tank, balancing himself, and raised his left foot unsteadily. Kelly took out a thin digital camera from his front pocket. He bent low, catching the toxic vapors as he lowered. He photographed the treading, or lack thereof, on the bottom of the man's well-worn soles. Kelly then pulled a small, rolled measuring tape. He held it alongside. A notation next to Blevins's name in his notebook read *left size 11*. Kelly repeated the process on the right. The shoe on the man's right foot was a different make and size. Photographed and measured with the odd notation of *right foot size 12*. Mismatched shoes for a mismatched man.

"Where can I find you if I need to reach out to you at a later date?"

"Here and there. In the cold months you can find me over at the UMass stop. Warm grates. Not too crowded. Not like downtown."

"Thank you, Mr. Blevins." Kelly pulled out a twenty-dollar bill and handed it over. A dirty hand with black-encrusted fingernails swallowed up the money eagerly.

"Buddy."

"What'd you say?"

"Buddy. My friends call me Buddy. Ask around; they'll know how to find me."

"All right, Buddy. I'll be seeing you."

Robert "Buddy" Blevins ambled away from Kelly. The shoe on his right foot was a size too big, held together by poorly adhered duct tape. Each step was accented by a flop and pop as his feet slipped in and out. Kelly watched the man take up the reins of his shopping cart and meander away from the scene he'd stumbled upon hours before.

"Ready to do this thing?" Kelly called over to the older crime scene tech.

"I thought you'd never ask. Get anything from our beleaguered drifter?"

"Nothing. Seems he stumbled upon her. He's not playing with a full deck."

"You don't say?" Charles spent thirty-plus years working scenes of departed souls and developed a palpable level of cynicism. Life took on new meaning when surrounded by the dead. "At least it doesn't look like dumb and dumber over there did too much damage to our scene." Charles eyed the two patrolman as he put white Tyvek booties over his sneakers.

Kelly retrieved a pair of his own from a small box in the back of the crime scene van. He leaned against the back bumper and slipped them on. Some scenes required more precautions, others less. This appeared to be one that would require less. The area inside the tape had already been contaminated by Russo and Lancaster's initial entry.

The rookie homicide detective had been on enough dead body scenes during his time on patrol to know they did nothing wrong. Every street cop's first instinct is to render aid to a victim. After it's determined life-saving measures are futile, the scene should be locked down. From Kelly's initial assessment, this appeared to be the case. Both patrolmen would give a detailed accounting of their actions upon first arriving at the body. One of Kelly's later responsibilities would be to fact check discrepancies, if any.

Kelly slipped on two pairs of latex gloves over each hand. After any contact with the body, or potential evidence, he'd remove the outer layer. It wasn't a perfect system, but if done right, greatly improved the likelihood for minimal transfer to the scene.

The two walked toward the barrier of "do not cross" tape. Kelly dipped under. He stopped just inside the scene. Jotting the time in his pad, he took a minute to take in the moment. Kelly allowed his senses to absorb his surroundings before stepping in deeper.

4

A dead body, regardless of the circumstances surrounding it, carries with it a uniquely powerful quality. Life is never more defined than in those liminal spaces where the living and the dead connect.

Kelly studied a rust-covered trencher. It likely hadn't been used in years. At the base of the construction vehicle's flat left front tire was an area of disturbed earth and gravel. In a shallow depression lay the form of a girl. Her right foot was outstretched. Guessing from Blevins's account for how he first located the girl, Kelly assumed this might've been the foot he'd seen when rummaging through the lot for copper.

"Let's get some overalls before we start in." Kelly knew Charles would do it without him needing to ask, but controlling a scene from beginning to end was a habit he couldn't turn off. Plus, every detective and tech had their own way of processing things. He'd worked with Charles enough in his short time in Homicide to know they took on a scene with a similar methodical approach.

The click of the Nikon sounded as Charles captured several photographs from the line. If the scene was extremely large, Kelly would request a drone overflight. From the initial observations that wouldn't be a necessary tool today. Kelly fanned out to the left, making a wide arc, skirting along the fence line toward the building's east side, each step taken with care, ensuring that no evidence was disturbed. Charles followed his lead, stopping to snap a photo every ten steps. Kelly took a couple photographs as well with his personal camera. He knew Charles would send him the photo file later, but Detective Michael Kelly liked having immediate access. It wasn't so much a matter of impatience, more of obsession.

Kelly stopped near a dumpster by the side exit door of the building. A trickle of water from the building's sump pump spewed out from the structure. The stream saturated the ground, turning dirt to mud. The slurry around green metal bins captured several fresh footprints.

"Let's get these. Not sure we're going to need to cast them, though." Kelly knelt, hovering above the markings. He laid his tape measure down. A click from the senior tech's Nikon. "Buddy."

"Huh?"

"Our tipster. These are his prints. See the smoothed-out soles and different sizing?" Kelly stood up and looked over toward the body. "Can you get a shot from here and direct it toward our Jane Doe?"

"Sure can. What're you thinking?"

Raymond Charles always liked to test the new detectives. Kelly was well aware the crime scene evidence expert already knew the correct answer. "I think this is the spot where our good Samaritan first saw our vic."

Charles nodded his approval and snapped the picture.

"Ready to close in?" Kelly asked.

"You lead; I follow."

Kelly made his slow and deliberate procession toward the body, careful not to step in Blevins's tracks. About ten feet from the body they noticed several other footprints around the area of disturbed earth. The deep grooved treads were most likely those of Russo and Lancaster.

The girl's right leg was the first feature Kelly could clearly discern. She wore a low-heeled shoe with black straps. Her exposed ankle was pale white and had a blueish tinge. As he stood a few feet from the makeshift grave, her sequined dress sparkled in weak morning light like a shattered disco ball.

The girl was face down, in a prone position, with hands down by her side. Her light brown hair was a tangled mess of dirt and rock. On his initial pass, Kelly didn't see any apparent injuries. No bullet holes or stab wounds.

Moving carefully, Kelly positioned himself up near the girl's head. He squatted low and reached out with his gloved hand. He worked his fingers along her neck and pressed his index and middle fingers along the girl's carotid artery, following with a silent ten count.

"Thinking Tweedledee and Tweedledum might've missed that?" Charles snarked.

"Did you work the Anita Tandy scene a few years back?"

"No, but I heard it was a bloodbath."

"Something like that, yeah. I was on patrol at the time. My partner, Danny, and I caught the call, but another unit beat us in. When we arrived, the other guys told us the mother and child were dead. I decided to double-check, knowing the report would be in my name."

Charles lowered his camera, intently waiting for the punchline. Kelly was happy to see the interest in the veteran tech's eyes. Telling war stories to somebody with Raymond Charles's level of experience was a slippery slope.

"Two things I learned that day—don't trust, verify. And always check for a pulse."

"Those are two very good lessons."

"The two hotshots who jumped our call hadn't cleared the entire apartment. Had they done an effective protective sweep, they would've located the doer hiding in the bedroom closet. He was still holding the damn knife when Danny and I snatched him up."

"I would've been pretty pissed if I were photographing a scene and the perp popped out on me."

"That wasn't even the worst part. While Danny and I were walking the guy out through the living room, a hand grabbed my ankle. I'm not going to lie, I screamed like a little girl. Here was this woman, sprawled in a pool of blood, believed dead, clutching onto my leg for dear life."

Charles chuckled. Kelly stood up from the girl's body and exchanged the outer layers of his latex gloves. "So, life lesson for me. Now I always double-check the pulse."

A rumble of tires across the dirt driveway of Sheffield Electric's parking lot caught Kelly's attention. He saw the oversized white van with the Medical Examiner seal on the side panel. "Hey Russo, let 'em know I'll be over to meet with them in a bit," Kelly hollered.

The stocky officer gave a thumbs up and walked over to greet the arriving van.

"What do you make of this grave?" Charles asked.

Another test. "Looking at the shallow depth, I'm going to take a guess and say it wasn't a planned event. I mean, why would you leave a body partially exposed?"

"Good point. I like your thought process on that."

"Thanks." Kelly downplayed it but was secretly pleased at receiving the compliment. "I'm guessing either the perp got spooked or was in a state of panic."

Kelly scanned the rectangular area of fenced-in property.

"What're you looking for?"

"I don't think this hole was dug by hand." He saw a slight break in the fence line leading out toward a sparse bit of land abutting the T's tracks. A couple buildings filled in the skyline beyond.

Without saying a word, Kelly slowly walked toward the small gap in the chain link fence. Reaching his destination, he bent down to survey the triangulated entryway. The fence had a gash approximately three feet high. The metal fence had been clipped and peeled open. He scanned the jagged pieces where the fence had been cut. Looking at the rust and grime on the cut ends, he didn't assume it was made by the suspect. Then he caught the shimmer of a few sequins attached to a small bit of fabric. The material was at the base of the fence near the ground.

"Ray, I think we found which direction the girl came from. I'm also guessing she didn't get here under her own strength. There's a bit of her clothing at the bottom part of the fence. I'm thinking she was dragged here."

"Maybe. Or maybe she crawled through."

"Look at this." Kelly pointed to the dirt around the fence. There was a smooth line approximately a foot and a half wide. More telling were the divots staggered on either side of the line. "If this girl crawled, the pattern would be more snaked. She would have shifted her hips to move. The line is relatively straight. Those marks on the outside of the line are indicative of the person pulling and digging their heels in."

Without waiting for instruction, the crime scene tech began taking photographs. He took pictures from various angles and distances within the areas of interest. Kelly measured the heel print. Although it was not a complete shoeprint, it was different in size from the mismatched shoes of Blevins or the boots of Russo and Lancaster. This heel print was definitely smaller.

Kelly looked out through the fence. His eyes took in pieces of the landscape one small swath at a time. And then he saw it. A red handle protruding out between some clumps of patchy grass. Spring, by the calendar's timeline, was still over a week away, but this was Boston and sometimes the warmer weather didn't hit until June. Had it been a month or two later, Kelly might not have seen the handle due to overgrowth. Not the case on this cool Tuesday in March. Kelly pulled out his personal camera and snapped a couple photographs in the direction of the handle.

"Looks like our doer left something behind." Kelly walked with purpose toward the crime scene tape, leaving Charles behind to complete his photographs. Kelly slipped under and noted the time he left the scene. He did this every time he or anyone else entered or exited. He knew by protocol Russo and Lancaster were tasked with keeping a running crime scene log, but Kelly believed redundancy was essential.

Kelly walked over to Sergeant Paul Massie's SUV. This time Massie didn't exit into the cold. He just rolled his window down instead. Kelly was bathed in the warm air pouring from the vents.

"Hey Paul, I forgot to ask. You didn't by chance happen to run a dog track?"

"I called for one, but the Staties and DEA were running some early morning drug raid in Mattapan and they were tied up assisting on that. Might be one available now if you still think it's worth it."

"Do that. Thanks."

Massie called in on a back channel and requested K9 support to the scene. Dispatch stated there was a unit available and the team would be en route. Kelly turned and began making his way back to the scene.

"Guess we're not getting out of here anytime soon?"

Kelly shot a glance over his shoulder. "Doesn't look that way."

* * *

Jane Doe had been face-down long enough that, when rolled, her skin carried the dimpled impressions of the gravel from her grave. Cold temperatures had slowed decomp, but Kelly had a window of time when the body could have been dumped. Sheffield Electric closed at 7 p.m. and the shop's foreman stated he'd stayed until 8 p.m. to finish up some purchase orders. The girl was buried between 8 p.m. on Monday and 4:17 a.m. today, the time when Blevins called it in to police. The foreman also admitted the surveillance cameras on the exterior of the building weren't working and hadn't been functional for quite a few months.

After rolling the body, Kelly confirmed no signs of bullet or knife wounds. There was a contusion on the back of the girl's skull and some blood in her matted hair. He'd have to get her on the table before he could determine cause of death.

Kelly bent to bag the girl's hands. If there had been a struggle, trace evidence could be contained under the fingernails. Before he did so, he grabbed a print card from his bag. Kelly took the girl's left hand, assuming by law of averages she had been a righty, and lifted a print from her left ring finger. He wanted to expedite the identification process. A print match was a long shot, but he figured breaking protocol might be worth the risk. The girl had no purse or identification. Hard to tell her age because of her condition, but Kelly guessed her to be a teenager. With the print lifted and then stowed, Kelly finished bagging the girl's hands and feet.

Sherryl Tinsley, an investigator with the Medical Examiner's office, wore khakis and a light blue parka with her title and name embroidered above the front left breast pocket. Her long black hair was pulled back into a tight ponytail. She had a serious look about her. Kelly had some experience with her from a month prior, working a previous case.

"Thanks for being patient with me on this." Kelly made a subtle apology for the hour-long delay she'd stood by while he did his initial scene assessment.

"I'd rather you take your time and get it right." Tinsley had a deep voice contradictory to her diminutive features.

"Sherryl, I know you guys are back-logged, but do you have any idea of when you'll be able to get her on the schedule?" Kelly had waited weeks for an autopsy in the past, but the process varied. He'd also been good about bringing a box of joe every time he made a visit. His hope was to keep in their good graces for times when he needed a favor.

"It's already on the schedule for tomorrow morning."

"Wow, that's fast."

"New management. They're pushing for a faster turnaround on any potential homicide. The office has pushed the overdose-related deaths to the back burner. We were getting killed on those lately. The rest of my team is working a multiple-fatality crash in the tunnel. Give me an assist on the lift?"

"No problem. Just me today on this one. I guess we're all running short this week."

Tinsley placed a large, clear plastic tarp beside the girl. All of the photographs and evidence around the body had been tagged, photographed, and removed. Charles was in the process of loading bags back into his van.

"I'll take the top and you grab her ankles." Tinsley squatted near the girl's head. She slid gloved hands under the front of her bare shoulders and looked up at Kelly, who took up a similar position by the feet. "On three."

They lifted the dead girl in unison. Her body was rigid, a combination of cold and the onset of rigor. The two experienced a bit of resistance. The sequined dress stuck to the cold ground as they hoisted her from her shallow grave. They moved the body to the tarp as gently as possible. The momentum used to extricate her from the hole caused the girl to roll over to her back.

Kelly had looked death in the face more times than he cared to admit, but it always gave him pause. The girl's ashen, rock-dimpled face had a twisted serenity when cast skyward. Her eyes were partially closed. The exposed parts were covered in clumps of dark brown dirt. Kelly didn't look away. In fact, the opposite occurred. He intensified his stare, etching every possible detail into his mind's case file. It was his job to speak for the dead. To do that effectively, he wouldn't shelter himself from any gruesomeness. To do so would be a disservice to the girl supine before him.

"Dog's here," Massie called from beyond the tape.

Tinsley set about her work, wrapping the girl's body into the tarp. She was careful to fold up the edges so no part got exposed during transport. The goal was to minimize the risk of contamination. Content with the packaging, she dusted herself off. Kelly and the death investigator hoisted the wrapped body onto a gurney.

The wheels squeaked loudly, and the metal frame jingled in a symphonic procession as Tinsley pushed the gurney toward the back of her van.

Kelly noted the time and followed Tinsley out beyond the tape's barrier.

* * *

"Davin Graver, how long has it been?" Kelly approached the man standing at the back end of a police cruiser. Even in the cool temps the door fan was running, circulating air for the four-legged tracker panting inside.

"Michael Kelly, Homicide detective. Never thought I'd see you in a button-down shirt. Always figured you for the street." Graver had a thick Georgia accent. A foreigner by Boston Police's norm, but Graver came to love the city during his years at Boston University and never left. His Southern charm and mannerisms were always treated as novelty when he responded to calls in the Southie. Kelly had worked with Graver for a few months after the death of Danny and prior to his transfer out of Patrol.

"I heard you took a K9 spot. Seriously, how long has it been?"

"I've had Biscuit going on four years now. It's been a spell, ain't it? How goes the fight?"

"Some days I'm up. Other days I eat the mat."

"Well, let's see if my partner and I can give you a win today. What d'ya got?"

"Dead girl was found early this morning in that ditch over there. Patrol called for K9 to run a track, but everybody was tied up. It works to my advantage anyway. I prefer to be on scene whenever a dog is used. Plus, I've got a good start point."

Graver opened the door and his four-legged partner leapt out and came to heel immediately. The German Shepherd sat unleashed next to Graver's right leg. The handler moved to the trunk, popped it, and brought out a water dish. Filling it, he stepped back, letting Biscuit lap it up. "It was a long morning for us. Multiple target DEA raid up in the North End. He'll be good to go in a second."

As if on cue, the dog stopped slurping and came back to a seated position next to his handler. Graver snapped a leash to the collar. "Ready whenever you are."

Kelly brought Graver and Biscuit to the taped perimeter at the edge of the fence line. He climbed a three-foot mound of dirt at the end of the parking lot and continued along the outer fence, rounding it until he came to the cut-open portion where he'd found a bit of the girl's dress. Graver and Biscuit followed close behind.

"This is the point of entry I believe our perp used to bring the vic inside the fenced area. There's a bit of clothing from the victim attached to that piece of fence right there. I wanted to leave it until your partner had a chance to catch the scent. I know it's been a few hours, but I'd like to see if we can pick something up."

Garver brought the dog close to the fence. "Seek, Biscuit. Seek."

The dark head of the shepherd dipped. The golden trail of fur along his snout ruffled as his nostrils flared and the tracker noisily drew in the scent from the bejeweled fabric. His head popped up and his ears perked into perfect triangulation. Looking up at his handler, he patiently awaited the next command.

"Find."

The dog began moving away from the fence. His head stayed low to the ground and bobbled back and forth from side to side. The limited K9 knowledge Kelly acquired came during the police academy over eleven years ago, but he remembered the instructor saying they moved back and forth because scent isn't cast off in a straight line, but in a cone shape. The dogs move along the bits and fragments they pick up, always seeking the strongest point of origin.

Kelly watched the dog move quickly through the patchy grass and uneven dirt mounds. The dog closed the distance toward the object of interest, the red handle becoming more visible as they approached. The dog moved to the shovel and sat, alerting Graver of his find. Kelly noted the time the item was located. He took a photo before moving on with the duo.

K9 Biscuit came to the T rails and paused. A gust of wind whipped across the open space, kicking up bits of dirt and debris.

"Did we lose it?" Kelly asked.

"Not sure. Let's give him a second. Biscuit's a good tracker, but at times I think he's got a bit of the ADHD."

A few moments passed where Biscuit meandered right to the track. Then, his ears perked again, and he redirected his attention back toward the rail. Biscuit gingerly navigated over the third rail and focused his attention on the opposite side's first rail, moving along to the right, occasionally dipping his nose on the metal. He came to a stop and sat.

Kelly approached, at first not seeing anything. Upon closer inspection, he noticed a dark spot on the outer edge of the rail. The rust on the steel camouflaged the mark. Kelly took a picture. He then photographed back in the direction of the fenced area, then in the opposite direction, out toward the buildings.

Kelly pulled out his phone. "Ray, we've got two more things to tag for processing. A shovel and blood. Follow the cut in the fence out to me. We can pick up the shovel on the way back."

"I'll see if Biscuit still has the scent."

"I'm going to stand by until Ray gets over here."

Graver gave a slight tug of the leash and Biscuit began his search in the next open field between the T tracks and a parking lot. Kelly watched as the dog stopped and redirected back in the direction of the railway. He then turned around again. Graver shouted over the wind, "He's lost it."

Kelly noted the time. And took a photo of the K9 team at their current position as Charles came huffing up.

"What did you find?"

"Some blood."

Charles withdrew a package. He opened it and removed a long, wood-stemmed swab. The end was moistened with purified water to assist in removing the sample. The tech bent down, groaning with a crack of his knees, and began vigorously rubbing the stained rail. The white cotton end became a dirty brown tinged with red. After extraction, the end was capped to preserve the contents and placed into an evidence bag. The tech repeated the process two more times.

Graver returned, with Biscuit proudly strutting by his side. Biscuit was a reward dog and had been playing ball in the field for the few minutes while the rail evidence got collected. The shovel, etched with the Sheffield Electric logo, was added to the evidence stacked in the back of the crime scene van.

Massie and his two patrolmen were still on scene holding the area's status quo.

"Your relief never came?" Kelly asked of the sergeant who now stood outside the warmth of his Explorer.

"Canceled 'em. The boys and I figured we'd make some easy overtime."

"Well, I think I'm wrapping things up on my end. Charles is going to take some overall pictures of the scene, documenting how we left it, and then I think we're good to go."

Kelly looked down at his watch. It was already close to noon. No way he'd be able to pick up Embry from school. Someday she'd understand, but he was certain it wouldn't be today.

5

"Smells good, *Matka*." Aleksander Rakowski walked into the back room of the Polina Deli.

"Aleksander, what did I say to you about smoking in our restaurant?" Nadia Rakowski swatted her youngest son in the back of his head. It was not as painful as the slaps she gave in anger. This swat was done with a more loving nature.

"In Poland people smoke in restaurants!"

"We're not in Poland anymore. And my customers complain." She pointed out from the kitchen.

Aleksander knew better than to continue this argument. He was tough, but his mother was tougher. He smashed the embers into a metal ashtray on the small circular table in the center of the room, then dipped his head into the steamy vapors escaping from the large pots. Memories of his childhood released with bubbles and pops from the fragrance of the red broth.

"You're home early. I thought you'd be sleeping in today," Nadia said.

"Things got a little crazy at work last night. Long night."

"I know. I heard."

Aleksander sighed. "So, what'd you hear?"

"This is not the time. I'm busy. Must make soup for the hungry customers. We can figure out your problem later."

Nadia Rakowski danced through the small kitchen, tending to the several dishes she prepared simultaneously. Aleksander leaned back in his chair and peered out through the gap in the privacy sheet separating the main space of the deli from the family area. There were only three people scattered between the tables, two who had probably been sitting there since the shop opened.

Aleksander remembered when his family had first come to America. He was fourteen. It had been a difficult adjustment. Learning English late in life proved to be a challenge. It was tough on his older brothers, but they were too old for school, so they didn't have to face the daily ridicule of classmates. Not much of a chance to make friends anyway. His mornings were spent prepping the shop and he returned as soon as school was done, working until close.

He never earned a dime. His mother told him there would be time for money. This was a family business and his payment came in good meals and a roof over his head. *Matka* was quick to remind him how things weren't that way for her growing up, and that he should be grateful.

Aleksander grabbed a bowl from the cabinet and served himself a hearty portion of potato soup. As was the case with all Nadia's recipes, its secrets had been handed down from generation to generation. He was told stories of how this soup saved them from famine when the family faced extreme poverty. Like the Irish, Polish families saw the sturdiness of the root vegetable and used it in a variety of ways.

Aleksander remembered when he first learned to make the soup. Those early lessons were always the most painful. His mother saw fit to use a sturdy wooden spoon for corrective punishment. It didn't take many whacks across the back of his hand for him to learn the importance of being vigilant with his care of the roux. A delicate balance of heat and movement kept up the combination of butter, flour, salt, pepper, and the slow addition of cream. He'd made the mistake of walking away from the pot during those critical few minutes, a blunder he made only once. The spoon of justice had been swift and incredibly painful. That day the lesson was simple, but one he never forgot. The roux is the foundation, and without it nothing can be added to fix it when done wrong. He'd applied the same philosophy to life and worked hard to build himself up slowly over time. Even though his current position was less than desirable, Aleksander knew his foundation was strong and would eventually pay dividends.

He gently blew over his spoon before putting it in his mouth. He savored the warmth and familiarity. Everything made in the kitchen was done by sight or smell, no measuring cups. His mother returned and gave him a smile. Even at thirty, Aleksander loved to receive her praise. If he was to be one hundred percent honest, he sought it above all else.

"Maybe it's time you get back to work and sort out the issue. You can't make things right while you sit here getting fat," his mother chided.

The glimmer of kindness was gone. In its place were the stern eyes of a driven woman, haggard and a bit weathered by life, but driven nonetheless. She'd been a real looker back in the day, not that Aleksander cared to admit it. Regardless, it was true. Life had taken its toll. Her once shapely figure had been replaced by a thicker, boxier version. The years of slaving in the kitchen had given her forearms muscles on top of muscles. At sixty-two, Nadia Rakowski could give construction workers half her age a run for their money in an arm-wrestling match.

Aleksander realized his mother's words were on a timer, and any delay in responding accordingly would most likely result in a swat from her dishrag. He tilted the bowl and let hot soup drain down the back of his throat, then placed it in the sink and gave it a quick rinse. His older brothers never had to clean up for themselves, but Aleksander wasn't afforded such luxuries. Unlike some families where the youngest was babied and doted on, he was treated harshly, referred to as the runt of the litter.

At six foot three, Aleksander towered over his mother. He leaned down low and gave her a peck on the cheek as she diligently stirred the soup, keeping it from thickening up. He stepped out of the kitchen and onto Dorchester Avenue. His dark-colored Audi A8 sat parked in front. Its tints were illegal, but he'd pay any ticket for the protection it provided. Most of the cops in his area knew Aleksander well enough to give him safe passage.

As was his normal routine, Aleksander walked the exterior of his vehicle and checked for any scratches or dents that may have occurred during the past ten minutes while he was inside. His car, named Priscilla after Elvis's ex-wife, meant more to him than anything, and he treated it accordingly.

Satisfied the vehicle had remained in mint condition while he was away, Aleksander got behind the wheel. For as much as he babied the car, he drove it like a madman. He accelerated out into the narrow streets and headed back to work.

* * *

Veronica paced back and forth inside the living room. His text said *we need to talk*. Knowing the man who sent it, the message could be interpreted in a multitude of ways. Her fingers played with the handle of the switchblade in her pocket. She hoped it wouldn't be needed, because regardless of the outcome, using it would mean a death sentence.

A rev of an engine followed by the chirp of a car alarm told her he was here. She tried to settle her mind. Six long years she'd been working her way up the ladder. Only a select few had ever made the steep climb and held her seat in the organization. Veronica Ainsley intended to keep that seat. Her name had long ago been abandoned when she'd been recruited. To those around her she was known as Slice. Not because of the blade she carried. Although, for the amount of times she'd put it to use, the moniker would've been appropriate. No, it was because she was told by her first handler that she was as nice as a slice of pie. She preferred the reference to the knife, blocking out those hard years of servitude.

The back door opened. An alarm tripped and the man disabled it by entering the code within the allotted time. The alarm wasn't designed to stop people from coming in so much as it was to stop people from leaving. Slice was the only resident who knew the security system's disable code.

"Slice, come in here and have a seat."

Aleksander Rakowski's voice was calm. It was a trait she'd come to deplore. There was no way of telling his mood. It was a maddening guessing game trying to discern his approval or disapproval.

She moved into the kitchen, where the tall man poured himself a large glass of milk. Slice dropped into a seat facing him. His back remained to her. She thought he might be testing her to see if she'd be willing to stick the knife in his back.

The man she'd once thought she loved placed the glass down on the counter with a clink and turned to face her. She was wearing a green tank top he'd told her brought out her eyes. It was his favorite color on her. Slice's mocha-toned shoulders were exposed. There was a time when the man standing before her used to take notice of such things. She thought at least if nothing else, the sight of them now would soften whatever blows might befall her.

"You made a mistake. One I was forced to clean up. I don't like to have to do those things. You know this, yes?"

The calm of his words unbalanced her. "It wasn't my fault. If your security had been monitoring the door instead of playing with the girls, this never would've happened."

"I don't want your excuses." Aleksander leaned forward. His large frame made the table look as though he were sitting at a child's tea party. "I will personally make sure security does not make another mistake. But your job is the girls. Do your job!"

"I tried to make it right. You've got to believe me." Slice's voice trembled. She refused to allow herself to cry, though her tears had long ago dried up.

"I want you to promise it will never happen again."

"I promise."

"You promise what?" he asked patronizingly.

"I promise I will never take my eyes off the girls again."

"Now it's time to fix your mistake. What do you do if your car is totaled?"

Slice found the question funny because she'd never owned a car. On a few occasions she'd been able to drive his, but it was under very strict conditions. "I guess you'd get a new one?"

"Smart girl. So that's what you're going to do. Do you understand?"

Slice nodded. She released her grip on the knife in her pocket and rubbed her moist palm against her pants.

"Is she ready?" he asked.

"She will be."

Aleksander Rakowski stood. He loomed over Slice and then leaned in and kissed her forehead. She could feel his warm breath and the years of servitude flooded her mind. The things she'd done for this man. "If she's not," he said casually, "then you can always fill her spot."

Without another word, he turned and left. She reset the alarm after the door closed behind him. Alex had given her a way of making things right again. Slice went to the stairwell.

The solution to her problem was on the second floor, sleeping in a locked room. Maybe if she did this thing, Alex would see her as he once had. Doubtful. But maybe. And the unbalanced hope canceled out reason.

* * *

The room was dark. The packed snow from the long winter never got cleared from the dilapidated rooftop. As the temperatures rose the heavy slush began making its way into the crevices, seeping into the building's interior. A leak dripped from several locations along the poorly maintained ceiling. To the man in the chair it was an unnerving sound. Another man stood nearby, behind the chair, but did not speak. It was frustrating since the two had known each other since childhood. But he knew the reason for the silent treatment. He knew what was coming. Radek Balicki knew because he was usually the man standing behind the chair. An unsettling turn of events.

He adjusted himself in the metal chair. The plastic drop cloth underneath bunched slightly around the legs and made a crackling sound. The restraints on his wrists and ankles were tightly ratcheted and left no wiggle room, not that Balicki had any delusions of freeing himself and fighting his way out. This was not the movies. No amount of theatrical kung fu would save him from his fate.

Balicki vowed to not grovel. He swore if his time ever came, he would face it unflinchingly. Today would be the ultimate test of his resolve. At least they didn't blindfold him.

The moment the girl disappeared from the hotel he knew it would not end well for him. Balicki had seen the determination of his employers in the past and was fully aware he'd be given no favoritism.

The building's location placed it at the southernmost point of Dorchester, north of Milton, where the Neponset River divided the city from its suburban neighbor. The area was a mix of industrial and residential, but on the corner of Medway Street the building owned by the Rakowski family was out of earshot of any residents. Balicki knew this because he'd inflicted pain within these walls many times before. Of course, the building had been purchased under a false name, unrelated to the family. No traces to them existed on paper except for the Polina Deli.

The boarded-up window and graffitied exterior were an eyesore to residents but also served to keep away nosy people. It looked as though you could get hepatitis by simply stepping onto the property.

A loud rapping at the door. The man standing behind Balicki crossed the poured concrete floor. Heavy deadbolts set at the top and bottom of the reinforced steel door thudded their release. A loud creak of the hinges gave way to a flood of gray mid-morning light, quickly lost as the tall Rakowski filled the void.

Balicki swallowed hard. As much as he thought he had prepared for this moment, being faced with its reality was devastating. His heart raced and he forced himself to slow his rapidly increasing breaths.

The door closed and the locks clicked back in place. Alex Rakowski approached.

"Radek, it's a very sad day for me. I never in my life thought we'd be having this conversation."

Balicki didn't speak. He was terrified any utterance would undo his barely contained composure.

"I've given a lot of thought to this." Rakowski flicked his eyes in the direction of the man standing silently behind Balicki.

A loud clang and a cart's wheels, squeaky and in desperate need of oil, rolled into view. The same mobile tray of pain he'd wheeled out several times before. The tools were always the same—pliers, hammers, a mini sledge, a few knives, and some pruning shears. An involuntary shudder ran down Balicki's spine. He prayed for a quick end, but from the looks of it, that would not be the case.

"You've assisted me in many such instances in the past." Rakowski picked up one of the knives from the tray and eyed the blade's edge. "What do you suggest I do?"

"It was a mistake. I will never fail you again." Balicki quivered as he spoke.

"I know." Rakowski put the knife down.

"Alex, we've known each other for over ten years. I've always been good to you. I've always been loyal to your family."

Rakowski held up a gloved finger to his lips. "I know. That's why I've found a solution that keeps everything in balance. I don't want to kill you, but I must make an example."

Balicki was no more relieved to hear Rakowski wasn't planning on killing him. Life after being in this chair was sometimes worse. "What solution?"

"I must take something from you, something others will see and be reminded of your failure." Rakowski gave a pensive scan of Balicki's body. "You like to touch my girls?"

"Alex, please. It was a mistake. I—"

"Enough! You like to touch my girls, yes?"

Balicki nodded, his heartbeat now drumming loudly in his ears. His breathing came in ragged bursts. He was no longer able to control his reaction to the stress of the moment.

"You're right-handed, yes?"

"Please."

"I'll take that as a yes. My gift to you is I will take your left." Rakowski stepped back and the large man moved into view, picking up the pruning shears. The enforcer stood at the ready and patiently waited for the final command.

Balicki wriggled against the restraints. And then, giving up, closed his eyes.

"One more thing. Since you're going to be somewhat limited in your services to me, I'm going to need an able-bodied replacement. I was thinking your brother could help."

Balicki's eyes shot open and anger momentarily overrode fear. "Jakub's only sixteen!"

"That's two years older than when I started."

"I don't want him in this life! I promised my mother I'd keep him away from it."

"Then you shouldn't have failed me." Rakowski leaned in close to Balicki's face. "Either your mother loses a son today or I gain an employee. But one thing is certain, you will not question my decisions ever again. Understood?"

Rakowski backed away and Balicki conceded, dropping his chin to his chest in defeat. He heard his employer shuffle away to the door. The latches released, the door opened and closed, sealing Balicki to his punishment.

He closed his eyes tightly and grit his teeth. Every ounce of energy fought his urge to scream. The large man was close by. He could feel it. The metal on metal scrape of the shears opening caused his body to shake.

6

"I made you a birthday present and wanted to give it to you." Embry Kelly's voice pleaded over the phone.

"I'm sorry, baby. I've got a very important thing I'm working on," Kelly replied.

"What's more important than me?"

"Nothing. But something really bad happened to somebody and I have to help. I'd much rather be with you."

Embry sobbed quietly. The pain in her failed expectation of delivering whatever "Embry Original" craft was ever-present. In the world of an eight-year-old, the disappointment was equivalent to finding out her best friend moved away, or her pet fish died. There was no balance in the equation. As an adult, Kelly knew this. As a recently divorced parent, his ex-wife knew it as well, and used it as leveraged guilt.

"Hey Squiggles, I'm going to make it up to you. Daddy-Daughter Date Night this week. I promise."

"Restaurant?"

"Of course, how could we do an official date without our restaurant?"

"Movie and popcorn?"

"You drive a hard bargain. Fair enough. We'll do the works."

Embry sniffled loudly. The consolation prize seemed to ebb her tears.

Kelly heard the muffled scratching as the phone got handed off. Samantha hissed, "Michael Kelly, don't you dare make her another promise if you don't plan on being able to keep it."

"Like the one you made to me when I put that ring on your finger?" Kelly regretted the words as soon as they escaped his mouth.

"Not tonight. I'm in no mood."

"Sorry. It just slipped out."

"Don't forget about her spring performance. Embry's been practicing every waking minute. Thursday at one o'clock. If you're not there, so help you God." She hung up.

Kelly sat back. Nothing was more draining than his adaptation to his new life. His support network had collapsed at a time when he couldn't be lower. Ever since, he'd been rebuilding it brick by brick. Sadly, besides Embry, the foundation was built on his ever-increasing case load.

He looked at the board. The red card: Doe, Jane 3/12/2019. Before things went further, he needed the girl's real name.

Kelly spun around in his chair. Sergeant Sutherland stood in the cubicle entrance, startling him. "Holy crap, Sarge. Are you sure you weren't a ninja in your previous life?"

"I'll never tell." Sutherland did his best attempt at Crane Technique. His bulk and bum knee made for a piss-poor rendition. Mister Miyagi would've been very disappointed. "Any updates on our girl? I'm heading to the sitrep meeting and I'd like to go in with something."

Kelly was used to his boss's need for continual updates. Homicide never knew which body was going to turn the department into a media circus, so the upper echelon did their best to stay informed.

"I'm about to head down and touch base with Charles to see if anything's popped up with the girl's print."

"You know they make this thing called a telephone?"

"I prefer to do things like this in person. Besides, I figure the more face time I get, the easier it'll be for me when I need some extra help."

"Fair enough. So, what do you have so far?"

"Teenager. Age still to be determined. She's got some blunt force trauma to the back of her head. I've got the autopsy tomorrow morning and should have a lot more in the way of cause of death. We've got a potentially good start.

Witness who found her is a homeless guy whose body is comprised of more alcohol than blood. But, at least I have an eight-hour window of when her body was dropped. It looks like the vic was injured on the tracks and her body was dragged to the back lot of Sheffield Electric. No suspect as of yet."

"Keep me in the loop on anything you find. I fear if the media gets wind of a dead teenage girl, we're going to be inundated with calls and FOIA requests."

"Will do."

Sutherland began his trek back to his office. Kelly left the cubicle and headed toward the elevators, taking his notepad with him.

* * *

Boston PD's Forensic Laboratory was located on the lower level of headquarters, a design plan to make case collaboration between investigators and the lab more accessible. The forensic analysts were not as pleased with this arrangement as the detectives. A group of people who prided themselves for performing hours upon hours of uninterrupted work were not accustomed to the unannounced arrival of guests, even if those guests were working toward the same end.

Kelly passed through the main doors of the lab and approached Karen Deschanel at the receptionist desk. She was the gatekeeper, a woman who wielded tremendous power, and it had been rumored she once turned away the mayor. Deschanel never confirmed or denied the truth of that claim.

"Good afternoon, Michael. I see you didn't bring a box of joe today?"

"Sorry, Karen, been one of those days."

"I heard. Young too. Never good to have a murder in the city. Even worse when it's a kid."

Kelly was always impressed with how Deschanel was able to keep track of the cases that came through the lab. For someone who'd never stepped foot in the field, she had the salt of the most seasoned detective. "Ugly stuff. Is Ray in?"

Deschanel chewed at the end of her pen. The dimpled end danced across her lips, coating it in the bright pink of her lipstick. "I believe so. Let me see if Mr. Crotchety is available."

Kelly had witnessed the two go back and forth in a live version of *The*

Honeymooners. They were openly rude to each other, but Kelly got the feeling the two actually liked one another.

She spoke into her phone. "You available? Or are you too busy taking one of your six hundred smoke breaks?"

Kelly couldn't hear the senior crime scene tech's response but could only assume it was equally gruff.

"It's Kelly. Here about the body from this morning."

Deschanel hung up the receiver. "All set, dear. You know where he's hiding."

A soft buzzer sounded, indicating the next set of doors were now open. Karen Deschanel, gatekeeper, had granted him access. Kelly strode down the long hallway. A strong antiseptic odor assaulted his nostrils. He stopped at the closed door with a frosted window embossed with the words: Raymond Charles, BPD Senior Crime Scene Technician. Kelly knocked.

"Come in," Charles called.

Kelly entered. The room was a small office. The walls were lined with built-in shelves filled with voluminous editions of medical books and journals, some Charles had penned himself. One of the technician's books was required reading at the basic academy. The wall behind his desk was filled with various degrees conferred over the years. Charles had printed a picture of a window's view, looking out onto a lake on a summer's day. Being in the basement, it was the man's attempt at creating a sense of normalcy. Kelly wondered how many times the tech had stared out this imaginary view.

"I've just finished processing the shovel. Maybe we'll get lucky and the digger didn't use gloves. That rough handle could be a treasure trove of DNA if that's the case."

"I know you printed the girl on scene. Any return on those yet?"

"I guessed her age to be between twelve and fifteen. So I hadn't much hope she would be in the system."

"And?"

"She was. Somebody did the child ID kit for her when she was nine. Probably at some school safety event. Regardless, she's in the database. Not sure how good the address information is, but our Jane Doe is Faith Wilson. Age thirteen."

Charles handed Kelly the printed file. Faith Wilson was listed as missing out of North Andover one year ago.

"I hate this part," Kelly mumbled. He stared at the photo from the missing person flyer. Faith Wilson's broad smile and dimpled cheeks showed a girl full of life.

"What's that?"

"Notifications."

"Never easy. I'll keep you posted if I get anything back from the DNA analysis."

"I know your investigative load is stacked, but can we give this case top billing and put it at the top of your priority list?"

"Already did."

"Thanks."

Kelly left the office and returned the same way he'd just come.

"That was fast," Deschanel said.

"Just the tip of the iceberg."

"Good luck with this one."

Kelly gave a faint smile. "Next time I'll bring the joe."

He departed the lab space and headed back toward the elevator. Kelly prepared himself for his next stop. North Andover wasn't a far drive from Boston, but for a thirteen-year-old girl it was a world away.

Michael Kelly needed to go back to the beginning in the hope of finding the path to Faith's end.

7

The mid-afternoon commute from the city to North Andover should have been quicker than the nearly two hours it ended up taking. But, as all good New Englanders know, road repair during the spring thaw is an arduous and never-ending battle. Entire political careers were built on the transportation nightmare.

Crossing into the suburban town was entering into another world for Kelly. The endless sea of concrete and cramped houses was replaced by open space filled with trees awaiting the first real kiss of spring. Each house he passed seemed bigger than the one preceding it. They each had something none of the lots in his hometown had—a yard with grass. The streets had wide lanes and the curbs weren't lined with cars. Most homes had detached garages. He'd been to suburban towns before, but each time took him a moment of adjustment.

North Andover was a far cry from the neighborhood of his childhood. He loved where he came from, but part of him always wanted to give his daughter something better. Maybe a town like this would give her more opportunities. Maybe not. That theory hadn't proven true for Faith Wilson.

On his drive in, he passed an elementary school. A group of children were outside enjoying a break from the freezing temperatures. There were pockets of kids chasing each other around an open field. *How did a girl growing up in these surroundings end up dead in a ditch in Boston?* As a cop it was disturbing. As a father to a young daughter, it was a nightmarish thought.

The Impala's heater sputtered out inconsistent bursts of heat, giving teases of comfort followed by blasts of cold air. Whatever malady the vehicle was suffering, it was no doubt terminal.

He'd called ahead and spoken to a Detective Vincent Chalmers, who agreed to make himself available when Kelly arrived. Kelly told him he was there to look into a missing persons case from a year ago and that the body of the girl had turned up. Chalmers sounded interested, almost giddy, at the prospect of assisting on such a case. Kelly understood this was an uncommon occurrence for the affluent Essex County town. A department about only one percent the size of Boston's meant a limited exposure to certain crimes, typically violent ones.

North Andover had seen five murders in the last fifteen years. Boston accumulated ten times that number in any given year. Not that the city's body count made him a better cop, it just made him more experienced. There was a distinction, though few understood it. And, because of this, Kelly didn't dismiss the smaller department as beneath him. In fact, there were times he envied the idea of shouldering a lighter case load. Still, Boston was his home and he knew the only way he'd be leaving it was in a casket.

Kelly parked in front of the red-brick building. It was small in comparison to BPD's main headquarters, but similar in size to his C-11 District HQ, where Kelly had cut his teeth as a rookie cop, patrolling the same Dorchester streets where he'd grown up. Over the years some of his childhood friends had gone on to make poor life decisions as adults, choices that forced Kelly into the uncomfortable situation of making the arrest. Some understood he was just doing his job. Others held a perpetual grudge, another reason policing in a suburban outlier held appeal.

He exited the busted Chevy and noticed the outside temperature was remarkably consistent with the poorly maintained climate of his unmarked. He shook off the chill of the day in the main lobby. Winter through spring, the lobbies of his city's district headquarters were filled with homeless trying to stave off the cold. It was a pleasant surprise to stand in the foyer of the North Andover building and not be overwhelmed by the smell of urine and body odor. It smelled of lilac. *Hell, maybe he'd need to reconsider the idea of making a transfer*, Kelly thought to himself.

He approached the three-paned, bay-window-style encasement housing the main desk officer. The heavy, bullet-resistant glass was now standard in most police departments, especially in recent years, when cops became targets for unbalanced citizenry. The thickness made it near impossible to communicate through, a minor pittance for safety. There was a phone attached to the side panel with a handmade sign taped to it reading *Dial 700 for main desk.*

Kelly did as instructed and could hear a faint ring penetrate the glass.

"Can I help you?"

"Detective Kelly, Boston Homicide, here to see Detective Chalmers." Kelly exposed the shield from inside his coat.

"Just a minute." The clean-cut officer behind the glass picked up the desk phone and spoke briefly into it. "He'll be down in a moment."

Kelly meandered about the lobby. There was a display case with turn-of-the-century photographs of cops. These nostalgic pictures could be found in most departments in the northeast. The lineage of these men gave policing a sense of history. Kelly liked feeling connected to something bigger.

A secure door adjacent to the main desk area opened and a middle-aged man with a soft gut stood in the doorway. He was wearing a mauve button-up shirt and khaki pants. The man's badge was clipped to his waist in front of the pancake holster containing his duty weapon. He waved over at Kelly with a warm smile. "Detective Kelly? I'm Vinnie Chalmers. We spoke on the phone."

Kelly shook the detective's hand. The man's soft exterior hid his strength. Chalmers had a firm grip which Kelly tried unsuccessfully to match. "Michael Kelly. Thanks for making time to meet with me."

Chalmers ushered Kelly inside, and the two walked a short distance to the elevator. "So, you said this was about Faith Wilson's disappearance when we spoke on the phone."

"I did."

"I pulled the report and took the liberty of doing a little digging into the case. The detective who investigated it is now retired."

"That's a shame. I was hoping to have a chance to sit down with him and go over it."

"Not sure it would do you much good. To be honest, it wasn't handled efficiently. But again, I'm looking at this thing in hindsight knowing she's now dead. It looks like it was chalked up as a habitual runaway and left open. There were some leads, but no clear notations as to why they weren't pursued. There was another issue I found."

"What's that?"

"Well, after Al Jeffries, the detective that worked it, retired, it looks as though the case got lost in the shuffle. It should've been transferred to some-body else, but it wasn't. There's only a handful of us in the detective bureau here and normally any open cases, especially a missing person case, would be handed off."

"You don't have a digital case tracking system?"

"We do now. The department recently went all-in in revamping and updating the technology side of the house. The chief used some seizure money to bring us into the twenty-first century. But we only got the system up and running six months ago. Faith Wilson went missing over a year ago and it slipped into our closed case section, so her case never made it into the new system."

The elevator dinged. "Okay. I still may have to speak with Jeffries and get some clarification on things. Is he local?"

"I think he splits his time between here and Florida, but I'll make sure I get you his info before you leave."

They walked to the door marked Criminal Investigations and entered. The workspace contained five desks neatly lined along a windowed wall. On one end was a lieutenant's office, on the opposite side was the sergeant's. Both doors were closed, and the cubicles were empty. "Nobody working today?"

"Just me. Everybody else is at a fundraiser luncheon at town hall. Between us, I'm glad I drew the short straw. I hate those things. Rubbing elbows and kissing ass is just not my thing."

"Same here." Kelly liked Chalmers. "All right, so let's see what we've got so far. Maybe those leads you mentioned can still be followed up on."

Chalmers walked to his cubicle, set in the middle. Everything was tidy and filed away. The only thing out on his desk was a manila file folder. The label on the upper lip had a case number followed by "Faith Wilson." Inside was an 8x10 glossy photograph of Faith Wilson at age twelve. It looked to be a school photo, taken at the start of her seventh-grade year. She had on a light blue summer dress, complementing the girl's eyes. The image before him bore no resemblance to the damaged creature he'd extricated from the hole earlier that morning. Kelly turned the picture over and quickly thumbed through the pages of the report. The initial investigation was documented by patrol. It detailed the last known sighting, lists of possible friends, description of clothing, etc.—the standard compilation of information for a missing report. Nothing out of the norm, and the wording conveyed the probability the girl had run away. Hindsight is 20/20.

Kelly came across the supplemental reports documented by Detective Jeffries. Chalmers was right. The case seemed to point to a possible connection with a teenager, Clive Branson, but it wasn't followed up on. Or, if it had been, there was no documentation. The case was left open, but the last notation stated no further leads and recommended suspending it until new information was presented. *Odd*, thought Kelly.

"I see what you mean about Jeffries dropping the ball on this one. Looks like he closed it to new information but failed to follow up on the lead he had. Definitely something I'm going to need to speak with him about."

"Sure. No problem."

Kelly flipped the folder closed. "Mind if I take this?"

"It's yours to take. That's a copy. I photocopied everything I could find from the original case jacket."

"Thanks. Did you make the notification to Faith's father yet?"

"Not yet. I wanted to speak to you first and get the details so that I could relay them to the patrol. We typically have our uniformed officers make notifications. Chief thinks it looks better for our citizens to see the shiny badge and uniform when we're delivering the bad news."

"I don't think this one should be done by uniformed patrol."

"Makes sense."

"In fact, if you don't mind, I'd prefer to go myself and be the bearer of bad news."

"You sure? Patrol does this all the time for fatal car crashes and the like. I'd hate to put you out."

"This is a lot different from a car accident. This little girl was murdered. I think it's best if it comes from me. Her father's going to have a lot of questions. I know I would."

"The address in the file looks to be current. I double-checked it through DMV records. I can go with you if you'd like."

Kelly could tell Chalmers made the offer with the hopes of being refuted. It was better he go alone anyway. "It's fine. I don't mind. Plus, no need to tie up the only working detective in North Andover." Kelly watched the relief in the man's eyes.

"You're a life-saver. I didn't want to have to tell my wife I'd be late tonight. It's our ten-year anniversary today and I promised her a long-overdue date night."

"Well, happy anniversary. It looks like you can keep that promise."

"Don't hesitate to reach out if you need anything on our end." Chalmers pulled a business card from his wallet and scribbled something on the back of it. "I put Jeffries's number here. Hopefully, he can fill you in on the gaps in the investigation. Go easy on the guy, his wife just left him, and from what I last heard, he's in a pretty rough spot."

"Him and me both. Thanks again for the assist on this."

Chalmers escorted Kelly back out to the lobby. The fragrant smell greeted him once more.

Kelly entered his car and took a sip of his now tepid cup of coffee. Hot was better, but he settled for caffeine in any form. When he and Danny were on patrol together, they had a simple goal each shift—get a cup of coffee. In the Dot, working the Eleven, the call volume was non-stop. They'd finished many a shift without accomplishing the goal. On other occasions, they'd manage to get a cup, but it grew cold by the time they were able to drink it. Kelly measured the pace of the day by the temperature of his coffee.

He punched in the destination of the next address into his phone. Only fifteen minutes away. Kelly used the time to prepare for the difficult task of telling a parent his child was dead. He'd done it too many times in his eleven years to keep an accurate count. No amount of repetition made it any easier.

Explaining death was never easy, and Faith Wilson's would be anything but, compounded by the fact that, as of right now, Kelly had more questions than answers.

* * *

The ride to Faith Wilson's home was a scenic one, bending along Great Pond Road. The lack of foliage in the early phases of spring's transition from winter left the trees relatively bare, giving Kelly a clear view of the water. Had the journey not come under such circumstances, it might have been enjoyable.

No two people reacted the same to learning of a loved one's passing. Kelly had seen people collapse to the ground. Some remained silent. One woman actually slapped him across the face. He remembered the painful sting of the blow and how his field training officer had laughed when they'd returned to the cruiser, saying he'd never seen that before. Kelly hoped today's encounter was less eventful.

He sat in the car and let his Impala wheeze and whine while he read over the missing person case file one more time. Kelly wanted to get the facts straight before speaking with Faith's father. The parking lot to the condo was nearly empty; most of the residents hadn't returned from work. He'd much rather speak with Faith's father in the privacy of his home rather than seeking him out at his place of business.

The Wilson condo was the end unit on the right. Kelly noted a bedroom window that opened up to a flat landing extending approximately four feet. A large, twisted branch from a nearby maple tree was close enough to grab if standing on the ledge. A perfect egress for a sneaky teen. *Had Faith used this window to exit her world into the one that cost her life?*

No security cameras. At least none visible on the exterior of the houses. The report noted a canvass of all the neighbors. Nobody reported seeing anything out of the ordinary on the day of her disappearance. One of the neighbors reported seeing her get on the school bus in the morning. Nobody saw her get off the bus in the afternoon. That didn't mean she didn't come home. It just meant nobody saw. The school said Faith rode the bus home and this was verified by the bus driver. There was no sign of forced entry. No theory of an abduction. It got listed as a probable runaway. His attention again turned to the window with the tree branch. *Why would she run from here?*

Kelly made the short walk to the condo's front door. The welcome mat on the stoop looked less than welcoming. It was covered with dirt and old leaves in various states of decomposition, obvious that Mr. Wilson hadn't done much upkeep before winter's arrival. The file had said he was a single father, but didn't go into much detail beyond that.

Kelly rang the doorbell twice. He heard a faint chime from within. Kelly listened. No barking dog. No sounds of movement. The blinds were drawn. Kelly was disappointed. He preferred to get this bit of nastiness over with fast, like ripping off a Band-Aid. Kelly opened the storm door. It creaked loudly. It seemed as though much of the Wilson house was in varying states of disrepair. Kelly banged loudly with his balled fist. The heel of his closed hand struck the white wood of the door three times.

He waited. Nothing. Kelly looked at the file for the work address and then at his watch. It was just past 4 p.m. If Gary Wilson was at work, Kelly would most likely miss him if he left now. Turning to leave, he heard a cough on the other side of the door. And then the deadbolt released with a thud.

The door opened. A man wearing a worn-out blue sweatshirt and stained jeans stood in the threshold. The top of his head was mostly barren, with only a few wisps of greasy black strands. One of the strands was flopped forward and hung over the man's left eye. He didn't seem to notice or care about the obstruction. "Whatever you're sellin', I don't want it."

Kelly squared himself to the man. "Mr. Wilson?"

"Who wants to know?" His voice crackled and he cleared his throat. He hocked loudly before spitting a loogie past Kelly. Milky phlegm landed on the W of the welcome mat, making it even more disgusting and less inviting.

Kelly slid his badge into view. "Mr. Wilson, I'm Detective Kelly with Boston PD."

"What's Boston PD want with me? Aren't you a little out of your jurisdiction?"

"I'm with Homicide." Kelly let the words sink in. He could smell from Wilson's emanations the man was on the downside of a six-pack.

Gary Wilson staggered back a foot. Kelly wasn't sure if it was the booze or the impact of understanding. Either way, Kelly seized the opportunity and closed the gap, placing his left foot on the lip of the door frame to prevent Wilson from slamming it closed.

"No! Not my baby!" Wilson sat back, landing hard on the steps. He folded his head inside his knees and began to rock.

Kelly stepped inside and closed the door behind him. The funk of the condo's interior left a sour taste in his mouth. Upon a quick scan of his immediate surroundings, he could see the interior was not in much better shape than the mat outside. Old newspapers and empty beer bottles decorated the floor. Kelly spied down the narrow hall to the kitchen and saw it too carried the same décor.

"When?" Wilson shot his head up. Tears streamed down his cheeks. The slight chub of his face was similar to that of his daughter. Kelly immediately saw the resemblance.

"She was found early this morning."

"Where? Boston?"

"Yes. In Dorchester. Mr. Wilson, would you be more comfortable in the living room or kitchen?"

Gary Wilson got up without speaking and walked to the kitchen. Kelly followed. A cigarette burned in an ashtray on the table. Wilson went to the fridge and pulled out a Miller Lite. He popped the top and sat facing Kelly. Wilson retrieved the cigarette and took a long drag.

Kelly looked at the chair nearest him and cleared off some crumbs before taking a seat.

"The maid's off this week," Wilson grumbled. His tears slowed with each sip of the beer.

"I'm terribly sorry for your loss. I can't imagine what you're going through. I'll do my best to give you what I know up to this point. Maybe you can help fill in some things as well."

"You're with Homicide? So, she was murdered?"

"As of right now we are still determining cause of death. I won't have an official confirmation until tomorrow when the autopsy is completed."

A flash of anger came across from the bereaved father. "That's not what I asked you. I asked you if my daughter was murdered."

"I'm treating it as such."

"How?"

"Like I said, we're still working on the how. From the looks of it she was struck in the back of her head. There was a visible injury on the back of her skull. As soon as I know for sure, I will tell you."

"Who did it?"

"Not sure. It's the early stages of the investigation."

"I'm hearing a lot of I-don't-knows and not-sures out of your mouth. I thought you city guys were better than this. You come here to tell me my daughter's dead and offer nothing else."

Kelly took the verbal blows in stride. He'd been through much worse. All in all, Mr. Wilson was handling the news of his daughter's death quite well. "I'm going to work your daughter's case until I have some answers for you."

"I heard that before. Detective Jeffries said something similar and look where that ended up."

Wilson got up, leaving the empty can on the table. He grabbed another and returned to his seat.

"So, what now?" Wilson sneered.

"Is there anything, looking back on Faith's disappearance, that you may not have thought important then that you do now?"

"I told Jeffries everything I knew. Faith was twelve. She kept to herself. Ever since her mother ran off two days before her eighth birthday. She had emotional issues. Faith ate her depression away. She suffered from low self-esteem. I probably didn't help, working at a grocery store. I brought home too many snacks. But, like I told Jeffries, she didn't have many friends. No boyfriends. None of that. So, as far as who could've taken her, I've got no idea."

"Did Faith ever mention a Clive Branson?"

Wilson took a long pull from his can and belched. He ashed out his cigarette and pulled another from the nearby pack, lighting it before answering. "No. Why?"

"Did Jeffries?"

"Like I said, the name doesn't ring a bell. Who's Clive Branson?"

"Not sure. But he was noted in the missing person case as a person of interest. Nothing further. I thought maybe he was a friend of your daughter. Maybe somebody I could talk to."

Kelly watched the man carefully. It was hard to gauge Wilson's reaction to this line of questioning. The alcohol and mental instability created by the news of his daughter's death made him a hard man to read.

"I see you looking around here. Judging me. You think I'm some drunk slob. No wonder my daughter ran away, right?"

"I'm not here to pass judgment."

"I wasn't always like this. Our house—life was better. I gave her—my Faith —a good, decent life. I was a manager at StarBrite Grocers when she disappeared. That little girl was my world. Ever since her mother left, it was her and me against the world. When she disappeared, I took a lot of time off from work looking for her. Too much. When I ran out of personal time, I called in sick. Eventually they threatened to fire me. My union rep got me a medical discharge, mental health stuff." Wilson tapped the near empty beer can against his head for added effect. "Pretty good compensation package too. By the looks of this place, you wouldn't know it, though."

"Would you mind if I take a look around your daughter's room?"

Gary Wilson sighed weakly. "Upstairs on the right."

Kelly could see the grieving father was not going to give him the guided tour. He climbed the stairs and nearly tripped over an empty bottle at the top of the landing, tucked by the banister. He rounded to the right and saw the unmistakable door of a pre-teen girl, "Faith" in brightly colored letter stickers surrounded by a rainbow.

Kelly turned the knob and the door swung inward. The room was bright pinks and purples. An obvious favorite of the girl. It was also clear Gary Wilson's depressive fall had not scathed the room's interior. The bed was made, and her dolls were neatly arranged on her bed and neighboring shelves. It was spotless. A moment frozen in time. In this room, Faith Wilson was still alive. Kelly moved inside.

His earlier conjecture had been right. The window with the tree escape ladder belonged to Faith. Kelly wandered to the window. He pushed up at the base of the sill. It resisted momentarily, then gave way. If nothing was touched since her disappearance, then she had most likely left through the window. Maybe she wasn't running away from something, but running to something. Or someone. *Who and why?* Those were the questions that needed answering.

"Find anything?"

Gary Wilson stood in the open doorway, his eyes downcast and his body rigid, as if he were physically incapable of entering the room, or even laying eyes upon it.

"You said she had no boyfriend?"

"She didn't."

"Then why'd she sneak out the window?"

"What do you mean?" Mr. Wilson looked up slowly.

"Window's unlocked. I'm assuming you didn't touch anything since she left.

So, I'm guessing she left out the window." Kelly pointed to the now opened window. "Usually, sneaking out means she was setting out to meet somebody in secret. From the report it appears her small circle of friends were all interviewed. None of them saw her after she was reported missing. My guess is it was a boy. My question is who?"

"Faith didn't have any boyfriends. Not that I know of, anyway."

Kelly closed the window and stepped out into the hall. Wilson closed the door behind him and this time guided Kelly down the stairs toward the door.

"I will do my very best to bring to justice anybody responsible for the disappearance and death of your daughter."

Wilson eked out a whimper and a tear rolled down his cheek. "She's dead. Not much matters now."

"It matters to me."

He stood and shook hands with Wilson. The father of Faith Wilson didn't show him out. Instead he sat on the stairs with his hand cupped around his beer can as if praying for an answer at its bottom, an answer Detective Michael Kelly hoped he'd be able to deliver.

* * *

The Impala sputtered out its glee at finally being free from stop-and-go traffic. Kelly walked up the back steps of the wraparound porch. As a child he'd often tucked himself under the steps in an effort to hide from his brother during one of their many games of hide-and-go-seek. As a teen, he'd used the same steps to hide his beer from his mother.

The floorboards creaked loudly and dipped slightly under his weight. The condition of the house was starting to slip. Since he returned home to live here once more, he intended to put in some sweat equity as soon as he had time.

The Dot's crime rate had risen significantly since his parents emigrated from Ireland in the fifties. Even so, Deidra Kelly refused to lock her doors. An area of contention between Michael and his mother, especially after Danny Rourke's home invasion.

"Ma, I'm home," Kelly called out as he entered.

"In the parlor."

Kelly entered the living room. His mother was watching *Jeopardy!*, a game show she'd become more fanatical about in her later years. Kelly knew his mother had a not-so-secret crush on Alex Trebek.

He leaned down and kissed his mother on the forehead. Her right leg was extended, a pillow tucked underneath. An icy fall during the last snowstorm of the year left her with a fractured right hip, but she was on the mend. Kelly took a couple weeks of leave during the first steps of recovery, but his caseload began to stack, and he had needed to return to work. The liquor store, normally overseen by his mother, was being managed by Reyansh Gupta, her best employee. Kelly had asked his younger brother, Brayden, to step up and help, but he was too busy with God knows what.

"My! You look like the devil's been chasing you." She turned to greet him. "Have a seat. It's getting close to the Daily Double. That young boy there is giving everybody a run for their money."

Kelly disappeared into the kitchen and grabbed a cold beer. He cracked the top and took a sip. "Ma, you want one?"

"I guess it's about that time."

Kelly brought his mother a beer and plopped down onto the couch beside her. He watched her watching the show. After each question was presented, his mother would inch forward just a bit. She'd then wait until the answer was announced and pretend like she knew it all along. Every once in a while, she'd actually get one right before the contestants. It usually came when the category had something to do with European history or geography. When she beat one of the contestants to the punch, she used to get up and do a jig. With her hip in disrepair, it would be a while before she resumed her celebratory dance.

"How's the leg today?"

"Good as gold. I'll be up and running in no time." She gave an exaggerated wink.

"I was in the neighborhood today." Kelly never talked about the cases he worked. He never saw fit to unload his burdens on people who hadn't worn the shield. There was always too much explaining, and something was always lost in the retelling. Plus, he never wanted to worry her. "I was planning on stopping by and checking in but got tied up."

"A bad one?"

Even though he never gave details, nor did she want them, his mother always made a point of asking. "They're all bad, Ma. You seen Brayden?"

She answered him by not answering him, turning her attention back to Alex Trebek. "Useless junkie," Kelly seethed. "I guess that's a no. He should be helping you with the store." Kelly shook his head. "He's an absolute train wreck."

"Michael Kelly, I will not have you speaking ill of family." His mother gave a stern look. "He's got problems."

"He's on drugs," Kelly snapped.

"That stuff's ruined him. He had such a bright future. Smart as a whip, that kid."

Kelly had gone around and around with his mother on this issue and the topic was an exhausting one. "You've got to stop supporting him. He needs to hit bottom and get help. No way he'll do it if you keep giving him money whenever he comes by. Stop feeding the cat, Ma!"

"He's not a cat. He's your brother." She muted the commercial in the background. "Sweet Mary and Joseph, we never turn our back on family. You know this. He's got a sickness and needs treatment. Why can't you help him get back on his feet?"

"I've tried. A million times I tried." Kelly slumped deeper into the worn cushion. "Every time he gets arrested, who's there to bail him out? Me. I can't even tell you how many times I've personally driven him to a treatment facility, only to find out he ran out the back door before I drove away. He isn't ready for my help."

"Well, let's hope he doesn't meet the good Lord before he gets it." Alex Trebek was back on the television and his mother reached for the remote. "Just promise me you'll try and knock some sense into him next time you see him."

"Family first."

"Family always." His mother gave a half smile and resumed the game show at full volume.

8

From the things he'd seen growing up in his neighborhood to the countless bodies he'd encountered during his eleven years as a member of the Boston Police Department, Michael Kelly had grown familiar with death. But his short time in Homicide had dramatically changed his perspective. If you ever wanted to see the meaninglessness of life, attend an autopsy. The manner in which a body gets evaluated will forever twist your understanding.

Kelly stood outside the pristine glass doors and arched entranceway to the Office of the Medical Examiner. He was a few minutes early, as always. Those quiet moments were critical to setting his mind right for the task ahead. A police officer's job didn't always afford that luxury, but when it did, he made sure he allowed for it. He noted the time and location in his pad: *Wednesday 0857hrs. ME Autopsy*. He'd note more as the morning progressed, but Kelly was thorough. In death, everything mattered.

He stepped up to the main doors and they parted with a whoosh. The sterile air of the lobby had a similar quality to a hospital, but the lobby wasn't littered with the sick and dying. It was quiet, except for a few personnel in medical coats talking in hushed conversations as they entered the secured area.

Kelly approached the receptionist. "I'm Detective Kelly, Boston Homicide. Here for the nine o'clock with Doctor Best."

"Have a seat, Detective. I'll page the doctor. She should be out in just a moment."

"Thank you." Just like Deschanel, this woman was the gatekeeper.

Kelly didn't sit. He hated to sit when he had work to do and equated it to laziness; he paced instead.

"Detective?" A thin woman with straight, shoulder-length blonde hair stood by the open door of the secured area. She wore a bleached white lab coat and carried a clipboard.

Kelly stretched out his hand. "Doctor Best? I'm Michael Kelly."

"Ithaca."

"Sorry?"

"Just call me Ithaca. I hate the doctor crap. Sounds too formal. Ithaca is my first name. And before you say anything, I know how bad it is to be a Bostonian named after a New York city. Family name. My grandmother's."

Kelly smiled. "It's nice."

The pathologist blushed a bit at the compliment before turning. "Shall we?"

"Lead the way."

The facility was capable of housing hundreds of the dead at any one time. There was a time when unclaimed bodies occupied so much of the space the facility was forced to use cold storage trucks as temporary onsite containment units. In recent years, and after several publicized cases of mishandled bodies, the funding increased to allow for more staffing. Since then, the opioid epidemic had created a tsunami of overdose-related deaths and the Office of the Chief Medical Examiner was again playing catch-up.

The air was always cold, and Kelly fought the need to shiver. Ithaca Best kept up a quick pace and her shoes clacked the recurrent cadence of each footstep.

"You're new?"

"Not to the PD but to Homicide. Been in the unit a little over six months."

"Where'd you come from?"

"I've bounced around a bit in PD. A gypsy so to speak. Did a stint in Narcotics before going over to tactical."

"A SWAT guy? Not a normal transition to the world of investigations, is it?"

"Well, I did the tactical stuff for a bit and then stepped over to the negotiator side of the house. Thought maybe I could talk some people down before it escalated."

"How'd that work out?"

"Not so good. And thus, my new path was forged." Kelly tried to pass off the statement with a touch of bravado, but knew it came up a bit short. Baxter Green's death still encircled his mind like a low-hanging cloud.

Best stopped at a closed door. She pulled up a lanyard and held it over the sensor pad on the side. The light above shifted from red to green and the door clicked loudly. She depressed the metal handle and pushed.

The room contained ten metal tables, columns of five on each side. The smooth laminate floor was dipped slightly, converging in the center, dividing the room. In the center of the concave floor were evenly spaced drains, similar to what you see at the base of a shower. The shape of the ground and the drainage areas were designed as runoffs for any fluids not captured by the tables' raised edges and prefabricated drain holes. It also made for a much easier clean-up and sterilization of the room at the end of each autopsy.

The last time Kelly had come into a room similar to this, nine of the ten aluminum beds were in use. It was a madhouse of sawing and cutting, like a scene out of an Eli Roth horror film. Today was different. Two techs stood by the one table occupied by the lifeless body of Faith Wilson. The girl's hands and feet were still in clear plastic bags.

A smell hung in the room, unlike anything most people could fathom. Most cops didn't have the opportunity to observe an autopsy. He'd known plenty of thirty-year veterans who hung up their gun without taking in this most private of investigative rituals. Kelly made attempts to describe it to others who'd never experienced it, but always seemed to fall short in conveying the experience. There was a musk of equal parts decay and chemical, like ammonia and a compost pile had a baby. The first time he'd smelt it, he almost turned and left.

The invisible forcefield of stink was too much for some investigators to handle. Some tried to mask it by putting Vicks VapoRub on their upper lip, under the nostrils. Kelly did not. He didn't shy away from the brutality of death. In fact, the opposite was true. He embraced it, fully and completely. To be the voice for the dead, he felt an innate need to embrace every gritty aspect of the case.

Best walked over to the table and introduced Kelly to the techs who'd be assisting in today's autopsy. Thomas Robichaud and Dennis Toomey were already masked up and ready to begin.

"Give me a second while I get my overalls and mask on. You can take your initial photographs if you want."

Today Kelly carried his department-issued Nikon, similar to the one Raymond Charles had used on the previous day's scene. He noted the time and then slipped his notepad into his back pocket. Kelly was by no means an expert with a camera, but had familiarized himself enough with it to know the basics. He'd put in a request to go to the week-long photography school, but it was still sitting on his lieutenant's desk. No telling how long until it would get approved, if ever.

Robichaud and Toomey stepped back, giving him a wide berth, as Kelly moved around the body. Kelly began at the head and moved clockwise, snapping photos from both table-level and overhead. Each aim point overlapped its predecessor and would give an overall continuity when he organized them later.

Faith Wilson lay on her back, naked, her skin a pale off-blue, like she was cast in a permanent moonlight glow. His original assessment seemed to be holding true. There were no discernable injuries sustained by gunshot or knife upon first pass. He'd wait for the roll to confirm, but it appeared the injury at the base of the skull was most likely what killed the girl.

Ithaca Best reappeared beside him in full gear. She wore protective glasses which muted the bright blue of her eyes, and her goldenrod hair was hidden beneath the disposable green cap.

"Ready to begin?" Best asked through her mask.

Everybody around the table nodded, including Kelly.

Best set a digital recorder on a tray next to the table and pressed the record button. "Today is Wednesday, March thirteenth, two thousand nineteen. I, Doctor Ithaca Best, pathologist for the Massachusetts Office of the Medical Examiner, will be performing today's autopsy of Faith Wilson, age thirteen. Pathology Technicians Thomas Robichaud and Dennis Toomey are assisting. Detective Michael Kelly of Boston Police Department's Homicide Division is in attendance and will be observing the procedure. Time on the clock reads zero nine eleven hours."

Kelly watched as Best moved around the body. She began at the right side, starting at the neckline and working her way down to the feet. Best moved and manipulated the girl's flesh, looking for evidence of trauma. She then did the same on the opposite side. Best then motioned to the techs. "We're going to roll her to the left side."

Robichaud stood on the left side and leaned over, grabbing the girl's right shoulder. Toomey did the same at the knee. "And roll," Best said.

Faith Wilson was rigid, her body stiff from the past eighteen hours in cold storage. The doctor moved her hand along the back of the girl's body. "No sign of any puncture to the girl's body below the neckline."

Best had the initial report from Charles's and Kelly's documentation up to this point. She knew about the trauma to the skull; the pathologist wanted to rule out any other prospects before focusing on the known. Best's hand returned to the base of Wilson's neck. Her fingers inched up to the skull. "Her neck is broken right here, at the base of the skull. Once I get inside, I'll be able to better pinpoint the extent of the damage."

"Do you think the broken neck killed her?" Kelly asked. He snapped a photograph of the area Best had indicated.

"Unlikely. It's very likely this injury may have had a paralyzing effect, depending if the spinal cord was severed."

"What about the blow to the back of her head?"

"Roll her back into position."

The two technicians pushed Faith Wilson into her original position. Ithaca Best leaned her slight frame in, hovering over the dead girl's face. She reached back without looking and grabbed some forceps off of the metal table behind her. The doctor then pried open the girl's mouth wider. Kelly heard a crack as the rigidity of the jaw gave way to the instrument's pressure. The sound caused his stomach to knot.

Best activated the light attached to the side of her protective glasses, enabling her to see more clearly into the dark recesses of the girl's mouth.

"What are you looking for?" Kelly leaned in for a better view.

"Look here." Best stepped back. Kelly took a small light out of his pocket and illuminated the interior of Wilson's mouth.

On the girl's swollen tongue were bits of dirt, similar to the covering over her half-closed eyes. Kelly snapped several pictures and then stepped back. "What do you make of that?"

"You said she was found in a shallow grave?"

"Correct. She was dragged from the rail."

"I'm going to have to look at her lungs when I take them out, but it looks like this little girl may have been buried alive."

Best began the Y-intersection of the girl's chest cavity, a brutal undertaking, gruesome to watch. One by one, the doctor removed each organ, labeling and weighing them. The lungs were heavier than expected, making the doctor's assertion more plausible. Dissecting them, the interior was coated in a dark gummy substance as dirt, moisture, and blood had mixed. The slurry had effectively suffocated the young girl.

The autopsy took a little over three hours to complete. When it was done, Kelly was emotionally drained. Doctor Best confirmed Faith Wilson's neck had been broken above the C4 vertebrae, paralyzing the girl from the neck down. The contusion at the skull was superficial, with no cracking of the cranial bone.

Best concluded that Faith fractured the vertebrae on the metal track, generating enough damage to cause significant paralysis but not enough to sever the spinal cord. Dirt could have gotten into her mouth if she was on her belly when dragged through the yard as he'd suggested. Impaired swallowing could have put dirt and possibly blood into the back of her throat, and she could have still had enough muscle function to breathe it into her airway.

Dumping her into the shallow grave would have most likely finished off the already damaged spinal cord, severing it. She would have died of suffocation because she could no longer draw a breath. Her brain would continue to function until starved of oxygen, and that would happen quickly. If she had been rendered unconscious by the fall on the rails, her attacker may not have seen her breathing. The dirt-filled lungs were the culprit. Asphyxiation was ruled as the causative factor in the teen's murder. Ithaca Best listed the manner of death as homicide.

Kelly's mind replayed all the images stored in his mental file set aside for Faith Wilson. The blood on the tracks, the torn fabric from her dress on the fence, and her final resting place. This girl was broken, paralyzed, and left for dead. He imagined the girl face down unable to move as she swallowed the earth around her until nothing was left.

Kelly sat in his car with the engine off. He stared at the building he'd just left and wondered how much damage seeing that body would have on his mind. He'd just watched all the contents of a young girl, once analyzed, get bagged up and stuffed back inside her chest cavity with the same care of someone packing for a last-minute trip.

His phone vibrated and he looked down at the text message. Samantha sending a reminder: *Don't forget Embry has her play today at one.*

Kelly looked at his watch. He had forty-five minutes to get across town to his daughter's school. With a little bit of luck, he'd make it. Seeing Embry would be medicine for his aching soul. After what he'd just witnessed, he needed her now more than ever.

9

The parking lot was packed, not one space available. He'd seen the latest text from his ex, asking where the hell he was, with wording that was not as pleasantly phrased. Kelly didn't waste time typing a response. The speed at which he sent text messages was comparable to a Neanderthal etching on a stone tablet. Plus, he was looping the block for a second time in search of a spot.

He gave up his futile attempts at finding legal street parking and drove his beat-up Impala up onto the grassy median between the sidewalk and the parking lot of Mercy Elementary. He knew his unmarked wouldn't get towed, or at least he hoped any self-respecting tow company would see the BPD insignia on the plate.

Kelly dashed for the doors, following behind an older couple carrying a bouquet of flowers. He realized he should've stopped for something like that. Kelly was positive Samantha would one-up him, or worse, her boyfriend, Martin Cappelli, would come in as the hero. He still couldn't believe she'd left him for Marty, of all people.

Snaking past the older couple, Kelly navigated his way into the auditorium just as a final announcement to take seats had been given. He scanned the stadium theater seating, a vast departure from the bench seats in the gymnasium of his childhood school. Samantha had somehow convinced him to send Embry to private school, a decision he regretted to this day, even more so now that he was eating most of the cost as part of the divorce decree settlement. He let the frustration reduce from a boil to a simmer as he caught a glimpse of the dark waves of his ex-wife's hair.

As if she could feel his eyes upon her, she turned and saw Kelly. She gave a relieved sigh and then flagged him over. As the lights dimmed, he deftly took the steps down to the center row. Kelly apologized as he squeezed himself across the already seated parents and grandparents. In situations like this, where a person had to squeeze by a group of people, Kelly was always plagued by the question—what direction should he face? Kelly gave the passing crowd a look at his posterior. Better than jamming his crotch in some old woman's face.

Kelly dropped into the vacant seat she'd held for him. Samantha was now bookended by her past and present lovers. The awkward trio faced the curtains as music played.

"What's that smell?"

Kelly dipped his nose to his shirt and inhaled. "Dead body." His senses were deadened to it and he could no longer smell the funk the autopsy room left on his clothes.

"You couldn't have changed?"

Kelly tried not to let the jibe take effect, but it was hard. "Came straight here from the body of a dead girl. You should just be glad I made it."

"It's not about me. It's about our daughter. And yes, smell or not, she'll be thrilled to see you here."

Kelly leaned forward and looked at Cappelli. "Hi Marty. Glad to see you brought flowers."

A second grader came to the podium and began his narration; Embry's second grade performance of *The Wizard of Oz* was about to begin. He had witnessed the practice his daughter had put into memorizing her lines as Dorothy, and his heart skipped a beat when he saw Embry traipse out on stage with a stuffed Toto cradled in a wicker basket. For a few moments, the thought of Faith Wilson pushed back into the recesses of his mind.

* * *

Polina Deli began to fill with the lunch crowd. Aleksander always tried to make himself available to help his mother with the lunch wave. His older brothers Bartosz and Darek couldn't be bothered. They'd explained to him that their time was much too important to be wasted on such things. Aleksander understood why they felt this way. They handled the heavy lifting of the other side of the family business. Being the youngest, he was still earning his place.

His brothers were in the back room, engaged in a heated conversation. Whenever the storage room door was closed, Aleksander knew better than to go sticking in his nose. Most of the time, their fights were over money.

Aleksander moved about the kitchen, quickly navigating the cramped space, grabbing spices. Having spent most of his life in and around the kitchen, he could probably have found what he was looking for among the cabinets and stovetops blindfolded.

Today was not just any ordinary lunch, not for the Polina Deli, and not for his mother. The mayor was going to visit. He'd proposed a recent initiative pushing the importance of mom and pop shops in the neighborhoods. Mayor O'Hara was coming up on re-election and somebody in his office must've thought it would be good PR to get out amongst the people, press the flesh, and eat some local cuisine.

The Polish community in and around the Boston area was a growing one that had been long established in the Dorchester neighborhood. Some pollster realized their vote mattered and could give him an advantage.

An entourage of suited men and women filed into the deli's main space, followed by cameramen and reporters. Within seconds, there weren't enough chairs to support the influx of bodies. The word had spread about the mayoral visit and a line had formed, crowding the sidewalk outside. Hands were cupped against the glass so peering eyes could catch a glimpse.

Aleksander's mother had put on makeup. It was the first time he'd seen the woman do so in recent years. She wore her cleanest apron, the one with a hand-stitched floral pattern. She moved about the counter area with a smile on her face, another thing he hadn't seen much of lately. It was like his mother had been taken over by aliens.

The large head of cabbage had been sitting in the boiling pot of salted water for several minutes. Some people used a timer, but not the Rakowski family. All food was cooked by eye and nose. Aleksander could tell the exact moment the cabbage was ready for removal. He tonged out the head and waited a few minutes for it to cool. During that time, he stirred the tomato-based sauce. In his youth he thought he pulled a fast one on his mother and used a canned tomato sauce. The welt his mother left on the back of his neck with the snap of a wet dishrag lasted a long time. The lesson, never to take the shortcut, was one he wouldn't forget.

The sauce needed to thicken before it would be ready to serve. The movement of the wood spoon was slow and steady. He could feel the slight resistance at the bottom of the pot, telling him he needed to reduce the heat a smidge more. Satisfied he could let the sauce simmer, Aleksander began the process of removing the thick, softened leaves. Today's cabbage looked extra hearty; he knew his mother had spared no expense on the ingredients for today's meal.

His mother entered the kitchen and opened the door to the back room. "Boys, I want you to come out there with me for a picture. The nice man with the camera said he would send us a copy."

"But, *Matka*, we're discussing business," Bartosz said.

"Don't talk to me of business." Nadia Rakowski pointed around the kitchen wildly. "This. All of this is business. You'll get out there now for a picture or I'll drag you out by your ear!"

All three Rakowski boys filed out into the eating area and smiled broadly. The cameras flashed and a news crew began rolling, capturing the interactions.

Mayor Shawn O'Hara shook the hand of each member of the Rakowski family, stopping and posing for the photographer each time.

"I love Polish food and can't wait to see what you and your mother have cooked up for us today." O'Hara was a refined politician who'd ingratiated himself to citizens of Boston during his first two terms in office. However, the latest polls showed he was slipping against an up-and-comer. His publicized affair with a twenty-three-year-old bikini model had not gone over well with the constituency.

"We are happy to have you as a guest in the Rakowski owned and operated Polina Deli," Nadia Rakowski said. Her voice carried, projecting over the mumbled conversations between the reporters. She fought hard to enunciate each word as she spoke. Aleksander knew she'd been rehearsing these canned phrases ever since hearing the mayor would be making an appearance. He'd heard her practicing in the bathroom that morning.

"My son, Aleksander, has been working on a family specialty from Poland — Gołąbki. Stuffed cabbage. And I think it will blow your socks off, Mister Mayor, sir."

Mayor O'Hara smiled broadly. "I'm just proud to be standing in what I deem the American dream. I've been told you came over to this country fewer than twenty years ago. Amazing what you've accomplished since coming here. From what I hear, your restaurant has been considered a mainstay in the Dorchester community ever since. Is that right?"

"Yes, Mister Mayor, sir."

"Shawn, Mrs. Rakowski. Please just call me Shawn."

Aleksander watched his mother gush. Beyond his most recent tryst with the model, O'Hara had long been known as a ladies' man. Many compared him to John F. Kennedy. Watching the brief exchange between the mayor and his mother, he saw why. The man exuded charisma.

"Come meet my sons." Nadia Rakowski ushered the mayor over to where Aleksander stood with his brothers.

The three Rakowski brothers again each shook hands with the mayor, pausing for individual shots of the exchange. Immediately following, a photographer corralled them into a cluster with Mayor O'Hara and his mother in front. Several more pictures were taken.

"It's a real honor to meet you all." The mayor took a bite of the wrapped cabbage coated in the perfectly thickened tomato sauce. "That's amazing! Before I leave, I've got to have that recipe."

"I'll never tell." Nadia Rakowski smiled broadly. "Some secrets we'll take to the grave."

This opportunity was good for his mother and, more importantly, good for the family business.

* * *

The play ended. The cast came up in small pockets to receive applause. Embry, as top billed, was the last to approach center stage. Her soft blue dress waved as she swayed, her stuffed animal Toto nestled under her arm. Embry took three short bows before blowing a wide kiss to the crowd. The eight-year-old received a standing ovation, and Michael Kelly clapped so hard his palms stung. The hour had flown by and he wished beyond reason that he could've stayed in that moment for a lot longer.

The crowd began to disperse, and families gravitated toward the stage to congratulate their performers. Kelly became lost in a sea of bodies.

Embry saw them approach and waved wildly. The excitement in her face was priceless and contagious. Kelly fanned his arms out to receive his little actress. She detoured at the last moment, hugging Marty Cappelli first. He tried to rationalize he'd been first in his daughter's sight line, but regardless, the blow staggered him. He felt temporarily lost, physically and emotionally distant from the girl he loved more than life itself.

She released Marty, taking the gifted flowers in hand, then embraced her mother before moving on to him. Each delay compounded his feelings, but he steadied himself. He reminded himself he was here for her, not the other way around. Embry filled the void and her tight grip around his neck made him forget the pettiness of his momentary lapse into jealousy.

Embry pushed back and wrinkled her nose. "Daddy, you smell."

"Sometimes my job stinks." Kelly smiled and kissed his daughter on the head. "Don't worry, baby, I'll shower before our Daddy-Daughter Date Night on Friday."

"You better." Embry pinched her nose and then blew him a kiss, in true exaggerated theatrical form.

Kelly looked at his watch. Out of the corner of his eye, he caught Samantha roll her eyes.

"Squiggles, Daddy's got to go. I love you and am so proud of you."

Kelly gave his daughter one last kiss before turning to leave.

Marty called after him, "Mike, don't forget we've got to meet tomorrow to go over your deposition."

Kelly gave him a thumbs up without turning as he bounded up the aisle steps. It still was an area of contention that his union-appointed attorney was now dating his ex-wife. An issue better left untouched at the moment.

The gusty March wind whipped across the lot as Kelly moved toward the illegally parked Chevy. Kelly bottomed out the small sedan on the curbing as he drove away from Mercy Elementary and toward another school. Clive Branson had been located, and Kelly was finally going to speak to the person of interest.

10

Kelly arrived to the lot of North Andover's elite preparatory high school, Saint Christopher's Academy. The irony was not lost on Kelly. The school had been named after the patron saint of lost travelers, and it was the same school housing a student who was somehow linked to the disappearance of Faith Wilson.

He'd pulled up a recent Facebook picture of Clive Branson. It took a bit of time, since his handle name was listed as PrinceBransonthefirst. *Who names themselves this way?* Scarier was the number of girls he befriended using a naming convention like that. His profile page was littered with posts about women, money, and drugs.

Kelly realized the significant opportunity to study this boy's lure if for no other reason than to prepare himself for the future. He was quickly becoming aware of the changing tide of threats presented to girls these days. The more he was able to learn from boys like Branson, the better he'd be able to protect Embry, if nothing else.

The students began to trickle out of the bricked cathedral-looking school. The Academy resembled Hogwarts on steroids in its design and scope. Ivy crept up the exterior stonework of the building. A few minutes of internet searching while he waited revealed the annual tuition was close to sixty thousand dollars, almost two-thirds of Kelly's annual salary, for a high school education. He'd read up on the amazing opportunities attending a school like this provided. It was almost a guaranteed entry into the Ivy League colleges, but the costs of tuition alone would put the average citizen in the poorhouse.

Kelly had learned from the teenager's Facebook account that he played soccer. From his timeline posts, he claimed to be very good at it. A world driven by clicks of a "like" button now defined a generation's self-worth.

Kelly exited the car. His Impala stood out amidst the sea of high-end sports cars and SUVs. *How would these kids ever learn the value of hard work without ever having to work for anything?* he asked himself.

He heard a whistle blow from one of the fields set behind the impressive school façade. Kelly saw a group of young men jogging around the goal in a warm-up routine. Too far away to pinpoint the boy, he approached on foot. The perfectly manicured grass was greener than it should be for the time of year, but Kelly surmised the amount of money dumped into this place could apparently counter mother nature.

Walking the campus grounds, he felt an odd sense of failure. Kelly was proud of the things he'd accomplished in life, but being in the presence of true wealth and its yield he realized he could never give his daughter an opportunity like this. No amount of hard work and subsequent overtime pay could get him close to the money it would take to attend a school like this. The harsh reality stung.

He saw a thin boy in an Academy-issued gray shirt and navy-blue shorts lollygagging along with a couple other teammates. A whistle blew again and the portly coach yelled, "Get your hustle on, boys. You're moving like you've forgotten our scrimmage with Suffolk is next week."

The three boys stuck up their middle finger and continued walking. The dejected coach turned away and began setting out cones. Kelly watched in disgust. He recognized one of the three bird-giving players from his profile picture as Clive Branson. He crested the small rise of the field and closed the distance.

"Clive Branson?"

"Who's asking?" The boy turned and squared his scrawny chest to Kelly.

"Me."

"And who are you supposed to be?"

Branson folded his arms and gave Kelly a smug look of pure arrogance. The pompous teen was bookended by his equally puny cronies. Odd world where the over-inflated machismo of untested youth thought to have some power to intimidate a man like Kelly.

"Detective Kelly with Boston PD."

"Is that supposed to mean something to me?"

"It should."

"Yeah, why's that?"

"Because I'm with Homicide, and I'm here to talk about Faith Wilson."

"I'll say it again. Is that name supposed to mean something to me?"

Branson's words conveyed confidence, but his body language told an entirely different story. The teen broke eye contact the moment Kelly mentioned the dead girl's name. His body shifted and the boy turned his foot outward. It was an involuntary subconscious response. The boy's mind said run.

Kelly devoured the teen's non-verbal cues and knew without a doubt this boy was worth talking to.

"You and I need to have a little talk."

"Nah, I don't think so. Do you know who my dad is? He owns the biggest chain of grocery stores in the state and he's personal friends with your mayor."

"Who your daddy is and who he knows has zero bearing on me."

"Then maybe you should speak to my lawyer."

Kelly didn't doubt the kid had an attorney on retainer. More likely for his father's business, but he was sure services had been rendered to bail out the misguided youth's poor decisions a time or two. The carefree wielding of power definitely meant this kid had crossed the criminal line with frequency, probably drug and alcohol related offenses. Being a juvenile, his record was sealed. Being a rich juvenile meant his record was probably spotless.

The coach approached. "Excuse me, sir. Can I ask you what you're doing talking to one of my players?"

"Kelly, BPD Homicide." He exposed his shield and flashed his credentials. "I need to ask Pelé here a couple questions. Shouldn't take long. Didn't look like I was interrupting much of a practice."

"Not sure you can do that. Don't you need a warrant, or something?"

Kelly was floored. The coach he'd just witnessed being treated like a second-class citizen now was standing up for the punk who'd flicked him off. "No warrant needed. All I wanted to do was have a little conversation with young Mr. Branson. No big deal. But he may have some information that can help me with a case."

Clive Branson held out his cell phone and smiled broadly. "Here. It's for you."

"Hello?" Kelly asked, assuming one of two people were on the other end of the phone, either Branson Senior or a lawyer.

"This is Lawrence Shapiro, attorney for the Branson family." The voice was curt and squeaked with a shrillness that caused Kelly's nerves to unravel. It also spoke volumes of the kid's family life. He chose to call a lawyer instead of his father.

"This is Detective Kelly with Boston Homicide. I have a couple questions for Clive that may help clear up some issues with a missing person case he was implicated in a year ago."

"What's Homicide got to do with the Wilson disappearance?"

"First of all, the girl is no longer missing. She's dead. And second, I never mentioned her name."

There was a stymied silence on the other end of the line. Shapiro cleared his throat. "You are not to speak to my client regarding this case. Is that clear, Mr. Kelly?"

"It's Detective. And yeah, we're clear. I'll leave my card with the boy in the event your client changes his mind and decides to cooperate with the case. It'd be a shame to see him implicated in a murder without giving me his side of the story." Kelly looked Clive Branson in the eyes when he said the last part, hoping the veiled threat was received. Again, the boy's body language spoke the truth. He was hiding something, and whatever it was, it had the cocky teen terrified.

"I think it's time for you to go, Detective," the coach prompted.

"I'm leaving. And good luck coaching them. Seems like you've got a real great group of players."

Kelly didn't need to wait to see the dejected look on the coach's face. He turned and began walking back in the direction he'd just come, leaving behind the only real lead he'd generated thus far.

Back in his Impala he realized an outside perspective on this case might be just what he needed, and he knew the perfect set of emerald green eyes to assist in that regard.

* * *

Even though the weatherman had called for an early spring thaw, Kristen Barnes had yet to see any sign of it. *It must be nice to be wrong ninety percent of the time and still keep your job*, she thought. The temperature in the early evening hours had dropped ten degrees since the sun slipped away. Bad night to be wearing fishnets and a hiked-up black leather miniskirt. At least she had on a light jacket, even if it was unbuttoned. Her clients expected that of her, and Barnes delivered in spades.

She never stayed in one spot for too long, but also never went very far in either direction of her block. It wasn't the nastiest corner she'd worked, but it wasn't the cleanest, either. She looked down at the gutter beneath her platform heels, littered with used hypodermic needles and the torn edges of dope bags. A sign of the times. Barnes had seen neighborhoods decimated by the opioid trade. Not her problem. She had her own world of crap to deal with and, in her humble opinion, it was far more important.

A car slowed as it passed. Sometimes it took these guys a few laps to work up the nerve to stop. Barnes lit a cigarette and blew out the first puff nice and slow in the direction of the older model Lincoln. Her head followed with the car's direction and she smiled coyly. *Maybe third time would be the charm?* she thought. Anything to get this night over with. She sought out her seventh customer tonight. That was the magic number her higher ups wanted to see. She didn't set the rules, tried like hell to follow them and, on occasion, broke them.

She heard the creak of the Lincoln rounding the corner. The sound of metal on metal grinding in the front axle filled the quiet night as the brown sedan jerked to a stop along the curb.

The tinted window jittered its way down, enough for her to see the man inside more clearly. Overweight with bad skin. His hair was a matted mess and looked as though it had been several days since a shower had got the better of him. The coke-bottle glasses completed the look. It was as if he went to a salon aimed at making people over into creeps.

"Hey baby, need a ride?"

It took this pathetic worm three laps to stop and that was the best line he could come up with? Barnes leaned against the passenger side of the car. "I haven't seen you around before, honey. You from around here?"

"Do you want to get in or not?" The man's voice pitched.

Barnes looked around and flicked her cigarette over the roof of the car to the other side. The embers cast up a glittery flicker as they struck the asphalt. She pulled the door handle and got inside, sinking into the worn gray leather of the seat. Something crunched underneath her. She lifted up to wipe free a crushed potato chip. The floorboard was littered with old wrappers, a who's who of vending machine edibles.

The man put the car in drive and accelerated away before Barnes even had a chance to fully close the door. The momentum slammed the door's armrest against her knee. "Hey man, relax. You're going to get pulled over, and I don't feel like going to jail tonight."

The man said nothing and took the first right.

"Where are we going? I've got a spot nobody goes to." Barnes looked in the side mirror. "You've done this before, right?"

The man said nothing except licked his dry lips. The Lincoln's front axle sounded as though it were held together by its last thread. Barnes had been around too long and knew something wasn't right. She was growing unnerved by the man's silence.

She clutched the small, bedazzled purse tucked under her right arm. She felt the weight of its contents and thought about unveiling them to the bloated man in the driver's seat. Barnes hesitated and patiently waited out his intentions. Seven and done, wishing her lucky number had been six.

Loose fat from the man's waist bubbled out from underneath his sweat-stained orange T-shirt. The man could have been a stunt double for Charlie Brown's Great Pumpkin, but his impressive girth could also crush her windpipe if given the chance. The space of the Lincoln suddenly felt cramped.

"So, what's your name, sugar?" Barnes asked, hoping the feigned sweetness of her tone worked to lighten the mood.

He grunted and then wiped his nose on his exposed forearm, leaving a slug trail of mucus along the wisps of dark hair. "Gavin."

"You know, I've gotta ask. And the rules say you have to tell me." Barnes paused for effect. "Are you a cop?"

The man chortled loudly. "Furthest thing from." He slid his right hand off the frayed sweat-stained leather of the steering wheel and gripped Barnes's thigh. "I'm your rocket ship, baby. And you're about to blast off."

She felt the moisture of his meaty hands dampen her torn fishnet and fought the impulse to jerk her leg away. It was part of the job. She accepted the repulsive touch. A nasty bit of business, but necessary if she were to close the deal. "What are you lookin' for tonight?"

"How much?" Gavin kept his eyes on the road and his hand on her thigh.

"Depends on what you want."

"I want it all."

"It'll cost you eighty for all of this deliciousness." Barnes ran her finger seductively from her lip to belly.

The man smiled, exposing the yellow-stained enamel of his teeth. His head turned, but not to Barnes. His eyes glanced behind her, toward the back seat, as he engaged the door locks.

Barnes followed his gaze and saw the end of a braided rope sticking out from beneath a roll of silver duct tape.

"Stop the car! Now!"

The man began to accelerate toward the upcoming intersection. The light transitioned from yellow to red. The Lincoln didn't slow, pushing forward with no indication of stopping, not until the through traffic entering the intersection forced Gavin to slam on the brakes. Both he and Barnes thrust forward at the sudden change in momentum as the car fishtailed, skidding wildly.

The driver took his hand off Barnes's thigh to brace himself against the dashboard. The disruption gave her the window of opportunity to reach for the contents in her purse. She unzipped the small bag and slid her hand inside just as the car came to a screeching halt.

Barnes found what she was looking for. Her hands seated around the end of her compact semi-automatic Glock 23.

As she began to pull the weapon free, the big man struck out his thick, greasy arm. Fat or not, the weight and sheer force of the man's blow to her chest was dizzying. She gasped, the wind knocked out of her.

A sudden flood of red and blue filled the interior of the Lincoln. The loud bang of fender- to-fender contact reverberated with a deafening crash. The car jerked violently forward, the driver's window shattered, and the loud commands of plain clothes officers with guns pointed at the driver replaced the sounds of the collision.

A hand reached in, manually unlocking the door and tearing it open. Gloved hands pawed at the oversized driver and ripped him from his seat. Barnes could hear the whimper of the man's smothered pleas as several blows were rained down upon the would-be rapist.

Barnes opened her door and stepped out onto the street. She stretched and rubbed her chest, taking a second to collect herself. The impact of his thick forearm's blow pulsed along her ribcage above the sternum.

"Are you all right?" Sergeant Winston Blake asked.

"I'm good. Told you we should've stopped at six."

"Sorry about the delay. Comms really sucked tonight. We only picked up bits and pieces from your feed."

"I checked for you in the side mirror, but you guys were way back."

"We didn't want to spook him by following too close. He didn't go to the spot."

"I think this sicko had an entirely different agenda this evening." Barnes thumbed toward the back seat.

"Well, look at that." Blake shook his head. "You definitely saved some poor girl's life tonight."

"After he's booked have somebody do a deep-level interrogation. I have a feeling there's a lot more to this guy's life that needs looking into."

"Agreed."

Barnes walked around to the driver's side of the car and eyed the man. He was cuffed, using an extra pair to accommodate the beefy circumference and limited shoulder mobility. A trickle of blood ran down his face from a small cut above his left eye. It looked worse than it was because it mixed with the sweat oozing out of the man's pores.

She kicked his foot to get his attention. The winded man looked up. No longer did the lustful intensity permeate his eyes as it had only minutes before. That look had faded into some assembly of weepy confusion.

Barnes pulled out an item from her purse. She pressed it out in front of his face. The red and blue strobes danced across the shield. "Detective Barnes, Boston PD. Looks like you picked the wrong girl to hurt tonight."

The heavyset man said nothing, just dipped his head low.

Number seven definitely earned her an early night. Seven johns in a two-hour prostitution sting was a decent number and would shut the corner down for a night or two. And then, as with all want-based crimes, the need would overwhelm the fear of arrest and the streets would resume its normal traffic of prostitutes and the johns who sought their services.

"Why don't you head in and get cleaned up? Grab Moynihan's car. We'll take the paper on this. Take the rest of the night," Blake offered.

"Sounds good." Barnes walked away and plopped into the driver's seat of Pete Moynihan's unmarked car. She reached up to shift into drive when her phone rang. Looking down at the caller ID, Barnes smiled. It had been a long time since that name had come up, but it was a welcome surprise.

"Saint Michael? Calling me? To what do I owe this honor?"

"Hey Kris, I know it's been a while," Kelly said. "But I could really use your help on something. You able to meet up?"

"It's been a hell of a day."

"You and me both."

"Let's do this over a cold one at Shep's."

"Shep's it is. Let's say half an hour?"

"Make it an hour. I've got to change out of my getup and remove about ten pounds of hooker makeup."

"I'll buy the first round. Sounds like you're gonna need it."

11
———

Shepherd's Flock, or Shep's as it was affectionately known by the townies who served as its primary source of patronage, was an old-school pub at the corner of Savin Hill and Dorchester Avenue. It had all the bells and whistles associated with an Irish-owned and run bar. The lighting was poor and the darkly stained wood was coated in a heavy lacquer, making it easier to clean up spills of both beer and blood. Depending on the night, both fluids were spilled in equal volumes.

Stephen McCarthy was born and raised on a farm in Kilkenny. His father had been a sheepherder. He'd come to America in his early twenties with dreams of being an architect. As things happen, the reality drifted far from the dream. Starting as a stock boy in a warehouse, Stephen put away enough money to put a down payment on what would become the most popular Irish watering hole between Bay Street and Savin Hill, which wasn't saying much, since it was the only pub on that area of the block.

McCarthy named the drinking establishment in honor of his father. And he'd managed to make a modest living keeping the residents of Dorchester inebriated. Booze was steady business in a predominantly Irish city. Regardless of the day, there was always a decent-sized crowd bellied up to the bar. The Kelly and McCarthy families had a long-standing relationship, mostly established through business. Lemuel Kelly, Michael's father, owned a liquor store around the corner on Savin Hill. Much of the booze lining the mirrored wall behind the bar was supplied by Kelly's Liquors, now run by his mother, in the wake of his father's passing.

Kelly shook hands with the doorman, Bill Cooney. He knew him from the neighborhood and was a grade above the thick-necked bouncer in school. The two never traveled in the same circles but each knew the other by reputation. Cooney loved a good fight and apparently found a job suited for an opportunity to pursue his passion. Kelly did too and was likewise rewarded by an occupation capable of providing its fair share of use for his skills. Although, the older he got, the more he sought for simpler resolutions to conflict.

Cooney also had a bit of a drug problem. He got snagged with coke and steroids a couple years back. It had been Kelly who saved him from eating the case. A little tit for tat and Cooney helped put Kelly onto a supplier higher up on the food chain. In return, the big doorman never saw the inside of a cell.

Kelly never held Cooney's misstep over his head. It was water under the bridge. Coming up the way they did, nobody was a saint, and nobody judged.

Cooney also moonlighted as extra muscle for Conner Walsh's crew. The Savin Hill Boys were an Irish gang borne out of the Savin Hill neighborhood of Dorchester. Although Walsh had long since expanded their operation beyond its borders, he still drew much of his talent from townies like Cooney. Walsh trusted the old neighborhood and the loyalty it forged. Kelly had resisted the temptation even though the carrot of money and power had been dangled in front of him many times during his youth.

"It's been a while." Cooney sized him up. "Heard you made detective."

"Nothing stays quiet for long."

"We keep tabs on our own. You know how it is," Cooney said. "Speaking of which, tell your deadbeat brother his tab is overdue by a month."

"You'll probably see him before I do. How much does he owe this time?"

"Two fifty."

"Why do you let him keep racking up the tabs?"

"He used to be good about paying his debts. Looks like that's not the case anymore. Not the same since your father passed."

Kelly nodded but decided to drop the conversation. In the seven years since his dad died, Kelly's younger brother, Brayden, had let his life spiral out of control. Kelly was tired of hearing about it. Tired of bailing him out. The thought of it now exhausted him. But regardless, for the Kellys, family came first. No matter what.

"He doesn't pay it..." Cooney shrugged his shoulders, a gesture that spoke volumes of his hands being tied, of him doing what he had to do, of Brayden either paying his tab or a hospital bill.

"I hear you." Kelly shrugged back. "Tell you what. How about you pay the tab."

"Huh?"

"You heard me. Before I leave, I want to see you pay my brother's tab."

"Now why in the hell would I do that?"

Cooney stepped closer to Kelly in a meager attempt to intimidate. But size was a minor factor for Kelly. He'd toppled much bigger opponents. His first move would be to the big man's knee, but Kelly hoped it didn't come to that.

"Because if you don't I'll haul your ass in for the pistol you keep tucked in your front waist."

"Don't know what you're talking about."

"You've gotten a little soft around the middle. The butt of the gun doesn't sit as flush as it used to." It was Kelly's turn to step closer. Although smaller, he was equally menacing, if not more so. "I know you don't have a license to carry that gun. That alone makes you up for a two-year minimum. But you're a convicted felon. You know how that works. It's an automatic five."

Cooney seemed to shrivel in stature but said nothing.

"Do you think you've got the chops to make it five years in Walpole?"

"Damn, Kelly, why do you got to be such a ball-buster?"

"Just stating facts." Kelly stepped back and relaxed his stance. He could see the implication of his words had delivered a punishing blow to the big man's overinflated ego. "So, what's it going to be?"

"I'll take care of it."

"See, that wasn't so hard?"

"Whatever."

"Good seeing you, Bill."

"Tell your Ma I said hello."

"Will do." Kelly walked inside. He remembered coming here in his youth and the air was laden with smoke. Even now, over a decade since the state banned cigarette smoking in bars, Kelly could smell the remnants as if the furniture had been so deeply permeated in those early years no passage of time would remedy the damage done.

He spotted a table with two chairs set back by a broken pinball machine. There was no waitstaff at Shep's. If you wanted a beer, you got off your butt and walked over to the bartender. Kelly tossed his jacket over the back of one of the chairs facing the entrance and did just that. He wedged himself into position at the bar between a thin woman of about sixty and a bearded man who smelled distinctly of fish.

Kelly flagged the bartender, a younger woman he didn't recognize. He ordered two Harp lagers with whiskey backs. Balancing the four items, Kelly gingerly navigated his way over to the table he'd scouted.

He placed the beers and shot glass on the small, round table. Kelly took a seat facing the door. The cool brick of the wall beside him dampened the air. Then he saw her. Kristen Barnes's bright green eyes were twinkling under the light above the entrance door as Cooney overtly flirted with her. He could see Cooney's immediate downturn at something she mentioned and thumbed over his shoulder toward the interior of the establishment. Barnes must have told the big bouncer she was here to see Kelly.

She gave Cooney a kiss on the cheek and moved inside.

Barnes stood in front of Kelly's table. "Why didn't you order anything for yourself?"

Kelly laughed, although he knew from past experience the girl standing before him was capable of going drink for drink with the best of them. "I see Bill over there still holds out hope."

"Nothing changes. He's been barking up that tree since you first turned me on to this place during our rookie year." Barnes looked back at the big lump. "Besides, he's harmless."

"Tell that to my brother."

"How is Brayden?"

"Same old."

Kelly's brother was a good-looking kid and always had a way around the ladies. He regretted introducing him to Barnes. The two had dated for a brief time, but Brayden's unbalanced life quickly proved too much. Kristen Barnes still held a soft spot for the damaged people of the world. She'd proved this time and again as a patrol officer, bringing food and clothing to the homeless on her beat, and she'd jumped at the chance to work in the Family Justice Division's Sexual Assault Unit, which handled Boston's most broken souls.

Barnes grabbed the shot glass and downed the amber liquor as she took her seat.

"Wow. Went for the whiskey first. One of those nights, I take it?"

The burn of the Jameson caused her eyes to water slightly. The effect was immediate. Her green irises glowed in their moistened state, refracting the emerald with what little light the barroom offered. "Yeah. Some perv went all *Silence of the Lambs* on me."

"I assume it didn't end well for him?"

"Never does."

Kelly laughed. He'd seen the woman, barely over five feet tall, lay waste to men much bigger than Cooney. She was a tightly packaged, ass-kicking machine. One time, a perp jumped Kelly while he was cuffing another. The man hit Kelly in the back of the head with a pipe. Kelly carried a seven-inch, jagged scar line ever since as a permanent reminder to always watch his six.

The initial blow rendered him unconscious, but the maniac continued his assault and managed to beat Kelly back awake. Danny Rourke was down the alley tussling with another one of the gangbangers. It was Barnes who'd arrived as backup. Kelly remembered watching in amazement as she went to work. Within seconds Barnes managed to knock out the pipe-wielding lunatic. That ferocious swing of her baton forever won the gratitude and respect of Kelly.

"You sounded pretty intense on the phone. What's going on?"

"I caught a body yesterday and I'm thinking you may have some insight on how I should proceed."

"Okay. How so?"

Kelly pulled his notepad from his back pocket and scrolled through it. Although most of his case was committed to memory, habit forced him to reference the pad's notes. "She was thirteen. Found dead in a man-made ditch."

"You're thinking she was a working girl?"

"Fancy dress for a kid. Found in a place she didn't belong. Your guess is as good as mine, but I'm leaning toward yes." Kelly pulled out his digital camera and scrolled through the photographs to find the one showing the girl's prone position within the shallow grave.

Barnes looked at the picture. She sighed but gave no overt reaction. Kelly knew she'd seen a lot of horrible things within the Sexual Assault Unit, much of which dealt with young children. Every once in a while, her unit's investigation crossed over into his. "Local girl?"

"That's the thing, no. She went missing from North Andover a year ago."

Barnes sat back, exchanging the camera for her beer. "A girl goes missing from suburbia and ends up dead in Dorchester a year later?" She took a long pull. "This has all the tell-tale signs of human trafficking. We see this a lot in my unit. Kids are mislabeled as runaways but are in fact being passed around by local pimps. Typically starts with weekend parties and eventually the girls get lost to the streets. Any leads?"

"I've got a prick-of-a-teen at a prep school in North Andover who may be involved, or at least knows something about the case. But he lawyered up while I was trying to get some info."

"That's a red flag. What'd the lawyer say?"

Kelly shrugged and took a sip. "Usual stuff. Told me not to go near his client."

"Maybe we can put a little pressure on him."

"We?"

Barnes smiled. "I figured you called me because you needed my assistance."

"I did, but I know you've got your own caseload to worry about. I really just wanted to pick your brain on this one."

"Who are you partnered with?"

"Solo."

"Michael Kelly, you've stepped in a great big pile of shit and you're going to need a little help. Give me a second." Barnes pulled out her phone and dialed. "Hey Sarge, I'm talking with Homicide. They're working a body of a young girl. Looks like it might have some ties to local prostitution or maybe even trafficking. Michael Kelly's assigned. I'm going to assist him on it." There was a slight delay as Barnes waited for the man on the other end of the line. She nodded to herself and then ended the call. She looked at Kelly. "All set, partner."

"I see who calls the shots in your unit."

"I guess after tonight's exploits with the creeper my boss was more than happy to oblige. Plus, I've cleared most of my caseload, so I'm all in. Let's see what we can find out about our young victim." Barnes reached across the table and tapped her glass against Kelly's. The two drained their remnants in unison.

Kelly looked at his watch. "Let's call it a night so we can get a fresh start in the morning."

"You're getting old. I remember times we'd walk out of this place as dawn was breaking."

"Lot's changed since those days. Let's plan on meeting at my office around ten."

"Ten? I thought you wanted to get an early start on this?"

"I do, but I've got to meet up with my union attorney to do some prep work for my deposition in the Baxter Green death."

Barnes winced. "I know you've taken a brutal beating on that one. I'm sorry. For what it's worth, I'm pulling for you."

"Thanks." Kelly drained his shot and stood. He walked over to the bar and flagged the bartender.

"You sure you don't want to do one more round?" she asked.

"I'm sure. I need to close my tab." He turned and went to the register. "I also need you to pull another tab." He hated himself for doing it, but family first.

"What's that?" the bartender asked over her shoulder.

"Pull Brayden Kelly's tab." Kelly looked over at Cooney.

She saw the amount and did a double take before adding it onto his. "Do you know how much he owes?"

"I do. Don't worry, Cooney's going to clear it." Kelly held the tab in his hand and waited until the doorman looked his way. Once he did, Kelly held it up and waved it. Cooney's broad shoulders slumped ever so slightly at the gesture, then he nodded at the bartender.

"Okay," the bartender said. "I've never seen Cooney pay somebody's tab before."

Kelly gave a laugh and smiled. "He and I go way back."

Kelly glanced back at their table. In the short interim it took him to close his tab, a drunken patron had made his way over to Barnes. Kelly's initial reaction was to ride in and be her knight in shining armor. But, deep down, he knew she didn't want his help, nor did she need it.

The man was in his early thirties, thick-chested, with the well-developed forearms of a construction worker. Kelly scanned the crowd and saw the guy's cronies huddled together by the jukebox. They were laughing, a crew of intoxicated day-laborers who had made some type of wager and goaded their friend to make a move on Barnes.

The man leaned in. He said something inaudible. The message was clearly distasteful by the furrowed brow and clenched jaw of Barnes. She pushed back her chair and stood to leave.

Then, the large man made a mistake. A big mistake. He grabbed Barnes by the wrist and tried pulling her closer.

Barnes sprang into action. Where she didn't match the man in strength, she more than made up for it in speed. Before he could count to three, Kristen Barnes had twisted free of the man's grip, spun him, and slammed his face into the nearby brick wall. That was a sound Kelly could hear, even across the noisy bar. Barnes held him there for a second, enough time for her to whisper something into his ear before she released him. The man cowered back to his friends like an injured dog with his tail tucked tightly between his legs. They broke into an uproar.

Kelly approached Barnes, who was beaming with well-deserved pride. "I can't leave you alone for a minute, Kris."

"What can I say? I attract men like flies to shit."

"I think he'll think twice before he tries that with another girl."

"That's my second creeper for the night. I think I've had my fill of idiots for a while."

Kelly and Barnes walked out together. As he passed Cooney, Kelly said, "His debt's settled, right?"

"Mikey, if you keep bailing him out, he ain't never gonna learn."

"When it's your brother, let me know what you do."

Kelly and Barnes walked out to the lot on the north side of the building. She broke the silence. "Some things really never change."

"You know better than most."

"I was hoping he'd figure himself out by now."

"He's the same man-child you dated seven years ago."

Barnes gave him a coy smile. "Well, his older brother was taken."

Kelly let the comment hang in the air, not sure how to react to it. They parted ways with the promise of reconvening their collective efforts mid-morning.

12

The office was small but immaculately maintained, each book neatly in its place in the one bookcase set beside the modest desk. A brass-based lamp with a polished green glass shade was nestled in the corner, near a framed picture of Kelly's ex-wife. Samantha looked genuinely happy in the photograph. It'd been a while since he'd seen her smile like that, longer since it was him who gave her the reason to do so. Seeing his replacement sitting behind the desk looking over paperwork, he couldn't help but blame himself for pushing his wife into the arms of another man. This man.

"Holy crap! I didn't see you there. Scared the bejesus out of me."

Bejesus? Who spoke like that? Who drank tea first thing in the morning? Kelly thought. He took solace in the idea Martin Cappelli was as boring in bed as he was at work. "Sorry, force of habit."

"Have a seat." Cappelli used the file in his hand to motion Kelly across his desk.

Kelly sat and pulled the chair forward so that his knees grazed the desk's wood backing. He couldn't help but feel like a child sent to the principal's office, a feeling he had much exposure to in his adolescence. But, sometimes the most troubled youth made the best cops. At least he told himself that, anyway. "Did you have a chance to read it?"

Cappelli looked up at him over his glasses. "I did."

"And?"

"I think you're throwing yourself to the wolves. You write, and I quote, 'Baxter Green died at the result of a decision I made.'"

Kelly nodded. "It's true."

"Doesn't matter. The other side will eat you alive if you say this."

"Look Marty, I made a decision after eleven hours of hard-fought negotiations. At the time we hadn't had proof of life the boy was still alive. Tactical wanted to force entry. I saw an alternative solution of directing the gunman, the boy's father, to the window. You've seen the transcripts. You've read my summation. In my experienced opinion, he was going to execute the kid. I saw our best and safest option was to direct him into the open so our sniper team could take the shot. Now, looking back, maybe tactical was right and a frontal assault and breach would've ended differently."

"Mike, you can't continue to second-guess your decision. Enough of that has been done with little to no benefit. I know you've been beating yourself up about this over the past year."

Kelly's eyes flashed with anger. "Oh, I know you know. My depression gave you a window to snatch my wife out from under me."

"Let's not go down that path again. Your deposition is tomorrow, and based on what you've written, you're nowhere near ready."

Kelly hated the fact his union-appointed attorney was also dating Samantha, but as far as pro-cop litigators went, Cappelli was the best. The two had first met after the Joe Rory shooting a few years back. Kelly had taken the life of a drug dealer during a gun battle that took place in broad daylight. It was a drug rip gone bad, and Kelly had been point on the takedown. It was clear cut. Thankfully, a traffic camera captured the incident in its entirety. Regardless, officer-involved shootings are terribly stressful, and Marty had taken care to not only argue on Kelly's behalf but monitor his mental well-being throughout the process. They'd become friends during the course of the case, and Cappelli had been over to the house for social calls on several occasions afterward. Maybe that's what hurt most, he'd opened the door to his home and befriended the man who eventually won over his wife. Or, maybe, he hated himself for not putting up the fight to win her back. Either way, complicated understated their relationship.

"Fair enough. So, what would you prefer I say on the stand?"

"I drafted this up for you to review. You can rephrase it to fit your natural way of speaking, but the emphasis should be made that you were the negotiator. SWAT took the shot. You didn't pull the trigger that ended Baxter Green's life, and to lay that burden at your feet doesn't do anything to help your situation." Cappelli slid the revised paperwork across the table. "You need to distance yourself from the shooter. The further away, the less this will damage you."

"Damage me? How so? Is it going to give me back my peace of mind? Is it going to fix the mistakes of the past year?" Kelly looked Cappelli dead in the eyes. "Tell me, Marty, is it going to give me back my family?"

Cappelli fidgeted with the eraser on the end of his pencil. "No. But it may help you come out relatively unscathed. It's an election year, and the mayor will be looking hard at the findings in this case. It's received a lot of media scrutiny lately."

"That's because Trevor Green is writing every legislator he can think of to plead his case. He's got the time to do it sitting in max up at Walpole." Kelly crinkled the papers in his hand. "He's the one who should be stepping up and acknowledging his role in Baxter's death. The bastard put his son in the situation to begin with."

"I couldn't agree more. But he's not the one being brought forth in the civil suit." Cappelli softened his expression, picked up his mug with both hands, and took a sip of his tea. "Everybody here knows you were trying to do the right thing. You've got supervisors, past and present, lining up to speak on your behalf. Sometimes the political nature of the beast overrides sound judgment. I just don't want to see that happen to you."

"Neither do I. But I've always been one to stand toe to toe and bang it out. Don't see much changing Friday when I take the stand." Kelly stood and turned to leave.

"Just read it," Cappelli pleaded. "If nothing else, take a moment and consider the slant I put on this."

"I'll take a look at it, but I'm not making any promises I'll use it."

Kelly walked out of the quaint office. It was nine-thirty. A half hour should be plenty of time to navigate the distance between Cappelli's office, located near Faneuil Hall, to One Schroeder Plaza. He knew Kristen Barnes well enough to know she was already at work, digging up any and all she could find related to the disappearance and death of Faith Wilson.

* * *

He'd made good time as far as he was concerned, arriving a few minutes before ten, and with coffee to boot. He sent a text, *I'm here.*

Kristen Barnes responded almost instantly, *At my desk. Come to SAU.*

Kelly took the elevator up to the second floor. The Sexual Assault Unit was down the hall from Homicide.

He walked the hallway. A pair of detectives assigned to Homicide with the sole responsibility of investigating fatal collisions passed by. They gave him a nod but were engrossed in conversation. Kelly only caught a piece as he briskly strode along, something about a DUI crash involving a patrol district captain. Kelly had heard grumblings about it a few weeks ago but was absorbed in his own messes and didn't pay it much mind. Rarely did an opportunity present itself for investigators to vest much energy in a case not assigned to them. That's why he'd been so caught off guard by Barnes's willingness to assist.

Kelly entered the main space of the SAU headquarters. It was about half the size of Homicide's, and less than that in staffing. The unit had long complained that more detectives were needed to carry the load, but at a time when budgetary cutbacks were the norm, it didn't look like it would be addressed in the near future. At least the unit was lucky enough to have an investigator like Barnes. She easily doubled—or tripled—the case productivity of her counterparts through her tireless work ethic.

Her brunette hair was in a messy bun atop her head. Kelly watched it wiggle as Barnes moved around the paperwork strewn about her desk. Martin Cappelli would have an aneurism if he saw the disarray in which she worked. Her back was to the door and she apparently hadn't heard him enter.

"Hey Kristen."

She spun in her chair to face him. "I've been busy pulling files from any recent locals falling under the missing and possibly trafficked category."

Kelly stood in awe of the pile of case files stacked on the desk and the floor around the file cabinet. "That's a lot more than I would've guessed."

"This is just from the last two months. I figured we'd start there. Probability says the trail will be fresher."

"What time did you get in?"

"Six. I wanted to have something together by the time you got here."

This was the reason Barnes graduated top of their academy class, and why she'd made Officer of the Year three of her five years on patrol—an unbridled work ethic, second to none. "What are we looking for?"

"I've crosschecked patterns in the initial reports to what your North Andover report documented. I looked at past history and any supplemental reports on girls located."

He set her foam cup down in a small clearing of paperwork. "Find anything?"

"As far as girls talking when they return home or are found by police, not much. These girls aren't known for opening up about their experiences. A little bit of a modified Stockholm syndrome coupled with the grooming they undergo. These girls are put through the psychological wringer, not to mention the physical abuse."

"Then why wouldn't they want to talk?"

"The people that do this kind of thing are usually very good about manipulation. Sometimes done with threats of force, but more commonly done by gifts."

Kelly knew a little about the sex trade, but admittedly steered clear of it. Raising a young daughter was scary enough without developing an intimate knowledge of the depravity out in the world. It appeared he was about to get a crash course. "You mentioned gifts?"

"Many of these girls either suffer from low self-esteem or come from extreme poverty. More times than not, both. The grooming process is designed to create loyalty and endear them to their handlers."

"Handlers?"

"Pimps, though the ones doing the prepping aren't always the ones doing the selling. You get a trafficking organization big enough and there's a division of labor. But yeah, handlers are more or less pimps. They make sure the girls are fed. They take them shopping and give them makeovers. Careful steps are taken to build their confidence."

"Makes me want to take Embry to some remote town in New Hampshire and raise her away from all this."

"It's there too. Just look at your girl from North Andover. It's pervasive and everywhere. The best thing you can do for your daughter is teach her to identify the warning signs."

"I'm glad I have your input on this case," Kelly said. "So, doing your initial comparison, did any look like potential starting points for a lead?"

"I've got five girls we should look hard at. I put them in this stack." Barnes pointed to the files stacked to the side from her mess of other case work. "The one on top should be our first stop."

"Why's that?"

"She was reported missing on Tuesday. The report listed her as a habitual runaway."

"Why her? Besides the fact she disappeared on the same day my body dropped."

Barnes opened the file and flipped several pages to the last paragraph of the narrative. The words were highlighted in yellow: *corresponding with a high school boy on Facebook. He goes by the username PrinceBransonthefirst.*

Kelly stared at the name. "It looks like our fancy new friend's got a little explaining to do. I think I'll give his lawyer a call."

"Already did." Barnes gave a sheepish grin. "Sorry, I get hot on these kinds of cases and I'm used to dealing with little turds and their lawyers."

"What'd he say?"

"Clive is on his way in now."

Kelly's eyes widened, impressed. "How?"

"I can be persuasive, especially when I mention the potential of trafficking. Even for a juvenile, if implicated, he could be tried as an adult. Looks like the attorney wants to get ahead of this thing before it comes to that."

"Nicely done."

"Don't thank me yet. The father's a bit pissed, to say the least, and he's well connected. There's a storm brewing and we're going to be at the epicenter of it."

"Nothing new there."

Kelly picked up the file containing the information on the recent missing person, Tabitha Porter. He devoured the contents therein and then did a comparison with the North Andover report. Kelly wanted all the ammo for his arsenal when he sat with Clive Branson. This time the cocky prep schooler would be on his turf, and Kelly wanted to make sure he capitalized on the home-field advantage.

He pulled his phone out. Kelly had one call to make before Branson's visit.

* * *

"Hello. I'm looking to speak with Alton Jeffries."

"Who may I ask is calling?" the thick, nasally voice on the other end inquired.

"This is Detective Michael Kelly with Boston PD."

The man cleared his throat. It sounded as though the call woke him. Being retired, a ten a.m. wake-up seemed pretty great.

"How can I help a fellow brother in blue?"

Kelly heard the tone immediately change in the retired North Andover detective. "I'm following up on an old case you worked."

"I'm living in Florida now. Well, at least part of the year until I can get out from under my house." Jeffries chuckled. "How can I help you? I'll do my best with whatever I can remember. For specific facts of a case, you'd have to pull the file. But assuming you got my cellphone number, I'm going to guess you've already done that."

"I did, you're right. I am calling about a missing person case you worked on, a girl by the name of Faith Wilson."

"Wilson? Yeah, I think I've got a vague recollection of the case," Jeffries said. "She pop up in Bean Town?"

"She did. I came across her Tuesday morning."

"Okay, that's good. What do you need from my end?"

"She's dead. If I failed to mention at the beginning of this conversation, I'm Homicide."

No words spoken. If not for the steady labored exhalation, Kelly would have thought Jeffries had disconnected. He waited. Silence acted upon the mind in strange ways. A person's natural need to fill gaps in conversation were an interrogator's tool.

"That's a damn shame." Jeffries coughed. "From what I remember, she seemed like a nice girl. Must've run off and got mixed up with the wrong crowd."

"Part of what you said is right. She definitely fell in with the wrong people. But where you're wrong, that girl didn't run off."

"What are you getting at?"

Kelly heard the tone change from placidity to aggression. He'd struck a nerve. "She was recruited. Enticed. Snatched. I don't know exactly yet, but one thing is for certain, Faith Wilson didn't just run away."

"Okay. I still don't see why you're calling me."

"You don't?" Kelly asked rhetorically. "Let me be more blunt. You dropped the ball, Jeffries. You had a lead and you never followed up. My only question is why?"

Jeffries exhaled loud and slow. Kelly heard the click of a lighter. "How much time you got?"

13

Clive Branson waited in the headquarters lobby with his attorney. Kelly had been notified by the desk sergeant ten minutes prior. He didn't mind making the prep school thug wait. In fact, he hoped it would have an alarming effect on the boy's psyche. The walk-in complaints that trickled into One Schroeder Plaza were as unique as the people presenting them. Kelly was sure Branson would have an earful as irate citizens of the city pled their cases through the heavy bulletproof glass of the main desk. Many of the most vocal of complaints came from the mentally ill seeking justice for the crimes, real or imagined, that befell them. Kelly hoped this introduction into city life would rattle the cocky teen.

Kelly and Barnes used the time to organize their pre-interview notes. They also set up the interview room to their liking. Kelly intentionally left the attorney's chair out of the room so the man would have to stand above his client while it got retrieved. He wanted Branson to feel isolated and alone. Minor manipulations sometimes paid big dividends in the long run of an interrogation.

The two had decided on using an interview room in Homicide rather than SAU. It would have more of a psychological impact on the boy. The buzz of the murder police unit's office space was an intimidating beast to behold, even for a cocky teen who thought he was untouchable.

Barnes accompanied Kelly on the short elevator ride down to the main lobby area. Kelly stepped out onto the shiny, rust-colored tile floor. "Mr. Shapiro? We're ready for you now."

The man seated next to Branson stood and bent to whisper into his client's ear. Shapiro wasn't exactly as Kelly had pictured when speaking to the attorney on the phone, but he was close. He was short, about five foot five, with a round middle. He wore a light tan trench coat over a dark-colored suit. Kelly didn't know much about fashion, but could tell no expense had been spared in the ensemble. He wore wire-rimmed glasses and his hair was closely cropped, thinning at the top.

The attorney moved in quick, choppy steps as Branson sauntered behind. Kelly could tell the boy was trying too hard at playing this cool. The overt nonchalant mannerisms were a mask covering his fear. No need to expose his weakness yet. There'd be time for that very soon.

Shapiro stuck out his stubby hand and Kelly shook it.

"Detective."

"Thank you for taking the time to come in today." Kelly guided them toward the open doors of the awaiting elevator. "This is Detective Barnes. She's been brought in from the Sexual Assault Unit to assist in this case."

Shapiro nodded and shook her hand as Barnes released the button, enclosing the group in the elevator's meager space. Kelly caught Branson give Barnes the elevator-eye treatment. Even under the duress of a criminal investigation, this conceited teen still had the balls to check her out. That familiar longing to punch the kid in the face arose again, but Kelly suppressed it. The only assault he'd lay would be done with words. And unlike the saying, Kelly knew better, and words could really hurt.

Nothing was said during the short trip up. No need for small talk. Shapiro would be looking for any angle to help his client and, unless Branson was advised of his rights under Miranda, anything discussed could be torn apart in front of a judge later.

The elevator arrived on the second floor and Kelly, acting as tour guide, led them down the hall to Homicide. Barnes brought up the rear.

Once inside, Kelly navigated the group past several of the clustered workstations to a closed room on the left-hand side marked Interview Room #3. Kelly unlocked the door and turned on the interior light. He stepped back, allowing Shapiro and Branson to enter. "Have a seat over there on the other side of the table. Mr. Shapiro, let me go get you a chair. There's usually an extra seat inside. Can I get you anything to drink?"

"We're fine, thank you." Shapiro stood awkwardly beside his client as Branson took his seat.

"Just so you know. The door will remain unlocked during our time here today." Kelly pushed the handle down a few times for good measure. In interviewing juveniles, it was critical to prove no level of coercion. Even a locked door could be construed by a good defense attorney as intimidation. "Also, I activated the camera system. Everything discussed in this room will be recorded by audio and video."

Kelly closed the door, and he and Barnes walked over to Sergeant Sutherland. "I see you're using the old missing chair trick." He chuckled. "Never gets old."

Kelly smiled. "Figured I'd pull out all the stops on this one."

"You know this case is getting a lot of prying eyes. This kid's dad has got some juice with the mayor. We've already been bombarded with requests to notify his office directly at the conclusion of this interview."

"Maybe the mayor should keep his distance from this one. Not sure he's going to be wanting to ante in on this kid's behalf. Especially during an election year." Kelly threw his hands up. "But hey, who am I?"

"Not my place to advise him. He just wants updates. What he does with them is on him."

"Mayor's going to be seeing my name a bit this week," Kelly said.

"How's that?"

"I've got the Baxter Green deposition tomorrow."

"That's right. Forgot about it. Hell of a week for you." Sutherland didn't wait for a response before he walked away.

Kelly turned his attention to Barnes. "Any final thoughts before we go in there?"

"Your show. I think we've got a good handle on how we want to approach him and where he fits in the scheme of things."

"Listen, sex crimes aren't my forte. I want you to chime in at any time you deem necessary."

"Will do." Barnes's eyes conveyed confidence. "Let's go in and have a little chat with our new friend, Clive."

Kelly dragged the extra chair behind him as he entered. It was an uncomfortable metal folding chair, not like the cushioned one his client was seated in. "Here you go, counselor. Sorry about that."

Shapiro eyed the chair but said nothing. Kelly was prepared to get him another, but wanted to test the attorney's comfort in asserting himself. Good sign, he was less so in person than he was during the phone conversation.

"Before we begin, I'd like to take a moment to advise your client of his rights." Kelly and Barnes sat side by side across from Branson and Shapiro. Only the rectangular table separated the opposing groups. Kelly fished out a single sheet of paper from his folder. "I want to ensure that Clive understands his rights before we engage in any conversation."

"I know it already. You have the right to remain silent. Blah, blah, blah." Branson leaned back in his chair and folded his arms.

"Not that simple." Kelly turned the form so Branson and his attorney could read along as he read. "You see, unlike on TV and in movies, you need to initial after each line I read to you. I'm going to want you to explain in your own words what each of your rights means to you so that I can gauge your understanding."

Kelly learned to not take anybody's claimed understanding for granted. He once asked a suspect what the right to remain silent meant and the man answered, "I shut my mouth when you talk." What made the pitiful explanation more daunting was, at that point, the man had been arrested over thirty times. Now, and especially when dealing with juveniles, Kelly verified.

The Miranda warning took close to fifteen minutes to complete, and with Shapiro's consent, Clive Branson agreed to talk about the Faith Wilson case.

"How did you come to meet Faith Wilson?" Kelly asked. Normally he would spend an additional block of time building rapport with the suspect and look at areas where they could connect and bond, but that would be a challenging road at best, considering their first interaction. Plus, Clive Branson had an arrogant aura, and feigning interest in the kid's already bloated ego would ring false. Kelly figured it was better to dive right in and grind out the case facts.

"Like I told you yesterday. I don't know any Faith Wilson."

"If this is where we are going to begin, then we might as well call it quits here and now. Mr. Shapiro, I assumed you briefed your client on the nature of this case and the evidence we have going forward with or without his cooperation?" Barnes asked.

"I did, Detective Barnes. I understand your position." Shapiro turned toward his client. "Clive, we discussed this."

"Fine. Whatever." Branson leaned forward and played with his Bieberesque hairdo. "I don't know what exactly you want me to say. She approached me on Facebook. That's it. No big deal. Not my fault she ran away afterward. Kids do stupid things."

"So, she contacted you? Are you sure you want to start going down this path with us?" Kelly tapped the thick file folder set on the table in front of him.

"What's that?"

"Detective Jeffries may have been afraid to go after you, but we're not." Kelly deadened his stare at the boy. He could read the discomfort in his smooth, unblemished face. "He did a search warrant for your social media account. I would think twice before you choose to answer with any more wasted lies."

Branson's cheeks flushed and the confidence dwindled like a candle deprived of oxygen. "Okay, so I reached out to her. What's the big deal? People do that all the time."

"And you told her how beautiful she was and that you wanted to meet up with her. Any of this ring a bell?"

"Not really, but I assume I said it if you got the records to prove it. Again, kids my age flirt like that. Nothing criminal about it."

"What if I told you she was twelve?" Barnes asked.

Branson looked as though he was going to be sick. "What? Twelve? Nah. I don't mess with girls that young."

"You did. And like you said, we have the records to prove it," Kelly said. He could feel the perceived advantage shift in their direction. All Barnes had told Shapiro was that we had enough evidence to proceed with a warrant for conspiring to solicit an underage girl for sex. It had been enough to get them in the door to deliver the real blow.

"I'd like to see those records," Shapiro requested.

"In good time." Kelly slid the file further away. "The real question is, do you and your client want to assist in helping us find who did this, or are we to assume Clive was in collusion? Either way works for us."

"Could you give me a minute with my client?" Shapiro almost stammered the question. A line of perspiration formed on the attorney's furrowed brow.

"Sure thing. Oh, and just so you know, we're looking at another missing person case involving your client."

Kelly and Barnes stood. Kelly took his file with him as they exited.

Before the door closed, Shapiro asked, "Please turn off the recording device."

* * *

Ten minutes later, Shapiro opened the door to the interview room and waved at Kelly and Barnes. They approached.

Shapiro closed the door behind him, leaving Branson alone in the room while he spoke with the detectives. "We'd like to discuss the option of brokering a deal. Full and complete disclosure in exchange for total immunity for my client."

"Total immunity for him? I guess he didn't explain his role in things." Kelly was starting to let his frustration get the better of him.

"He did. Well, at least I've got a good idea of things and can fill in the details on the rest." Shapiro wiped at sweat with a red handkerchief he pulled from his breast pocket. "I think you're going to have a tough time proving this in court. But, beyond that, my client's father is a well-respected businessman within the commonwealth and doesn't want his son's name dragged through the mud. Also, if we do this, there will be no recording, only what you write in notes. My client's father doesn't want a soundbite of his son being leaked to the media."

"Maybe he should have thought of that before he let his son run around the state picking up girls," Kelly hissed.

Barnes put a hand on Kelly's shoulder. The contact immediately soothed his building rage.

"Mr. Shapiro, give us a moment to confer with prosecution," Barnes said.

Shapiro re-entered the interview room.

Kelly and Barnes retreated to his cubicle. "What do you mean 'talk to prosecution?' You think we should cut this little prick a deal?"

"Mike, I'm just saying his attorney may have a point. I've worked these cases before. Having a bunch of messages and pictures from a social media profile looks bad in front of a jury, but a good defense attorney is going to eat us alive. There's no definitive proof." Barnes's green eyes pleaded with him. "This might be our first real bit of usable information. If nothing else, maybe we get a lock on where Tabitha Porter may be."

Kelly sighed and picked up the phone.

Chris Watson, prosecutor with Suffolk County District Attorney's Office, answered on the second ring, "Michael Kelly, is this about the Wilson case?"

"How'd you know?"

"My boss has already received a call about some teenager you're interviewing."

Kelly rubbed his temples. "I'm meeting with him and his attorney now. They want to broker a deal. Full confession in trade for zero backlash."

Watson grumbled something. Kelly liked the prosecutor and was glad when he heard Watson had been assigned the case. Big cases always had the early ear of the DA's office. It helped having them involved from the start so that they weren't caught off guard with a big, steaming pile at the end. "Not much else to go on until we get some forensics back. I say take the deal. Offer immunity for the exchange."

"Will do."

"And Kelly, make sure you drain this kid for every last drop of information. I've got to run. Keep me posted if I can be of any assistance. You've got my cell."

The call ended and Kelly looked at Barnes. "Let's go chat with young Mr. Branson."

The duo returned to the room and assumed their respective seats. The smug look on Branson's face seemed to have dissipated a bit since they'd left. Whatever attorney-client privileged conversation took place in their absence seemed to have leveled the teen's overinflated ego.

"I've spoken with the Assistant District Attorney Watson with regard to your request and he will support it as long as your client holds up his end of the deal."

Shapiro gave a stern eye to the boy. "You will have our full cooperation."

"So, let's get back to where we left off. You claimed our girl contacted you. Let's set the record straight on that and then move forward," Kelly said to Branson.

"I hit up lots of girls. It's what I do. And yeah, I reached out and messaged that girl."

"So, you messaged Faith. And then what?"

"We talked a bit. This and that."

"I actually have no idea what you're talking about." Kelly shifted and addressed Shapiro. "If your client doesn't want to clearly state the facts and speak using his expensive prep school education, then I'm going to start losing my patience with this cat-and-mouse game."

"Clive, this is not a game. We talked about this. Cut the crap and tell these detectives what they need to know," Shapiro scolded the boy. "Your father is expecting my next call to him will be one in which I tell him your issue with the police has been resolved. I'd hate for it to be anything but."

Branson sighed, his face teetering on a temper tantrum. Kelly watched the boy in amusement and wondered what horrible punishment would await the spoiled brat. Maybe his dad wouldn't buy him a Lamborghini for his birthday. Kelly let his mind wander to more suitable consequences if the prep schooler had come up in his neighborhood, the thought of which gave the detective a moment of mental bliss before reengaging his interrogation brain.

"Okay." Branson huffed. "I talk to girls. Lots of them. I use a variety of social media accounts to connect. Most of these girls I've never met before. But when I get a girl that's interested, I mean really interested, then I have her meet me at the spot."

"What's the spot?"

"I got the address in my phone. It's in Dorchester. A house where I take them."

"What happens there?" Kelly asked, dreading the answer.

"We party. That place throws the sickest parties. Run by some Polish guys."

"Names?"

"I don't know."

"How did you ever meet up with these people?" Barnes asked, leaning in, very interested.

"My dad."

Shapiro shot the boy a worried glance.

"Your dad?" Kelly asked.

"Nothing like you think. My dad's a powerful man. He knows lots of people.

Throws an annual BBQ around the Fourth of July. This Polish guy was there. I guess his family runs some restaurant my dad supplies. I really don't know. Anyway, the guy approached me and asked me if I wanted to make some good money."

"A rich kid like you needs money?"

"Everybody needs money." Branson smiled. "He gave me a thousand dollars for bringing girls around to his parties."

"A thousand dollars to bring girls to a party and you didn't think anything was off with that?" Barnes asked through clenched teeth.

"My client is being very open and honest with you, detectives. I'd appreciate if we lowered judgmental questions to a minimum," Shapiro admonished.

"What happened to the girls after you brought them to this spot?"

"Don't know. Never asked."

Kelly clicked his pen and waited while Branson retrieved the information from his phone. He looked over at Barnes. She was teetering on the edge of her seat like a mountain lion prepared to pounce on its prey. Her disgust toward the teenage hustler had peaked.

"We're going to be needing that address."

14

The storm door was unhinged and set aside on the porch. There was a busted couch on the landing. The gashes and exposed coiled springs of the cushions seemed more a home to rats than a comfortable place to sit, but the cans littered with cigarette ash pointed to the contrary, indicating the front porch of Tabitha Porter's foster home was commonly used as a hangout.

The doorbell had a strip of tape over it that read *broke*. Kelly knocked loudly, giving three good raps across the lightweight door. He and Barnes stood waiting.

"Who is it?" The woman barked the question with a tone conveying her dislike for unwanted visitors.

Kelly noted the black trash bags covering the windows. Could be a poor man's shades, but more likely, based on his time in Narcotics, it was done to conceal some low-level drug operation. "Boston PD. Detectives Kelly and Barnes."

"You ain't got no business barging in my house," the woman said through the closed door. "Need a warrant to come up in here."

"We're here about Tabitha."

There was a silent pause, a creak of a floorboard, and then the sound of several internal locks being released. The door opened a crack, providing an inch gap from the frame. An older, dark-skinned woman peered out. Her eyes squinted at them. Kelly positioned his badge so she could see it clearly.

"What'd that girl get herself into now?"

"Not sure. We're here to figure that out and thought maybe you could help us along."

"You ain't found her yet? What good are ya if you can't find a dang loud-mouthed teenager? DCF's been breathing down my neck about it ever since she went missing." The woman lit a cigarette and blew the smoke out the door, not at them, but there was no way to avoid the acrid blast. "That girl's been more trouble than she's worth. Only been with me four months and already got detectives at my door. That one ain't worth the money."

"Mind if we come in and talk?" Barnes asked.

"Like I said before. You need a warrant to come in. We can talk just fine from where you're standing."

The strong odor of marijuana confirmed Kelly's suspicion that Tabitha's foster mom had a side business in the drug trade. "Is there anything you may have left out when speaking to the patrol officers the other day?"

"Not that I can think of. I told him she was talking to some skinny white kid. Gave them the boy's info from her account."

"It was mentioned at the time of the report that Tabitha left with her cell phone, but you didn't have any account information." Barnes leaned in. "Were you able to locate any of it?"

"I did. Let me get it for you." The woman retreated deeper inside and closed the door.

"Sweet lady," Barnes snarked.

"Let's see how helpful she is. Otherwise, I may have to place a call to one of my former Narcotics buddies. Pretty sure she's running a grow."

A few moments later she returned. "Here you go." She handed over a sheet of paper. It contained the iPhone's number and password to get into her cloud account.

Kelly was impressed. "This will be helpful."

"I did that 'find my iPhone' application and saw her phone was on until yesterday around noon. Hasn't updated since."

"Thank you. We'll be in touch if we locate her."

"Don't bother. I already told DCF to take her back. You'll need to talk to them if she's found."

Kelly and Barnes walked down the rickety landing to the sidewalk. "Great system. Borrow a kid, get a paycheck. Return said kid if you're not happy with her."

"Been broken for a long time. But they're not all in it for the money. Not sure where I'd be if it weren't for my foster family." Barnes gave a contented smile. "I definitely wouldn't be wearing a badge. That's for sure."

"Sorry, I totally forgot." Kelly felt like putting his foot in his mouth. "They ended up adopting you, right?"

"Yeah. During my senior year. I'd been living with them for two years at that point and after getting through some rough patches, we felt like family." Barnes cleared her throat. "But seeing them stand up before the Family Court judge during my adoption ceremony was the single most important day in my life, with a close second being the day we pinned on our badges."

Kelly took a moment to appreciate the woman getting into the passenger seat. Her involvement in this case was exactly the perspective he needed.

* * *

She'd never felt prettier in her whole life. Tabitha Porter did a pirouette in the mirror hung from the back of the bedroom door. The seafoam green skirt and matching top looked amazing against her skin. She didn't feel fat or frumpy, no matter what her foster brother had called her. Well, he hadn't used words so kind, but she liked to lessen the impact when recalled. That had been a lifetime ago. She had a new family now, one that actually took her shopping, then to a salon.

Tabitha held up her newly painted acrylic nails. The deep pink shimmered against the diamond decals. They even bought her a pretzel. *What a life!* she thought as she flopped back onto the bed.

Slice told her to put on her new outfit. She said tonight would be special. Tabitha couldn't believe it could get any more special than it already had. Maybe they'd take her out for a fancy dinner before the party? There hadn't been time to meet anybody else yet. But Slice said everybody was really nice.

There was a knock at the door. It opened a second later and Slice appeared in the doorway. "Are you ready?"

"I am. How do I look?"

Slice rolled her eyes. "Let's go. Everybody's already waiting."

Tabitha was a little hurt by the sudden curtness. "Okay," she mumbled.

"Drink this." Slice held out a plastic cup of red juice.

Tabitha took it in hand. "What is it?"

"Just drink it. It'll take the edge off." Slice gave her a wink. "Trust me, everybody needs a little liquid courage in the beginning."

Tabitha didn't argue. She knew they were going to a party, and she wanted to fit in. She tilted the cup and chugged its contents. It tasted like cough medicine and grape juice. She smacked her lips together trying to get rid of the tart aftertaste. "Yuck!"

"You'll thank me later." Slice put a hand on Tabitha's back and gave a gentle push out of the room and into the hallway. She then walked ahead at a hurried pace. Tabitha did her best to keep up but wasn't used to walking in raised platform shoes.

At the bottom of the stairs the floor felt as though it shifted under her feet. Tabitha placed a hand on the wall for balance. Slice turned and looked at her. She said something but the words were garbled. Tabitha staggered forward and felt like she just got off the tilt-a-whirl at the Bolton Fair.

She heard a strange beeping sound as she swayed into the kitchen. Then the back door opened. Her mind skipped forward. The next thing she knew, she was bouncing in the backseat of a large van. Techno music was pulsing in her ears, and another girl next to her bobbed her head to the tune. Tabitha felt like she was watching everything from outside her own body. Unable to gain control, she gave in and let go.

15

Ithaca Best had left a voicemail to call her back while Kelly was in with Clive Branson.

"Ithaca?" Kelly asked upon connecting.

"Hey Mike. I did an expedite on the sex kit I performed on our girl from yesterday. I got prelims back."

"Anything?"

"CODIS hit. Apparently one of the four male specimens found inside the girl matched a previous offender."

"I'm sorry, did you say four male specimens?"

"Not uncommon in prostitutes."

Kelly stopped his mind from swirling around all of the awful things. "But she was thirteen."

"I emailed you the hit. It returns to a Phillip Smalls, age forty-two. His DNA was taken in a rape case from four years ago."

"I'll see what pops on my end."

"I got the tox screen back, too."

"Anything unusual?"

"Nothing other than the girl was pumped full of drugs. Heroin was the front runner, though. Looks like she was a sniffer. We didn't see any track marks on her arms or feet during the autopsy."

"Thanks. I appreciate you pushing this forward. I know how long it can typically take. I'll be sure to make it up to you."

"I may cash in on that."

Kelly hung up and looked at Barnes. It had been a while since anybody had flirted with him. He wasn't even sure if that's what had just happened.

"Anything good?"

"Good's a misstatement, but we've definitely got somebody to go after. Faith's rape kit came back with several specimens, but only one identified. Phillip Smalls."

"Not that turd. No way he could already be out," Barnes fumed. "I arrested him a few years back. Actually, it was my first case when I'd come into SAU."

"Didn't stick, I guess."

"The vic was a prostitute. The prosecution wasn't overly sympathetic toward a working girl getting raped. They joked it was a theft of services." Barnes rolled her eyes. "I've spent a lot of time with corner girls. Enough to know their life is no bed of roses. It takes a pretty tragic event for one of them to come forward on an assault."

"What do you remember about either him or the case that might help us now?"

"I remember he was transient. It took me months to track him down last time. He bounced from shelter to drug den to back alleys. Almost impossible to find."

"Great." Kelly sighed. "We may have another angle. It's a long shot, but might be worth a try."

"What's that?"

"Faith Wilson had heroin in her system. I didn't see tracks at the ME's. So, the drug side wasn't on the forefront of my brain. I should've assumed."

"Pretty common nowadays, especially among trafficked girls. Their handlers don't want to present girls with marks up and down the arms. The johns look at them as damaged goods. If they dose 'em, it's usually snorted."

"Makes sense in a sick sort of way." Kelly jotted the time and new information into his notepad. "I know a guy who might be able to shed some light on this."

"Before we do that, let's check out the address Branson gave us."

"He did say the place runs all day and night. The bigger parties happen at night, but who knows, maybe we'll get lucky."

Barnes laughed.

"What's so funny?"

"Get lucky? Nice choice of words, Mikey."

* * *

The gray, triple-decker house was quiet. It was a little past one p.m. The two detectives sat with the car off. They'd opted to take Barnes's Caprice, since the brass apparently liked her better and gave her a car made within the past ten years. Each had a cup of Dunkin' coffee in their hands, warding off the cool afternoon temps while giving them a much-needed jolt of caffeine.

"Not much happening here today." Kelly took the lid off his cup. He hated drinking through the small opening. "Maybe we should come back later tonight?"

"Give it a few. The after-lunch crowd will be arriving for their quick release before returning to cubicle hell."

"You've really got this stuff down to a science, huh?"

"Spend enough time dealing in sex crimes, you start to see the underbelly of society for what it is." Barnes sipped at her coffee. "Honestly, I wish I could erase from memory half the crap I now know. Can't go anywhere without noticing some skell."

"If normal people had an inkling of what was swirling around them at any given time, they'd probably lock themselves inside their homes and never come out."

A light blue sedan pulled up along the curb in front of their target. The driver remained inside the vehicle.

"Looks like our douchebag teen's intel might've been right after all." Barnes jutted her chin in the direction of the newly arrived car.

"Let's hope so."

Kelly watched as a middle-aged man exited. He was tall and thin. His dark hair was slicked back, and the man wore a windbreaker over a collared shirt. He had on neatly pressed slacks and shiny brown shoes. He looked more like a banker or accountant, and maybe he was, but this particular area on the west side of Dorchester wasn't known for its commerce, unless you happened to be in the drug trade.

"For a guy who seems a bit out of his element, he doesn't look too nervous," Barnes said. "Probably means he's stopped by here before. Maybe daily."

The man gave a casual scan of his surroundings and then proceeded up the dilapidated wood steps leading up to the first-floor porch. He opened the door, disappearing inside.

"What's the play?" Barnes asked.

"We could wait until he comes out. Or we could stop in and pay a visit."

"I like option B."

"I figured you would."

"Doing exigency?"

Kelly smiled. It was as if she read his mind. "I'm pretty sure I just heard somebody scream. Let's call it in."

Barnes keyed up her radio. "Detectives Barnes and Kelly at the corner of Millet and Wheatland on a possible disturbance. Investigating."

Kelly and Barnes exited their vehicle and picked up a slight jog as they trotted across the street to the triple-decker. Moving in tandem, the two crested the rickety stairs quickly. The warped wood creaked loudly.

In the upper right-hand corner of the covered porch was a security camera. The blinking red light was an indicator that if somebody was monitoring, their element of surprise was now compromised. Kelly looked to Barnes as he withdrew his service weapon and bootlegged it along his right thigh. He gripped the doorknob. Barnes tightened her body close to his and nodded.

"It's unlocked," he whispered.

"Now or never."

Kelly turned the knob and shouldered against the door, bringing his weapon up to a low ready as he entered. The door opened to a stairwell on his left and narrow hall to his right.

Kelly announced their presence. "Boston PD!"

A large man in a soft gray track suit stepped out from a door ahead of them. "What the hell is this?" His voice sounded layered in a thick Eastern Bloc accent.

"Hands!" Barnes barked.

The velour gorilla raised his hands slowly, as if each inch came at some great toll to his ego.

"Down on your knees!" Kelly closed the gap and holstered his gun, exchanging his Glock for cuffs. He brought the big man's hands to the small of his back while Barnes provided cover. With the man secured in a seated position outside the doorway, he withdrew his pistol again and visually cleared the room the giant had come from. It was empty. A small television played in the background and a cigarette burned in an ashtray by the kitchen sink. "Where are the girls?"

The man said nothing. He spat on the wood floor next to Kelly's foot. Kelly fought back the urge to pistol whip him. Then he heard the sound of a door opening and closing on the second floor.

Barnes ascended the stairs two at a time while Kelly moved to the bottom of the staircase, monitoring his partner while keeping an eye on the handcuffed detainee.

"Get on the ground!" Barnes yelled. Her voice was loud, but in total control. She was a pro and could handle situations like these, a proven point of fact from her early years working these same streets.

"What you got?" Kelly called up as he heard the familiar ratcheted click of her cuffs locking into place.

"One male. Sending him down."

Kelly heard the mumbled commands given to the man upstairs. He descended the rickety stairwell with hands behind his back. The man wobbled; restraints disrupt equilibrium. Once at the bottom, Kelly directed him to sit on the floor next to the man in the jumpsuit.

The businessman listened, but as he passed by muttered, "You're making a big mistake. You don't know who you're messing with."

"I'm sure we'll get to know each other soon enough. For now, why don't you sit down and shut your mouth."

Barnes appeared at the top of the stairwell with three girls in tow. One, a younger looking girl, was more disheveled than the rest, and worked at straightening her shirt as she crept down the stairs.

"I cleared the remaining rooms. These were the only ones I found." Barnes shrugged. "Lunch wave wasn't as busy as I thought it would be. Maybe we should've waited for tonight."

"Let's see what these two have to say first."

Kelly called in for patrol assistance using his portable. In the fifteen minutes it took for two cruisers to arrive, they'd had an opportunity to identify the three girls. None were minors. The youngest looking girl was eighteen.

The businessman was identified as George Puzzo, an aide to the mayor. The man began to weep openly when he realized Kelly didn't care to whom he held political connections. The brief machismo displayed early on was now completely washed away. Kelly couldn't tell if the man was more worried about losing his job or his wife if the arrest came to light.

The velour bodyguard, Aleksander Kowalski, didn't speak at all. He showed no trace of emotion, fear or otherwise, as he was led away by the patrol officer assigned to his transport.

A small crowd had gathered on neighboring porches to watch the free episode of *Cops* play out live on their street.

Puzzo continued his steady sobbing as he was escorted to the rear of the awaiting cruiser. He looked back over his shoulder at Kelly and Barnes. "Can't we work something out?"

"Depends what you feel like telling us."

"Anything you want to know. Just don't tell my wife." An officer guided Puzzo's head low, ducking him into the backseat.

"Bring him up to Homicide after he's been booked," Kelly said to the young patrolman.

The patrol officer nodded. "What charges you want me to put on this one?"

"Let's start with solicitation of prostitution. We'll see where we go from there."

"Should be done booking him within the next hour or so."

"Thanks." Kelly banged on the roof of the car and gave a mock salute to the man in the backseat.

"Maybe he knows more than he looks like," Barnes said.

"Worth a shot."

"We've got a little bit of time. I want to look at another angle on this."

16

"How much?" The man looked around, then over his shoulder nervously as he asked. His hands shook. Even in the cool temperature, sweat poured from his body.

Art Devers knew all the signs. It was part of the job description. Know your client, know your price. The sweaty man was dopesick. That fact alone jacked his cost up a few bucks per bag. The other factor weighing into the onsite monetary adjustment was frequent flyer status. Just like the airline industry, the world of drugs worked in a similar fashion. The more often you bought, the better the price. But this guy was an out-of-towner. Never seen before around Dot Center. Not a cop either. His sickness was way too real. Plus, Devers did his homework. He knew all of the narcs and most of the patrol faces in Boston's C-II.

Devers did his mental calculation, quickly adding in all of the life taxes imposed on a junkie. "Seven a bag."

"Man! Are you outta your damn mind? I could get it for half that somewhere else!"

"Then go there." Devers called the doper's bluff.

The man bent down and pulled up his frayed jeans. He dug into his socks, which at one point were white but now were a disgusting yellowish brown.

Devers shuddered to think what fluids had contributed to their condition. The dopesick man stood awkwardly and stuck out his closed fist.

Devers took the crumpled money, moist from the man's bodily excretions, and thumbed through it to verify the count was correct. Two twenties and three tens. It was always best when they had exact change. It made everything faster and less obvious to those around.

He turned away from the man and retrieved a tightly wrapped bundle from inside the lining of his sweatshirt. Many a pat down had missed Art Devers's creative hiding places. He handed the product over. The man scurried away around the corner.

Devers stuffed the man's money into his right front pocket. He pulled out some sanitizer from his back pocket and doused his hand in the clear liquid. He hated the filth associated with his job, but loved the money. He'd never once used his own product and was hoping he'd soon prove himself worthy to move from the corner to an office. That's where the real money got made.

He sat down on the stoop and pulled out a cigarette. It was a fresh pack, so he banged it against his thigh, tightening up the loose tobacco. He cupped his hand around the end to protect from wind as he lit it. A car pulled up, coming to a stop in front of where he sat. He recognized the man inside. It was a face he hadn't seen in quite some time, but Art Devers never forgot a face. Especially a cop's.

"Art freakin' Devers! It's been a long minute since I've seen your ugly mug."

"You're bad for business, Kelly." Devers blew out the smoke from his first drag.

"You know those things will kill ya?"

"What won't?"

Kelly walked up on the step and towered over the man. He looked around for eavesdroppers. "I need your help on something."

"If you're going to do it, make it look real. Lot of eyes on me. Lot of eyes whose mouths will whisper in ears of people I can't afford to cross," Devers whispered.

Kelly gave a barely perceptible nod. Devers reacted, flicking his cigarette to the side and jumping up as if to run. Kelly snatched the small dealer by the collar, yanking him into the air. He brought him to the ground, doing his best to control the impact with the concrete. "Try to run from me?" Kelly yelled. "Cuff this prick!"

Barnes dropped down beside the two men and clicked a set of handcuffs into place. Kelly righted Devers and brought him to his feet. Once standing, Kelly shoved him toward the awaiting Caprice. Kelly pressed Devers against the rear quarter panel of the passenger side of the car and kicked his legs wide. He ran the outside of the dealer's clothing starting at the top right shoulder and working his way down to the ankles. He repeated the same motion on the left. Once complete, he opened the rear door and shoved Devers inside.

Kelly entered the front passenger seat. Barnes took the wheel, and the car pulled away in dramatic fashion.

"When I said make it look good, I didn't expect you to go all Terry Tate Office Linebacker on my ass."

"C'mon, Brush. I've hit you harder than that before." Kelly turned and smiled. "Remember the first time we met?"

"How could I forget. I've still got the scar to prove it." Devers canted his head, exposing a large scar in his hairline.

"Hey Barnes, what do we say about running from the police in the Eleven?"

"If you're gonna run, we better not catch you," Barnes recited.

"Cause catch you comes with a price," both detectives said in unison, a mantra indoctrinated into them early in their careers working District C-11.

"Enough whining from you. Don't forget, you still owe me," Kelly said.

"I know. Can you at least take these off? Wonder Woman cranked these things on tight."

Devers bent forward, exposing his wrists. Kelly released the restraints, and the man sat up, rubbing his wrists and inspecting the damage.

"So, what can I do for Boston's finest?"

Kelly pulled out a picture from his file and handed it over to Devers. "Ever seen this girl before?"

Devers shook his head. "Nah."

"Take a good hard look and think," Kelly said. "We could just hang a u-ey and drop you off where we found you. I'll make a real big show of how cooperative you've been. I'm sure the neighborhood appreciates a snitch."

"Yo, that's messed up. Do me dirty like that?" Devers looked genuinely hurt by the comment. "I ain't never did you wrong before."

"You're saying you've never seen her?"

"On my mother's grave."

"Your mother's not dead. She's locked up."

Devers sucked his teeth. "She's dead to me."

"Fair enough. So that's a no?"

"I'd tell you if I did. You know I got a good eye for people." Devers handed the picture back. "What'd she do anyway? Run away from her rich daddy?"

"She's dead." Kelly handed Devers another picture. "What about this girl?"

"Damn. She dead too?"

"Just take a look and tell me if you've seen her."

"No dice, bro. Sorry."

"She's still alive. If you see her while you're out doing your thing, call me. If for some reason you can't reach me, call my partner, Detective Barnes. She's a Dot Rat like us. You can trust her." Kelly handed him a slip of paper with Barnes's work cell.

"A'ight bet." Devers studied the neighborhood they were passing through. "Hey, let me out behind KFC."

Barnes came in off of Park Street and pulled between two cars parked in the rear lot of Kentucky Fried Chicken. Devers looked around for a minute and then, using his drug-dealing- Spidey senses, determined it was safe to exit. Without saying a word, Art Devers hopped out of the car and disappeared inside the fast food joint. Barnes pulled out and back onto Park, leaving the spry dealer to navigate his way back to his home turf.

"You keep an interesting assortment of friends," Barnes jested.

"Narcotics crosses into shades of gray and connects you to the likes of people you'd never normally associate with. Devers was a good informant. He'll keep an eye out for Tabitha Porter now that he knows we're looking."

"You said he owes you?"

Kelly sighed. "Yeah, I helped his cousin out of a bad spot a while back. Good kid, just got caught up with the wrong people. Devers asked me to set him straight, and I did. Last I heard, he was applying to college."

Barnes looked over at him as she drove. "You're a good man, Michael Kelly."

His phone vibrated. It was Sutherland. "Hey Sarge, what's up?"

Kelly had to hold his ear away from the phone, but he could still clearly hear his sergeant's angry voice venting on the other end. "Are you trying to get in a personal sparring match with the mayor? Are you out of your mind? First, you bash some rich kid whose dad is golfing buddies with our elected leader. Then, you go and arrest one of his aides in some local brothel."

"I'm just going where this case is taking me. I don't really care who the mayor knows or what he thinks he can do to me."

"Did you forget you've still got the Baxter Green deposition tomorrow? If you keep pissing in the wind, you're bound to come out smelling like urine."

"Thanks for the fortune cookie advice."

"I'll see you when you get in."

17

The normal energetic buzz of the Homicide unit at work was subdued. It wasn't complete silence when Kelly and Barnes entered, but there was a distinct hush. Kelly walked to his desk.

Sitting in his chair was a man he'd never seen before.

"You mind telling me why you're sitting in my seat?"

"I'm Roy Clark. I am a liaison for the mayor."

"You're sitting at the desk of a Homicide detective working an active murder case." Kelly's face reddened and he spoke through gritted teeth. "Not sure who let you in."

"Let me cut you off before you say something we both regret," Sergeant Sutherland said. For a big man with a gimp leg, he could sneak up on his own shadow.

"Seriously, Sarge, what's the deal here?"

"I think you should let Mr. Clark speak."

"Let's hear it then." Kelly folded his arms and leaned back against his cubicle's divider wall.

"I heard you picked up one of the mayor's personal advisors. He's apparently made some bad choices recently."

Kelly shot a glance over at Barnes. She too stood in a guarded stance with arms crossed.

"We want you to know that the mayor is in total support of the fine work being done here by this unit, and in particular your handling of the Faith Wilson case."

"But?"

The outer corners of Clark's eyes creased, and his face brightened slightly. "I can see you're a perceptive one, Detective Kelly. Yes, there is a but to this conversation. The mayor would like to ensure no record of his aide's arrest is mentioned anywhere. Ever."

"I guess the mayor must be in quite a tizzy this week. First, his friend's son is involved in recruiting young girls into the sex trade, and now one of his own is out tasting the merchandise. Not a good week of PR for the mayor's re-election campaign."

"It's a delicate matter, and we would like you to see that. The mayor did not know of Branson's son's escapades. Nor did he know his advisor was frequenting a whorehouse during his lunch hour." Clark, still sitting in the detective's chair, leaned in toward Kelly. "But, even though he didn't know, or have any part in either incident, the release of such information would be terribly damaging. As you noted, this is an election year."

"So, you want me to just let Puzzo go? No questions asked?"

"We do want you to let him go. Your sergeant has already arranged to have his charges vacated from the arrest log and the report expunged."

Kelly stared at his supervisor and shook his head in disgust. Sutherland just shrugged.

"But, to show you that the mayor is in full support of your investigation into the tragic death of the young girl, I've made Puzzo available for you to interview him. Trust me, he will fully cooperate with any and all questions asked of him."

"I'm guessing everything is off the record. Nothing admissible at a later date?"

"Come, Detective. You seem like a resourceful fella. I'm sure you'll find a way to use anything you discover."

Kelly realized Clark must've heard about the entrance made into the brothel. Smart man. No wonder he was the mayor's clean-up guy. Made him wonder what other messes he'd mopped up for the city's highest official.

"Where is he now?"

"Interview 2," Sutherland said. "Told you to hear him out."

Clark stood up and extended his hand. Kelly hesitated in shaking it, but felt he'd made his point, and didn't want to push whatever luck he had left with the mayor.

"Keep up the great work, Detectives." Clark moved past the two. Sutherland followed, escorting the mayor's handyman out.

"Ready for another round in the interview box?" Kelly asked.

"Of course." Barnes smiled.

The two grabbed their pads.

* * *

"Mr. Puzzo, I don't know if you remember me and my partner?" Kelly paused to evaluate the man. "You were in a pretty emotional state when we met."

Puzzo maintained his focus on the table in front of him. His eyelids were a deep shade of irritated red, connecting to his blotchy cheeks. In the simplest of terms, he was a hot mess. "Of course, I remember."

"Good. Then we can skip the pleasantries and get down to brass tacks." Kelly slid his chair out and took a seat across from Puzzo. Barnes did likewise.

"Not sure what I'm supposed to tell you. It was my first time ever doing something like this."

Kelly smirked. "Let's get something straight. My boss made the deal to cut you loose, not me. If you waste my time, I'll drag you back down to booking and start the process all over again."

"You can't do that. A deal's a deal."

"You're not the one calling the shots. Understand that." Kelly softened his tone slightly. "And, you're right. A deal is a deal. So, you best hold up your end, which means telling us everything you know about the operation."

Puzzo's head sank lower. "I don't really know much. They've been running that house you found me at for a while. I'm actually surprised the cops haven't busted it before."

"What about the girls?"

"What do you mean?"

Kelly slid the photo of Faith Wilson across the table, the one from her missing person flyer, the innocent twelve-year-old immortalized by the school photographer two months before she disappeared. Puzzo leaned forward, hovering over the glossy finish of the picture.

The mayor's aide slowly shook his head. "I don't think I've ever seen her before."

"You think or you know. In our world those are two very different things."

"She looks a bit young," Puzzo added.

"That's because she is. Or was." Kelly slid the next picture, the one depicting the girl at thirteen and face down in a ditch.

"My God!" Puzzo's body began to quake. "Why would you show me this?"

"Look at the dress. Ever seen a girl wearing it before?"

"No!" Puzzo pushed the pictures back toward the detectives. "I don't touch young girls. I've got a daughter around her age."

"You don't touch the young girls, but you've seen them?" Barnes asked.

Puzzo made eye contact for the first time since they'd entered the room. He didn't verbalize his answer, only gave a single nod of his head.

"This girl?"

"I don't remember her. But, that's not to say she hasn't come through there. The girls rotate quite a bit. Only a couple regulars stick around. I'm not sure where the rest end up."

Kelly tapped on the picture of the dead girl. "I can tell you where she ended up."

"What do you know about the operation? Now is not the time to skimp on details," Barnes prompted.

"I usually only stop in once a week. I pay up front, and whoever's working security takes the cash. I assume the guys at the house are just the muscle. They don't talk much, if at all. They rotate too. There's not a lot of traffic during the daytime hours. I heard from one of the girls that night is a totally different scene. She told me they rent hotel rooms and hold large parties."

"How do you find out where the parties are?"

"Not sure. I didn't ask because there was no way I could ever attend. It would be too out of character for me to leave the house at night. I'm a family man."

Kelly almost choked on the man's words. He had thousands of insults loaded in his verbal catapult, but fought the urge to unleash them.

Puzzo must have noticed Kelly's disdain, because he offered up a conciliatory attempt. "Listen, maybe asking the big guy in the jumpsuit or one of the girls might help. I'm sure they'd have a ton more info than a guy like me."

"Not happening. The Polish gorilla lawyered up, and the girls are too scared to speak." Kelly sighed. "That's why we're having this conversation."

"Detectives, I truly wish I could be of more assistance."

Kelly reached into a white box he'd brought in with him. He removed two paper containers each roughly the size of a pencil. He then slipped on two pairs of latex gloves over each hand.

Puzzo gave Kelly an inquisitive look. "What's all that?"

"Part of the deal is you give me everything I ask for. I'm asking for a voluntary sample of your DNA." Kelly held up one of the packages. "These are buccal swabs. I'm going to rub them on the inside of your cheek and remove some skin cells from the interior of your mouth. It won't hurt."

"What are you hoping to find?"

"If what you told us is true, then nothing." Kelly peeled open the packaging, exposing the soft applicator tip. "But, if you're lying, then no amount of political pressure can stop me from coming after you."

Puzzo swallowed hard.

"I can call Mr. Clark and let him know that we've run into a bit of an impasse with you. Maybe he can come back and explain the way this is supposed to work."

"That won't be necessary." Puzzo leaned forward and opened his mouth.

* * *

Kelly finished tagging the sample and walked it down to Charles in Forensics. He asked him to see if he could get it to the lab and into Ithaca Best's hands as soon as possible. She had some male specimens to compare it against and Kelly needed to know if George Puzzo was a match.

"Our little interrogation of Puzzo didn't open up much for us," Barnes said.

"Let's attack the Tabitha Porter angle from a new perspective. We should check out the last known point the girl's phone was showing before it went offline."

"I assume I'm driving?"

"Unless you'd prefer the soothing comforts of my four-wheel death trap?"

The two headed out of Schroeder Plaza and back to Dorchester.

"As much as we've been in the Dot this week, we might as well have been reassigned back to the Eleven," Barnes said.

She rode the bumper of the car in front of her, leaving no room for error should the person suddenly brake. A classic masshole technique of ensuring no other driver could slide into position. Lane changes were made without signaling. Another sign of weakness, of which Barnes showed none. For being born and raised in the area, Michael Kelly never adhered to the driving principles seemingly intrinsically passed from generation to generation. He gripped the handle above the passenger window and pressed his foot against the floorboard in a futile attempt to magically slow or stop the car.

"Look at the tough Michael Kelly white-knuckled in my car. I thought nothing scared you?"

"Your driving has taken years off my life."

"Gosh, Mikey, you say the sweetest things." Barnes accelerated and shot across into the left lane and around the car in front. The movement jostled Kelly from side to side, and his grip tightened.

"At least we're making good time." Kelly kept his eyes on the cars around him because he got the terrible feeling Barnes either did not see them, or if she did, didn't care.

They arrived in the area of Dorchester Ave where Tabitha Porter's phone had last indicated she'd been. It wasn't a perfect match to a specific spot and the grid coordinates had a margin of error, but it was a good starting point.

Barnes parked the car. Her ability to quickly parallel park, wedging her unmarked between two cars into a spot that, upon first impression, looked too small for a Smart Car, was as impressive as it was stressful. Kelly swore he'd felt her tap the bumpers of both vehicles ahead and behind, neither of which even registered on Barnes's radar. She threw it in park and gave him a knowing smile.

"I'll drive tomorrow." Kelly released his grip from the handle and grabbed his notepad.

The two surveyed the area. Kelly looked for a spot that rang of teenage runaway. A place where a young girl would go. There was a bakery and hardware store on the side of the street where they stood. Food maybe. Tools not likely. Kelly spotted a Vietnamese nail salon across the street. Barnes had keyed on it too and nodded.

They hurried across and went inside. The Nail Palace was quiet, except for the light instrumental music chiming over the hushed conversations of the masked nail professionals speaking in their native tongue. Kelly wondered how many times they mocked their clientele as they worked their beautification process. The air smelled of citrus, but was overwhelmed by the chemical smell of the lacquered polishes.

One of the nail technicians left her elderly client with her hands under the purple-hued drying lamps and approached Kelly and Barnes.

"How may I help you? Mani-pedi?"

Kelly exposed his badge from inside his windbreaker and then stuck it back into the recesses of his jacket. Her eyes widened a bit. Police presence was not always welcome in places like this, and he didn't want to make too big a show of their position. Local police were often confused with their federal immigration counterparts. The fear of deportation left many victims' crimes undocumented. Kelly hoped to mitigate any barriers to her cooperation.

"We're here about a missing girl. She may have come into your business a few days ago," Barnes said. She held up an image of Tabitha Porter on her phone.

The nail specialist squinted at the picture. "When she here?"

"It would have been Tuesday around noontime." Kelly watched for a reaction in the woman's face.

She pursed her lips. "I no work Tuesday."

"Anybody else here who was working then?" Barnes asked.

The woman turned and spoke in the fast-paced cadence of her native tongue. She broadcast what could only be assumed as Barnes's question. A small woman stood up from the foot-washing station in the back of the parlor. She dried her hands and hesitantly approached the front of the store.

Barnes showed the picture to her. "Do you recognize this girl?"

"She came in here around lunch time. She had a friend with her." The younger employee clearly enunciated each word. Although her command of the English language was better than her older counterpart, Kelly could tell it still took great effort to articulate her thoughts.

"Can you describe the friend?"

The girl hesitated. "Not sure. But I can show you."

Kelly and Barnes looked at each other. "Show us?"

"We got robbed last year. My mother put in security cameras." The girl pointed to the front of the store.

In the corner, where the yellow painted wall met the glass of the front façade, a small black orb was affixed.

"Can you access the footage from Tuesday?" Kelly asked.

"Yes. Follow me to the back." The girl turned and said something in Vietnamese to the older woman, who Kelly surmised to be the mother, and then walked purposefully to the back door, guiding aside beaded drapes.

The heavy woman whose foot bath had been interrupted gave Kelly a smile. He eyed the stubby toes and snarled nails protruding out of the bubbling water. The detective, who'd seen a lot of disturbing things in his career, immediately found a new level of respect for the young girl's profession.

Through the beads and to the left was a small office space. Hung from the wall above the monitor was a framed dollar bill. Incense burned on the desk beneath it, giving the room a sweet smell of lavender and rose. The girl sat and began typing on the keyboard. A moment later the screen came to life and a live image of the storefront came into view. She went to work manipulating the date and time. It only took a couple of minutes before an image of two girls appeared, standing in almost the exact spot Kelly and Barnes had stood only moments before.

Tabitha Porter was clearly visible as she stared up toward the camera. By all accounts she looked happy. The girl with her had wavy black hair. The footage scrolled by, and Kelly asked to fast-forward to their departure.

At no point in the surveillance recording did the camera capture a clean shot of the girl with her. The manicurist stopped the footage at the point where the girls opened the door to leave. "Did this help?"

"Are there any cameras outside of the store?" Kelly asked.

"No. I'm sorry," the girl said, disappointed. "We only bought one camera."

"Can you keep playing? It looks like your camera catches a bit of the street," Barnes said.

The image started up again. Tabitha and her friend exited the store. The camera provided enough coverage to show the two standing by a dark-colored sedan. Tabitha got into the passenger seat and, a few seconds later, the car drove off. From the angle, Kelly couldn't make out a license plate, or even the make or model.

The only thing he could tell was that as of Tuesday, 1:27 p.m., Tabitha Porter was still alive. He hoped that was still the case now.

18

The commute time doubled on his return to the office. Kelly transferred his case notes from his pad to computer. It always helped him to do so before he left for the night, a way of organizing the highlights of his investigation into a clear and cohesive format. He stared at the screen, double-checking the information one last time before logging off. The clock on the wall read 7:45. If he pushed it, he could still make it back to Dorchester in time.

Kelly was the last to leave. All of the other workstations were dark. The motion light activated when he stood up, casting the quiet office space of the Homicide unit in an eerie glow. He looked back at his Murder Board. He had crossed out Jane Doe on the red card, replaced by Faith Wilson. One minor piece of the girl's death resolved, while a host of others lay in wait.

Kelly left the office feeling wholly unfulfilled. He navigated the busy rush hour traffic at a much slower clip than Barnes had earlier in the day. Unlike the other commuters battling their own bouts of road rage, Kelly took solace in the drive. He didn't listen to the radio. It didn't work even if he'd wanted. On a good day, he'd pick up static and classic rock on 100.7 WZLX. More times than not, he embraced the isolation and was glad to have a reprieve from the spoken word. The only sound, besides his Impala's rattle, was the symphony of horns and profanity provided by other motorists.

The beat and rhythm of any case held its rises and falls. During the academy, there'd been a guest speaker, Detective James Flaherty, or Jimmy Smokes as he was affectionately known around the department. A man known for always having a cigarette in his mouth, even after the department evolved into a more health-conscious era. There were tons of classes and instructors who espoused their wisdom upon the recruits, but something Flaherty said stuck with Kelly to this day.

The raspy Irishman had been talking about working a murder. He spoke about it not being sexy and glamorous. The depravity witnessed wore at a man's soul and played out in the mind long after the files were closed. Solved or unsolved, once you worked a body, they never left you. Like some cosmic connection, life clinging to death, or the other way around. But above all else, Kelly remembered one thing Flaherty said: *In the quiet of an investigation sometimes the dead speak. If you have the talent for it, and few do, the dead will whisper to you when all seems lost. Their weak and distant voice will call out from the darkness and guide you forward.*

He remembered the recruit next to him giggled. Kelly did not. There was something in the way Jimmy Smokes delivered his message, an intangible weight to the words. Kelly always meant to seek out Flaherty after and dive deeper into the man's wisdom, but never had the opportunity. The opening in Homicide that Kelly filled was created when Flaherty, facing retirement, stuck his duty weapon in his mouth and pulled the trigger. Maybe it was facing life after the badge, or maybe the memories of the dead finally took its toll. That's the thing about death, especially suicide, it left the living with more questions than answers.

Faith Wilson hadn't yet whispered in his ear. He was still grasping for answers into the disappearance and death of the suburban teen.

* * *

Kelly finally arrived in the neighborhood where he'd grown up. He pulled the Impala into the back lot of Pops's Gym, Kelly's second home. Pops had served as a surrogate father after the early passing of his own.

He changed into his workout clothes, consisting of a T-shirt and shorts. No fancy Dri-FIT Lycra fabric for him. Just plain old cotton. Hard to change the conditioned years of simplicity. Kelly grabbed his duffle from the trunk, buried under a spare ballistic raid vest and other police-related accouterments, his two worlds heaped together.

The familiar buzzer sounded from inside the gym, announcing the last ten seconds of a round. *The Hard Ten,* as Pops called it, when you unloaded everything left in the tank, exhausting the reserve, knowing the one-minute recovery period was just seconds away. Many a match was won and lost in those critical ten seconds of fight.

The final bell dinged as Kelly opened the back door, always unlocked, even though it was nestled in the heart of Dorchester, just off of Dot Ave. Pops refused to listen to reason, stating his door was always open. Kelly didn't need reminding of seeking the gym's refuge during difficult times, and he knew it continued to serve a similar purpose to this day for many of the young boxers it housed.

"Oh my! Boys, lookie what the cat dragged in!" Bobby McDonough, standing ringside, yelled from across the room.

A mix of leather, sweat, and blood bathed the warm air of the gym. There was no heat or air conditioning. The climate was solely powered by human exertion. Pops always said, "You want to get warm, put in work. You want to cool off, then sweat."

Walking across the wood floors to his childhood friend, Kelly dropped his bag and pulled out his hand wraps. He hooked the loop to his thumb and began the ritualistic wrapping. Always four turns around the wrist before Kelly started his zigzag pattern, interweaving the canvas strap between each of his fingers. It was the first thing he'd learned when his father walked him through the doors of the gym.

Kelly had been eight years old, same age as his Embry, when his father caught him fighting in the street against a neighborhood bully, Antonio Marino. Fat Tony, as he was affectionately known to his victims, stole Brayden's bicycle. Fat Tony was three years older and about thirty pounds heavier than Kelly, but none of that fazed him. He'd been raised to stand up for family and never back down from a fight. Both principles, firmly ingrained, still held true today.

All the heart in the world didn't matter without skill, and at age eight, Kelly lacked much of the latter. He took a beating unlike any kid had seen, punched and kicked by the obese pre-teen. To those witnessing the assault, Kelly earned legend status for being able to take a beating. Each time Fat Tony knocked Kelly down, he got back up. Bloody and half-unconscious, Michael Kelly stood his ground.

His father showed up after Brayden had run to the family liquor store a block away and explained what was happening. Kelly remembered the look in his father's eyes when he arrived, a twisted combination of pride and pity. His father snatched the bike from Fat Tony's hands and gave the hefty boy a kick in his thick ass, sending him on his way. Nowadays his father would've been dragged away in cuffs for handling the scuffle in such a manner, but things were different back then.

On the evening of that same day, bruised and battered, Michael Kelly got walked through the front doors of Pops's Gym. His father brought him directly over to the lean black gym owner and said, "He's got the heart of a lion but the mitts of a kitten." Kelly remembered Pops's simple yet powerful response. "Heart, I can't teach. Everything else can be learned."

It started that day and continued to the present. The skills forged in the sixteen-square-foot ring served him throughout his life. Kelly had been the reigning middleweight Golden Gloves champion for his last three years of high school, one of the toughest weight classes in boxing. In a state known for its prowess in creating pugilistic artists, it had been a near-impossible feat. Pops prided himself on developing fighters from the inside out. His methodology had apparently worked because Pops's Gym housed more local champions than any other in the area.

"I thought you weren't going to show," McDonough chided. "I know how much you hate punching the priest."

"Well, you know he is a saint. At least that's what I've heard," Father Donovan O'Brien said. He was out of breath from a round of jumping rope.

"You sure you want to do this, Donny? You're looking a bit winded." Kelly sealed his wrap, adhering the Velcro end. He punched his hand into his palm, checking to ensure the wrap was tight enough to keep his wrist from flexing on impact. Satisfied, he began the same ritual with the other hand.

"Just remember to keep your guard up. I don't want to mess up your pretty face."

"I'm not the one who's got girls throwing themselves at me all day." Kelly laughed.

Edmund Brown gave his deep baritone laugh. In Dorchester's early years, it had been primarily Irish Catholic and predominantly white. Edmund had been the first African American in Kelly's school. The boys became fast friends and Kelly never saw race as an issue. Others were not as open-minded, and Kelly had fought shoulder to shoulder with Ed as they stood their ground against the ignorant. In those fights, they'd formed an unbreakable alliance.

Ed Brown was a genius, academically lapping all of them in school, and eventually earning a full-ride scholarship to Harvard. But he was, like all of them, forever connected to the neighborhood, and returned after graduating to serve as a schoolteacher in the same school they'd gone to as kids.

"Seriously, Donny, how do you turn down all those women throwing themselves at you?" Brown asked.

"You really need to share some of your confessional stories with us." McDonough punched the priest in the shoulder, then made a sign of the cross in mock repentance.

"Mikey, you might want to say your prayers, because it's going to be lights out for you in a minute." Donny bit at the laces of his gloves, ratcheting them to his wrists.

Kelly laughed as he stepped between the middle and top rope of the ring. "I hope God doesn't smite me when I lay out one of his favorite servants."

Kelly bounced up and down on the canvas flooring of the squared area. The minimal cushion and spring underneath had long since been stomped out. The stains of sweat and blood had woven a unique tie-dye of various shades of brown, a testament to the years of use. Not that it was unhygienic, but some stains never seemed to come completely out. Pops ensured the gym was scrubbed clean at the end of each night, a task left to the most junior members as a rite of passage every night except Thursdays, when the four childhood friends always put in the cleanup work as a way of thanking their old mentor for the hard-fought lessons and continued support.

Kelly rested against the worn covering over the corner turnbuckle. He rolled his neck from side to side, loosening it from the strain of his last few hours hunched over his computer, entering the notes of Faith Wilson's death investigation. The muscles were tighter than usual tonight, but nothing a couple rounds wouldn't fix.

Father Donovan O'Brien entered the ring. For a man of the cloth, he was cut from stone, more likely to be modeled for some Greek gladiator monolith than a humble servant of God. His chiseled chest and six-pack abs were a contradiction to the gentle work of his calling. "Somebody ring the bell," he said, his words muffled by the mouthpiece surrounding his upper teeth. The mouthpiece was black except for the small white cross painted onto the front.

The buzzer sounded, indicating the start of the first of two three-minute rounds. The group always fought two rounds unless the match was left undecided. Then, an additional would be fought. Long gone were the days when they'd move and swing for ten or twelve grueling rounds. They were not the men of their youth, but battled hard to maintain a shadowy resemblance of that time. Each week the sparring partners would rotate. McDonough and Ed Brown had already fought before Kelly arrived. He was disappointed he'd missed it; their bouts were epic. From the size of the swelling underneath McDonough's eye, it looked as though Ed took the win.

Kelly shuffled toward Donny and the two engaged in the ritualistic feeling-out dance, as each man sought to find their range with testing jabs. Nothing too heavy usually came in the opening moments of a match. It wasn't like the days of Tyson, when he'd enter the ring and toss an all-out haymaker to end the fight before it began. The boys of Pops's gym were taught the finer points of the trade and demonstrated the skills learned both inside and outside the ring. Kelly and McDonough were the only two who still found use in their day jobs, but for totally different reasons.

Donny shot a hard jab that struck Kelly square in his forehead as he dipped. His reflexes were a bit off, his mind still back at the gravesite of Faith Wilson. The shot to the head snapped him out of his mental malaise, and he appreciated it. Kelly slipped low and to the side, unleashing a flurry of body shots to the priest's muscle-encased rib cage. Kelly was a body blow fighter. It was his trademark. Work the body hard enough and long enough so an opponent's hands dropped. Once down, he'd take his time and pick away on the defenseless and exposed head with surgical precision.

The priest didn't take the abuse lying down and sent a barrage of short hooks toward Kelly's head. The detective slipped most of them by bobbing side to side, rolling with each punch as it came. It was a smooth defense, and was working well to deflect the punishment, when Kelly was suddenly caught off

guard by a surprise uppercut. The impact buckled his knees and sent him stag-
gering backward.

Donny's eyes widened. Kelly watched as his friend approached, his shoulders tightly drawn up, and his gloves extended a few inches in front of his face.
It looked like Donny was trying to end the bout early, seeing his opportunity
with Kelly off-balance and rocked by the previous attack.

Kelly shuffled until his back found the ropes. He leaned into the rubber-
encased top rope. Donny moved in quickly. Once in range, Kelly used the
springy ring's barrier to launch himself forward. The immediate change in
distancing threw Donny's planned assault off-course, and Kelly seized the
opportunity, slamming his gloved fists up and down his friend's body and
head. When he was a Golden Glove Champion, the paper had called him
the Irish Hurricane for his memorable onslaught of combination attacks.
During those times, he had more in the tank, and could release them at will.
Now, not so much, and Kelly was actually surprised he was able to do so
tonight.

The whaling sent Donny backward several feet. Kelly let up and watched
his friend wobble. He waited, evaluating the extent of his efforts and, if he were
to be completely honest with himself, waiting for the wind to re-inflate
depleted lungs.

Donny fell forward. He caught himself by stepping out with his left foot.
His body dropped down, and the fighting priest knelt like a squire readying
himself to be knighted. He placed his gloved hands on the mat for balance.
Then he held up his right and waved it slowly in the air. The match was over;
Kelly immediately went to his friend's side.

"You all right, Donny? Sorry. I didn't even know I had one of those combos
left in my arsenal."

"Whew!" Donny laughed. "I think I saw God for a minute there."

"I'm not going to lie, when I saw you take a knee, I thought you were going
to call in a lightning strike or something."

The two sat back on the moist mat, freshly saturated with their contribu-
tion of sweat, and laughed.

McDonough rolled water bottles to both of them. "Hydrate. We've got some
drinking to do. I assume the good priest has brought us something pleasureful
for our heathen palates?"

"Seriously, I steal from a liquor store when I'm fifteen and you guys make me buy the beer every Thursday for the rest of my life? Seems a bit harsh."

"Father, it's your atonement. You're a Catholic priest. You must be burdened with guilt. We're just trying to help you." McDonough loved to chide Donny. "But, seriously, what'd you bring?"

Donny slipped his gloves off and pointed a wrapped hand in the direction of the cooler by the back door. "Look and see."

"Mikey, I haven't seen that combo from you in a while, son. Nicely done." Pops leaned his elbows onto the mat.

"Didn't know I had it in me."

"Donny, what'd I tell you about getting overconfident? Never go in for the kill that early. Especially when you're facing off with Mikey."

"I know, Pops, I just thought I had him this time. Saint Michael here is getting a bit old. He did just turn thirty-five."

Pops smiled faintly and shook his head. "You boys take the drinking to the back lot. I don't want this new generation thinking I condone that amongst my fighters."

Kelly gave Pops a gloved thumbs up. Pops gave them the same warning each and every Thursday. Kelly hoped one day the old man would join them for a cold one. It hadn't happened yet, but all four boys felt it was overdue.

The cold air felt good on Kelly's sweat-soaked shirt. He cracked open the IPA and swallowed hard. There was something about the first swig of beer after a good fight, an intangible and unquantifiable experience that only a small percentage of the population ever shared.

"I really thought I had you tonight," Donny said. "You seemed a bit distracted. Figured I'd try to get a win under my belt."

"You definitely caught me good with that uppercut."

"So, what's eating at you? Work?"

McDonough cracked his second beer. "Father, maybe our good friend Mikey doesn't feel like going to confession tonight."

"It's okay. I don't mind." Kelly took a pull from the can. "I caught a bad one the other day. A young girl, just turned thirteen, turned up dead in a ditch."

"Where at?" Ed Brown asked, his face etched with concern. He taught kids in that age bracket and Kelly knew he was concerned it might be someone he knew, or a possible former student.

"Close. Over off Von Hillern."

"That's in our backyard!" McDonough slugged back his beer. "Why didn't you tell me?"

"I just did. You know, Bobby, you're not always the first person I call when there's a crime."

"Was she local?" Brown asked. His face looked strained as he sipped his beer. Ed Brown only allowed himself one beer during these nights. It was the only alcohol he'd consume during the week. He prided himself on clean living and would nurse the beer until the night was over.

"No. Suburban kid. Ended up on the wrong side of something."

Donny O'Brien placed a gentle hand on Kelly's shoulder. Kelly didn't know if he was doing it as a concerned friend or consoling priest. The lines of those two roles had long since blurred. Either way, the gesture was appreciated.

"I don't have much to go on yet. Hopefully, tomorrow I'll know more."

"I'll do a little digging too and let you know if I hear something," McDonough said, crushing the beer can in his hands.

If Ed was the teetotaler, then Bobby McDonough was the yin to his yang. Kelly witnessed his friend demolish the upper side of a twelve-pack in less than an hour. What was more astonishing is the lay person would never be able to tell the man had taken a drink. Tolerance was the word for it, but Bobby claimed he had a magic liver, a gift from the homeland.

Bobby McDonough and Michael Kelly were interchangeable as youths. The McDonoughs lived two doors down. At times it was impossible to tell who lived where. Both mothers treated them as their own, bandaging cuts and feeding them on a constant basis. Bobby's first legitimate job was as a stock boy in the Kelly family liquor store. It didn't last long, and was probably the only legitimate job he'd held.

Many thought the two were brothers. More times than not, Kelly felt closer to McDonough than his own kin. The two had plans of conquering the world together. That was until Conner Walsh intervened.

Bobby McDonough was also a wrong place, wrong time kind of kid. He got sucked in by the fast money of being a runner. Walsh recruited heavily from the neighborhood and thus Kelly's best friend became the newest member of the Savin Hill Boys.

McDonough's real break came when he was making a cash drop at one of the bars run by Walsh. It was a front to wash the money from drugs and guns. Bobby Wrong Place, Wrong Time McDonough walked into the back room as Conner Walsh pulled the trigger, killing a local thug named Joseph Gillespie. Conner Walsh was rumored to have dispatched many a rival into the great beyond, but very few had ever witnessed his acts of violence firsthand. As far as Kelly knew, his friend Bobby was the only living witness to such a crime.

In that moment Walsh let McDonough live. Each day after a gift, and Bobby knew it. The bond between Walsh and McDonough solidified over the years as Bobby never spoke of the incident to anyone, at least as far as Walsh could discern. Bobby had told one person and one person only. Michael Kelly.

Kelly had tucked that secret deep, knowing to expose it would mean certain death for his friend. In the eleven-plus years Kelly served the City of Boston he was never able to close a case against the Irish kingpin. Joseph Gillespie was still listed as a missing person. No body. No murder. But Kelly knew. And some day he planned to right it. Maybe it would free his friend from his indentured servitude, but many years had passed since the days of old. It was unlikely Bobby would ever leave even if he could. Still, Kelly's loyalty to his friend had no expiration date.

"I don't know if I want anybody from Walsh's crew sniffing around my case. Even if it's you."

"Well, Connor's not going to like hearing a young girl ended up dead on his turf. You know the rules around here, Mikey. You know 'em better than most."

Kelly didn't answer his friend. McDonough was right. If something happened in Dorchester, then Connor Walsh took notice. A dead girl from out of town would bring an unnecessary amount of heat down on the area, and that would be bad for business.

Secretly, Kelly was glad McDonough now knew about the case. Bobby could work in channels off-limits to one of Boston's finest, even if that cop came from the neighborhood. The badge created barriers.

19

She was shrouded in the binding weight of a thick comforter. Tabitha was aware she was on a bed, but for the life of her couldn't figure out how she got there. The last distinct memory she had was in the van. There was no accounting for the lost time. The clock on the nightstand read 1:13 a.m.

Tabitha Porter sat up, or at least tried her best to assume a position that could be described as sitting. Gravity worked against her, and the room spun wildly with her effort to resist it. Her right leg broke free from the restraint of the sheets and a cool draft worked its way up her body. She realized she was naked. The seafoam green skirt was strewn across a chair.

A toilet flushed, and the suddenness caused her to turn toward the bathroom. The quick movement increased her vertigo and she closed her eyes in an effort to bring about some equilibrium.

The bathroom door opened, and a bright light fell across the red shag carpeting of the floor. The glow was dashed by a shadowed silhouette. The clearing of a throat, deep and weighted, told Tabitha it belonged to a man.

A middle-aged man stepped into view. He wasn't threatening or scary. On the contrary, he looked like your everyday average Joe. She guessed him to be in his mid-to-late thirties. He wore jeans and a black T-shirt. There was writing on the shirt, but her eyes were still adjusting, and she couldn't make out the details. Same went for the man's face. It was difficult to make out any features, except he had dark eyes and similarly matched hair color.

The man gave a smile and placed some money on the dresser closest to him. "Here's a little something extra just for you."

The words, although gentle in delivery, were confusing. None of this made any sense.

He walked out of the room and closed the door behind him. Tabitha slid off the bed. Crawling across the floor, she followed the trail of undergarments. With great effort, she slid her bra and panties on. She was sore but didn't allow her mind to ask the question she already knew the disturbing answer to.

Tabitha pulled herself up onto a padded footstool. She stepped her feet into the soft fabric of the skirt and began inching it up toward her waist. Unsteady, she had to stop several times to correct for her lack of balance.

Successfully zipping up her skirt, she reached behind to grab her top. The door to the room opened, and she instinctively covered her chest with the small garment in her hand.

"No need to cover up, baby. Your night has just begun." She had never seen this man before, and the coldness with which he spoke was a far cry from the man who'd just left.

He crossed the room quickly and stood over her. In the poorly lit room, the tall man was a menacing sight. Tabitha assumed, even in the light of day, this man would intimidate most. She cowered back, sliding into a chair.

"Do you know who I am?"

Tabitha shook her dizzied head.

"Good. Better for you it stays that way." The man pulled out his cellphone and swiped his finger across the screen, casting his face in an eerie glow. He looked like somebody telling a campfire spooky story.

He pushed the screen toward her face. The light was blinding, and it took a moment for Tabitha's eyes to adjust. The image was of a girl. That she was sure of. The rest took her a bit to decipher. She was wearing a sequined dress. Silver shimmers had bounced off the flash when the picture was taken, giving the girl an angelic glow. Then, as her eye traced the outline of the body, she noticed the fancy-dressed girl was face down, surrounded by dirt.

"Do you know this girl?"

Tabitha, entranced by the disturbing image, shook her head.

"Do you want to be this girl?"

Tabitha looked up, eyes wide in terror. Her heart pumped faster, and she could hear the blood pounding in her head. A deafening, rhythmic thumping overwhelmed her ability to think.

"Good. Then you understand."

Without saying another word, he walked to the door. As he left, a familiar face replaced his.

Slice walked over and sat on the edge of the bed. Tabitha looked at the girl who'd taken her shopping and bought her new clothes. She sought an answer to the madness in her friend's eyes. The hazel eyes staring back held none of the kindness she'd seen earlier. No compassion or worry. Only coldness.

"You understand how this works? You're with us now. We'll take care of you as long as you take care of us." Slice was devoid of emotion.

"Take care of me?" Tabitha whispered the words and feared the reprisal.

Slice stood. Tabitha tucked herself into a defensive ball. "I'm not going to hit you. The customers don't like bruised fruit, especially when it's as sweet and young as yours."

Tabitha unfolded herself only slightly.

Slice held open her hand. There was a small bag with a cocoa brown powder lining the bottom. She gave the bag to Tabitha and handed her a cut orange straw. "Snort this."

Tabitha winced at the thought. "I don't want to."

"Trust me. You're going to need it if you plan on getting through this night."

Tabitha didn't resist any further. Terrified at the meaning behind the words she sniffed the contents of the package. A taste of chocolate filled her mouth.

"I'll be back later." Slice got up and walked to the door. She looked down at the twenty-dollar bill on the dresser. "All tips come to me." She snatched up the money and opened the door.

Three men stood in the doorway. Slice allowed all three to enter and walked out without looking back.

Tabitha watched the men approach. These guys didn't look kind. They had thick gold chains and baggy pants. She caught the glimmer of a gold tooth in the wicked smile on the man in the rear. The thought of what was coming sickened her. They started shedding clothes as they advanced on her.

Tabitha Porter closed her eyes and willed whatever magic powder she'd just inhaled to take her mind as far from this place as humanly possible. Regardless, she knew that when she opened them again, her world would be forever changed.

20

Sleep had never come easy, but over the years, as the mental plaque of accumulated experience built up, it had become an entirely elusive concept. Kelly found ways to compensate. Drinking to a numbing level was one solution he'd tried. He quickly deemed it unsustainable. While alcohol knocked him out, his sleep was anything but restful, and he found his ability to operate at full capacity the following morning greatly diminished.

White noise, in the form of an old wobbly fan, turned out to be the best remedy for his insomnia. Although, even with the whirling hum, Kelly usually only managed four hours. Occasionally he would start his day with six hours of shut-eye under his belt. Those were rare days indeed, and he cherished them.

Tonight, apparently, would not lead to one of those days. He stared at the Red Sox clock above his dresser mirror, tucked amidst the posters of legendary southpaw Sean Mannion. Coming to America at the age of seventeen, Mannion fought his way through life with the same tenacity he faced his opponents with in the ring. In his fifty-seven professional bouts he was never knocked down. Although Kelly couldn't claim a similar feat, he could count the number of people who'd sent him to the canvas on one hand. Mannion was Kelly's childhood hero, made even more real because he lived in Dorchester.

His mom had kept his room the same as he'd left it when he moved out. The clock had a jittery second hand that put a lag on time's accuracy. Every few days, Kelly needed to adjust it to the correct time. He compared the clock to his digital watch. 2:07 a.m. He would need to reset his wall clock in the morning.

He fluffed his thin pillow for the hundredth time and tried to find a comfortable position on the twin mattress. Then Kelly heard a sound above the rattle of the fan. The front door creaked. Sometimes the wind would blow it open, but it was usually followed by a slam. This was not.

Kelly leaned over and pulled the chain to the rickety fan twice. The noisy whirl slowed to a stop. In the following silence, Kelly listened. A creak, and then the distinct sound of someone trying to conceal a cough. The muffled rasp carried throughout the colonial. His father always said, "This house has got good bones. Like mine, they tend to creak a bit with age."

He sat up slowly, trying to minimize the squeak of the springs. Kelly moved across the room with soft steps on his bare feet. No need to bother turning on a light. He knew the house like the back of his hand and could navigate it wearing a blindfold. He tucked his Glock into the waistband of his sweatpants and cinched the drawstring tight. Kelly then grabbed a baseball bat from his closet.

Kelly slowly turned the knob and opened the door. He stopped when it was half-open because the hinge was in desperate need of some lubricant and would yelp loudly if he went any further with it. He slid his body sideways, navigating the small opening, entering onto the second-floor landing.

Heel to toe, his bare feet took the progression to the stairwell carefully. Kelly wanted to catch the perp off-guard and give himself the best opportunity to overwhelm the intruder.

As he moved down the stairs, he heard the cough again. This time it came from the kitchen. Once at the bottom, Kelly could see the light from the kitchen pooling out into the living room. *What self-respecting burglar turned on the lights?*

He paused along the wall near the hall entrance to the kitchen. He waited and listened, trying to pinpoint the exact location of the perp before making his entrance. Then he heard the suction release as the fridge door was pulled open. Kelly seized the opportunity.

Kelly spun into the threshold connecting the narrow hallway to the kitchen, bat held high. He could see the rear end of the man sticking out from behind the refrigerator door.

Kelly wielded the bat, leveling it onto the exposed buttocks of the unaware prowler. The blow's contact was deflected slightly by the impact with the door. Regardless, it was enough to cause the man to arch back and scream.

Kelly prepped himself for a second swing. He stopped midstream as he recognized the disheveled man standing before him.

His brother gave him a pained look as he rubbed the left side of his butt wildly. "What the hell, Mikey?"

Kelly felt like giving his brother another whack for posterity. "Who comes in during the middle of the damn night? Are you outta your ever lovin' mind?"

Brayden didn't answer; he turned back to the fridge, fishing out a beer and some leftover lasagna, plated and covered in plastic wrap. "I'm hungry."

"Hungry? You show up at two in the morning to grab a bite to eat? Ma and I haven't heard from you in weeks."

His brother sat at the table. He cracked open the beer and took a long pull. Brayden Kelly pulled off the plastic and forked a large piece of cold lasagna into his mouth. He groaned in enjoyment as he devoured the first bite.

"You're killing Ma. You know that? You're all she talks about."

Brayden smirked. "The golden child, Saint Michael, is feeling left out?"

Kelly didn't give in to his brother's goading. He put the bat down, in the event anger got the best of him. "What happened to you?"

Brayden stuffed another piece in his mouth. "Life."

"Don't give me that load of crap! We were raised in the same house. Under the same rules. You just chose a different path."

"Maybe. Or maybe we're just cut from a different cloth." Brayden winked.

"Cut the crap, Brayden. I just cleared your bar tab. Two hundred fifty!"

"I didn't ask for your charity."

"Next time I'll let Cooney settle it his way."

"That no-neck son of a bitch ain't gonna do shit to me." Brayden put down the fork and pulled a loose cigarette from his breast pocket. He played with it, twirling it between his fingers.

"I don't know how to help you."

"Not everything needs your fixing. Ever think of that? You're not a super-hero. God only knows you've got enough problems of your own to worry about without spending time on me."

Kelly sat in silence. Sadly, his brother was right.

"Maybe it's time you knew the truth." Brayden slipped the cigarette behind his right ear and took a sip of his beer.

Kelly eyed his brother hard. "The truth about what?"

"Enough from the both of you!" Kelly's mother caned her way into the kitchen. Kelly had been so focused on his brother he hadn't heard her approach.

"Ma, sorry I woke you. Brayden decided to pay us a late-night visit."

"Hi Ma." Brayden stood and walked around the table to give his mother a kiss on the cheek.

Kelly caught wind of his brother as he passed by to return to his seat, and he was days past due on a good lather. Brayden spun the fork on the flowered porcelain plate.

"What is it you think I need to know?" Kelly asked, resuming the inquiry his brother had started.

Brayden looked over at their mother.

"You shut your damn mouth, Brayden Kelly!" As a woman who rarely swore, her sudden verbal explosion was unexpected. She turned to Michael and immediately softened her expression. "Michael, go back to bed. You've got the hearing tomorrow. You can't be facing those folks unrested."

Kelly knew she was right. In a few hours he'd be speaking about the Baxter Green death and his role in it. He and his brother would finish this conversation at a later date.

"Wait! Before you two go your separate ways I want to hear my Kelly boys say it."

Kelly looked at his brother. There was an underlying disdain in Brayden's expression.

In a softly delivered unison, they recited their family mantra, "Family first. Family always."

21

The courtroom was small. The criminal trials took place a floor below and were designed with a larger audience in mind. Civil litigation most often took place behind the scenes, with settlements reached absent the media spotlight. That was not the case in the Baxter Green civil suit. The shooting had made national news and sparked the ongoing debate about military tactics deployed in civilian law enforcement situations.

Most of the general public viewed SWAT with jaded perspective. They saw the military-styled personnel carriers as they occupied an area under threat. The operators, in heavy vestments, carrying automatic rifles, often gave rise to questions of excessiveness. The counter side is quite simple, but rarely understood. Deploying law enforcement tactical elements, more times than not, greatly reduces the injury or likelihood of casualty to both criminals and police by statistically drastic numbers. Kelly waited in a room down the hall. Marty Cappelli had stopped in to check on him before running off to handle some unrelated administrative union flareup. He promised to be back in time for the start. Kelly watched reporters pass by, wondered if they would cover both sides fairly, whether they had already made up their mind as to what happened the day Baxter Green died.

The days before Kelly's testimony were lined with tactical's accounting for the facts and circumstances leading up to the tragic death of the seven-year-old

Baxter Green. Kelly was the closer, so to speak. After his deposition was given, the judge would retire to counsel and make a determination of fault. The family, in particular Trevor Green, had waived a jury in the hopes of expediting the decision by the court.

The re-written accounting of Kelly's eleven hours of negotiation was in his hand. The majority of the first ten hours remained unchanged. It was Kelly's last hour Cappelli had deemed a problem. The wording was wrong. Kelly, although without authority to do so, had maintained control of the operation when it should have shifted solely to Captain Lyons's shoulders. Kelly was given wiggle room to come up with an alternate resolution as he guided the decisions of the tactical element. Kelly read the suggestions made by Cappelli and pocketed the papers.

Cappelli knocked and entered without waiting for Kelly to respond. "Are you ready, Mike?"

"As much as I'll ever be."

"Did you have a chance to read my suggestions?"

"I did." Kelly didn't offer anything further as he followed Cappelli's brisk pace down the corridor to the courtroom.

"And?" Cappelli asked over his shoulder.

"I know what I'm going to say."

Martin Cappelli stopped short, at a door marked Courtroom C1. "I really don't like the sound of that."

"Not your place to decide my fate." Kelly eyed the doorknob. "Let's not keep the judge waiting."

Cappelli opened the door and guided Kelly to the stand. There was a slight rise to the open-gated box where Kelly would be speaking. A wooden-backed swivel chair was set inside, and an adjustable long-stemmed microphone was centered on a ledge, facing out. The judge sat in his dark robe and turned to greet Kelly as he took the stand.

"Detective Kelly, would you please remain standing while I swear you in?" Judge Coleman instructed.

"Yes, Your Honor." Kelly stood and squared himself to the judge.

"Please raise your right hand. Do you swear that the testimony you shall give, shall be the truth, the whole truth, and nothing but the truth, so help you, under penalty of perjury?"

"I do," Kelly said.

"Please state your name and occupation for the record."

"Detective Michael Kelly, Boston Police Department. Currently assigned to Homicide."

"Thank you, Detective. You may take a seat."

Kelly did so. He scanned the crowd. No cameras were allowed inside the courtroom at the request of the family. A sketch artist peeked out from behind a large pad. Kelly locked eyes with Trevor Green. He was in a red jumpsuit, the color indicative of his current assignment in 10 Block, an area of the prison assigned to dangerous inmates. Of the sixty cells set aside for isolation, Green occupied one. His eyes were thirsty for interaction with the outside world. He was seated in a separate section of the room accompanied by a court security officer. The year of incarceration had only added to the bereaved father's intensity.

"Detective, you understand that you will not be directly questioned by counsel today? And that your sole purpose is to provide your verbal recollection of the incidents that took place on February twenty-fourth of last year?"

"I do, Your Honor."

"Then whenever you're ready, you may proceed."

Kelly cleared his throat and leaned forward to bend the microphone closer to his mouth. He felt the thickness of the folded paper pressing through his pants pocket. He ignored it and sat up straight.

"Last year, I was assigned as a negotiator with our department's Crisis Negotiation Team, or CNT for short. Around twenty-three-hundred hours our unit was notified of a Code 99, an armed barricade situation, in the Jamaica Plain neighborhood. My partner, David McElroy, and I were on call that day, and arrived on scene about an hour after the barricade situation began. We immediately attempted to establish communication with the subject, Trevor Green. He did not pick up, or refused to answer his cellphone, so we deployed a throw phone. The phone was tossed through a bedroom window. It has the ability to receive transmissions even when not in use, although we prefer to use it as a direct link to communicate with a subject. I was able to establish contact and took on the role as primary negotiator, while my partner, McElroy, served as recorder. Trevor had described killing his wife and another male when he'd come home early from work. His seven-year-old son was home asleep at the time."

Kelly sipped from the cup of water provided. "Trevor was not planning on coming out. He'd made several comments about knowing his situation and the subsequent future waiting. As time progressed into the early morning hours, Trevor Green began making statements about not letting his son fall victim to the system. Based on his display of emotional volatility demonstrated by the killing of his wife and her lover, we, both CNT and tactical, decided that negotiations had stalled and were proving unlikely to bring an end to the standoff."

Kelly looked out in the audience at Lyons, who'd decided to stick around for Kelly's retelling of events. He'd worked under the man when he was a member of SWAT, and always felt he wore his emotions on his sleeve, a man easy to read. But this morning, Kelly couldn't make heads or tails of the tactical leader's take on his speech thus far.

"Captain Lyons had drafted a plan to make a dynamic entry on the dwelling. I was concerned that, without knowing the exact whereabouts of the hostage, entry could prove dire. I suggested an alternative solution, one in which I would negotiate Trevor Green to a window and expose him for a sniper shot. I saw it as a safer plan of attack. Lyons allowed me the opportunity to attempt my plan. Although the captain was technically in charge, I was in control. After several failed attempts, I was able to reestablish phone contact with Trevor. I asked him to bring his son to the bedroom window so that we could visually verify the boy's well-being. He eventually complied. During the verbal exchange with me from the window, I gave the green light for the shot which was passed on by Captain Lyons to the sniper team located across the alleyway."

Kelly had not retold this story aloud to anyone, and the telling of it now caused him to choke up as he saw the young face of Baxter Green fill his mind's eye.

He drained the remnants of water and set the plastic cup on the railing in front of him. "At the point the shot was taken, Baxter Green changed position and hugged his father. The bullet struck the boy in the back of the head, killing him instantly." Kelly made eye contact with Cappelli, who subtly shook his head. "I, Michael Kelly, take full and complete responsibility for the decision to make a sniper-initiated assault, the result of which took the life of Baxter

Green. I greatly apologize to the boy's family and, for what it's worth, there isn't a day that goes by that I don't think of that moment."

The judge turned and surveyed Kelly carefully. "Thank you for your time. Is there anything else?"

"No, Your Honor."

Judge Coleman addressed the small crowd. "If there's nothing further, we'll recess, and I will have my answer once I've had an opportunity to review all of the testimony from this week. I'll notify counsel once I've rendered my decision." The judge then turned to Kelly. "Thank you, Detective. You may step down."

Kelly stood and stepped out of the witness stand. Cappelli met him at the rear of the courtroom and the two walked into the back hallway.

"You just couldn't hold back. Not even a little? Do you think falling on your sword is going to help the department out of this mess?" Cappelli turned a shade redder.

"I said what happened and I took responsibility for the way things broke. I own my mistakes."

Kelly walked away. He exited into the main lobby of the courthouse. Kristen Barnes was standing by the information desk and smiled when he approached.

"What are you doing here?" Kelly asked.

"I thought maybe you'd need a friend. Can I buy you a drink?"

"Kris, it's like eleven o'clock."

"Coffee, silly." She smiled. "Now, if it was noon, that might be a different story."

Kelly chuckled softly.

The weight of the deposition was finally lifted. Regardless of the outcome, at least he'd spoken his mind. He could focus his energy back where it belonged.

22

The kitchen was loud. Tables had been pushed together and chairs brought up from the cellar. Aleksander yawned. Close to noon, it was still early after the late night he had pulled. He stirred the pot and checked the oven temp.

The sound of screaming girls overrode the laughter of older men. His young nieces ran into the kitchen, almost pulling the plates off the table. Their game of tag quickly came to an end when his uncle, Stanislaw, intervened with a firm hand. "Take it outside, girls!" he commanded. The two children disappeared out the back of the kitchen as quickly as they'd entered.

Aleksander looked over at his uncle. "Girls and their silliness. Am I right?"

"If I recall you were pretty wild as a child, too." The man sipped his iced vodka and chuckled. "But look at you now. Helping your mother with the family business."

Aleksander's mother entered the room. "He's learning. My Aleksander is not too shabby around the kitchen, either." She patted the back of his neck as she passed by. "Stanislaw, now why did you send those girls outside? It's raining."

"In Poland, we played out in the rain. Don't you remember?"

"Of course, but times are different now. We are in America. Kids don't play in the rain." Nadia Rakowski peered out the window. "And they are in their pretty dresses, too. Call them in now."

Stanislaw, her mother's youngest sibling, bowed to her command and yelled for the girls to come back inside, speaking in his native tongue.

"How long until it's ready, Aleksander?"

"Not long." He gently poked the pierogis with a fork, checking the tenderness. His technique was gentle enough to depress the exterior without puncturing. The resilience of the doughy casing told him their readiness. "Five more minutes."

"Good. Let's talk."

Aleksander followed his mother into the family room, or salon, as she commonly referred to it. "What is it?"

"I worry that this job is too much for you." She patted his cheeks tenderly. "You need a little break. What do you think of running the restaurant for a bit?"

"I am not a baby. Stop treating me like one."

His mother cuffed him in the ear. The blow was delivered with the speed and accuracy of a trained fighter. "Then you stop moping about. Get a handle on things and keep your nose clear. Is what I say understood?"

Aleksander rubbed his ear and nodded.

His mother walked back into the kitchen and made an announcement. "Let's all eat the wonderful food prepared. My niece only turns six once." She clapped her hands twice, with the impact of a cannon's blast, and the family appeared from the various nooks of the house.

* * *

She had no watch, and there was no clock. Tabitha was back in the room at the house. There was no way of telling what time of day it was. She went to the window and tried to lift it without success. Long, heavy-duty screws secured it to the wooden frame. The window was coated in an opaque paint, the color of dingy dishwater. Maroon blackout curtains added the final layer of visual isolation from the outside world.

She felt the clothes on her skin. A day ago, the soft green skirt and matching top gave her great joy. Now they were a reminder of the night's passing and all the intermittent memories that would forever haunt her. Tabitha started to undress when the exterior latch to the door clicked. Startled, she returned to the bed.

Slice peeked her head inside. "Shower time."

Tabitha sat up, but refused to look at her. She edged her feet off the bed and let them dangle for a second before planting them on the floor.

"Let's go, girl, or your five minutes under the water will be down to three." Slice had a meanness to her tone that had been absent during their day of primping. "I know you're going to want as much time as you can get to wash off the stink of last night."

Tabitha moved with her head down toward the door. Slice put a hand on her shoulder and nudged her into the hallway. She followed the tattered carpet runner leading down the hall to the bathroom. All of the other doors were closed, and Tabitha assumed they were locked, as hers had been.

She stepped her bare feet onto the cool dampness of the tiled floor. Steam hung in the air and the mirrored cabinet above the sink was fogged over.

Slice stood behind her. "I'm going to be waiting out here. You can use one of those towels when you're done. You've got five minutes." As she pulled the door closed, she added, "Not sure how much hot water is left. You're the last one."

A gray hand towel hung from a rod and was stained in a brownish red she assumed was blood. Whether it was the thick humid air or the combination of whatever she'd ingested during the night, Tabitha's head spun, and her stomach lurched. She launched herself toward the toilet and vomited. The acidic bile burned her nose.

Feeling no better but knowing she had limited time, Tabitha forced herself to stand. Using the side of the tub for balance, she turned the shower faucet handle all the way to the right. The water cascaded down. Slice was wrong; there was still hot water left. Tabitha was glad for it. She wanted to burn away as much filth as she could.

Stepping inside, the water poured over her head and body. Tabitha Porter wept silently. She found a withered bar of green soap and set about scrubbing at her skin. The frothy lather of her efforts built up around the puddle at her feet, but nothing could remove the filth. She would feel forever tainted. Her body ached and had a tenderness to the touch. It only caused her to scrub harder. She noticed strange bruises on her arms and legs, the cause of which she had no recall. It was like being transported to another body.

Tabitha Porter didn't exist anymore. What was left was a shadow of her former self. Looking down, she saw a cheap disposable razor resting in the corner of the tub. She picked it up and started pulling at the plastic casing covering the blade. Tabitha nimbly navigated her fingers, avoiding unwanted cuts. After a few moments of toil, she freed the blade. Holding the paper-thin metal, she looked down at her wrist.

Guiding the sharpened edge to the inside of her left forearm, she held it there as water trickled down her back. Her heartbeat thumped wildly as she contemplated the option.

"Time's up!" Slice called through the closed door. "Wrap it up, sunshine."

The sound of Slice's voice ripped her from the desperation, shattering her commitment. Tabitha had another idea. She slipped the blade into her mouth, carefully resting it between her cheek and gumline. Slowly biting down, she closed her mouth. Tabitha grabbed the cleanest of the used towels from the discarded pile, wrapped it around her chest, and stepped out into the hallway.

"Let's get you back to your room. You're going to need your rest for tonight."

The thought of what that meant sickened her. She fought back the urge to release the contents of her stomach again.

Tabitha entered the room and flopped atop the bed. Slice closed the door. The door's exterior deadbolt made its distinctive thunk. She closed her eyes in the hopes the experience of the past twelve hours was just a terrible nightmare. Deep down she knew it was only the beginning. Spitting the razor blade into her hand, Tabitha looked down at her possible escape plan.

23

With the morning's Baxter Green hearing complete and the stall in the Faith Wilson case, Kelly took advantage of the break and decided to make good on a promise.

He waited on the front steps of Mercy Elementary as droves of kids emptied out in excited anticipation of that weekend's prospect of being curbside at Sunday's St. Patty's Day Parade. Rarely did the parade land on the 17th, but when it did, there was a contagious, intangible vibe. Kelly celebrated the day in a different way, one with less fanfare, but nonetheless important.

Kelly saw Embry before she saw him. Her long auburn hair swung in a ponytail from side to side as she bounded down the concrete steps, giggling infectiously with one of her classmates. The hardened cop inhaled these moments, tucking the memory deep in a protected mental reserve from which he pulled when all else seemed lost. His daughter had saved his life more times than she'd ever know. He thought of Jimmy Smokes and wondered if he'd had an Embry would he have stuffed that gun in his mouth?

Her pace doubled when she saw him. Airborne off the last step, she dove into her father's arms, smothering him with much needed affection. He wondered how long these hugs would come to him. How much time did he have before she was too old to show her feelings? He let the thought slip away with the sound of her voice. "Daddy! You're here?"

"Of course, Squiggles. I couldn't miss an official Daddy-Daughter Date Night, now could I?"

"Dinner at Sushi Mama?"

"Wouldn't be complete without it."

Embry turned and said goodbye to her friend. She slipped her hand into his and they walked away toward his unmarked, this time parked legally in a spot.

* * *

Dinner was fantastic. Embry filled him in on all of the amazing things happening in the world of a second grader. She gave animated retellings of conversations with friends. The most seemingly insignificant discussion about an argument she had with Shelly DeLong about why dogs were better than cats got absorbed with a strange fascination. Kelly envied his daughter's innocence.

On the way home, they stopped by a Redbox and picked up *The Meg*. Ever since his daughter was younger, she had been fascinated with all things big and scary. It started with dinosaurs and had apparently migrated to giant man-eating sharks. He hesitated on making the selection, but she made a pretty good argument about it being a film about a prehistoric shark. Kelly was in no place to battle with his daughter's sound points.

When Kelly arrived home, it was already dark. The light flickered in the living room and, judging by the time, his mother was several minutes into her nightly love affair with Trebek.

"Ma, I'm home. I brought you something." Kelly always made a point of announcing his presence, and had done so for many years, ever since his mother's hearing started to fade.

"Is it ice cream?" she yelled back.

"Something sweeter."

Embry ran into the living room at full speed. "Nana!"

"Oh my sweet baby girl!" She opened her arms wide.

"Embry, be careful of Nana's hip."

"Now don't you go worrying about me. Get over here and give me a hug."

Embry navigated the injured leg and snuggled up into the recliner. She laid her head on her grandmother's chest and gave a gentle hug.

"And to what do I owe this honor, my dear? Are you back from sacking the castles and laying waste to dragons?"

Kelly always laughed at the imaginary world his mother and daughter spent much of their time in.

"I rescued the prince from the evil queen." Embry beamed.

"I'm sure you did, my love." His mother gave Embry a peck on the cheek. Kelly noticed a light smudge of lipstick and wondered if his mother had gone through the efforts of putting on makeup to impress her favorite talk show host.

"Can we make popcorn?" Embry asked.

"I'm on it." Kelly disappeared into the kitchen. He returned a few minutes later with an oversized Tupperware bowl filled with salty, buttery goodness.

Kelly's mother clicked the button on the remote, switching the television's input to DVD mode and cutting Alex off in mid-sentence.

"Ma, I'm shocked. What will your boyfriend do?"

She laughed with a childlike sweetness. "He can wait until tomorrow. Tonight, we have a special guest."

Kelly set the popcorn down and slid the DVD into the player. He took a position on the couch, and Embry whispered something in his mother's ear. Kelly didn't hear the question, but heard the response. "Of course, dear. Go sit with your father. My leg could use a rest anyway."

Embry scrambled up onto the loveseat and tucked herself under his arm. There was no place he'd rather be. He settled in with the bucket now between them as the movie began. Just then his cell vibrated. The caller ID said the incoming call was from Art "Brush" Devers. Embry stirred and gave him sad eyes.

"Dad, please don't leave. We never get to do date nights anymore."

It wasn't so much the words but the way she said it. His new life in Homicide was consuming him and he knew it. Worse, he was honest enough with himself to know that he allowed it. Ever since Samantha left him, he'd been putting more time into the job. An unhealthy position.

"Not tonight, my sweet." Kelly reached over and shut off his phone. "Tonight it's just us."

24

She'd just got back from her nightly run around the Charles River. She ran the seven-mile loop from her one-bedroom apartment on Gainsborough Street, darting through the crowded sidewalks until she found her rhythm on the trail that shadowed Storrow Drive, over the Harvard Bridge, around MIT, and returning back along Memorial. She moved at a smooth seven-minute and thirty-second pace, nowhere near the pacing of her college years, but strong enough to get in a good burn while taking in the sights. Running was a fun way to people watch, one of Barnes's favorite pastimes aside from solving crimes.

Barnes shed her damp clothes and tossed them in her hamper. She was about to hop in the shower when her work cell rang. Barnes looked down at the number. She didn't recognize it. Not a name in her contact list.

She answered it just before it went to voicemail. "Barnes."

"Detective?" the male voice asked cautiously.

"Yes. Who's this?"

"It's Art Devers. Kelly told me to call if I had something. I tried to reach him, but he didn't answer."

Barnes knew Kelly was spending some much-needed time with his daughter. "What you got?"

"He told me to call if I found anything about those girls." He coughed and cleared his throat. "I saw her. The girl from the picture."

"Where?"

"At a hotel party. Um...somebody ordered up. They had me come into the room to make the exchange. It was quick but I saw her sitting on a bed with another girl."

"You sure it was the same girl?"

"Like I said, I never forget a face."

"How long ago was this that you saw her?"

"Maybe a half hour. Sixth floor. Room 612. The guy I sold to is no joke. Do whatever you got to, but leave my name out of it."

Barnes jotted down more information from the informant. She often thought it strange to turn a blind eye to the fact the man had openly admitted to a cop that he'd just dealt drugs. But the lifeblood of a detective was information, and the source of it wasn't as much an issue as its veracity.

She stepped into the shower long enough to rinse away the salty layer of sweat. Barnes decided against calling Kelly. She figured if he didn't answer for Devers, it was for good reason. Plus, she'd learned long ago never to trust information without verifying it first. Having only met Devers earlier that day, her need to check his claim before wasting Kelly's time felt important.

Barnes dressed and slipped her compact Glock 23 into the concealed holster in the small of her back. She set out for the hotel.

* * *

She sat in the parking lot of the Bayside Hotel. A few people came and went, but no sign of the girl. Barnes decided to get a closer look.

Stepping out of the car and into the cold night air, Barnes shuddered, and tucked her hands into her fleece-lined jacket pockets. She stepped quickly toward the main entrance. Her legs quivered, still tingling from her earlier run.

The lobby broke the wind, immediately raising the temperature ten degrees. She shook off the chill as she took a moment to scan the area. An older man sat in a lounge chair reading the newspaper. A couple was checking in at the main desk. To the right of the elevators was a stairwell.

Barnes ascended the stairs. There were two flights between each floor. She stepped out on the fifth floor and walked along the corridor. Even numbers were on the right, odds on the left, with the doors facing directly across from each other. Six rooms down from the stairwell's access was room 512. Barnes wanted to have an idea where the room above was situated.

She returned to the stairwell and climbed the remaining flight to her destination. Barnes waited by the closed-door entrance to the hallway. She listened for any signs of movement.

It wasn't long before she heard the ding of the elevator and the voices of two men as they exited. Barnes heard their voices drift away from her and down the hall. She opened the door and peered out through the gap. She watched them stop at the target room. The men knocked, a sign they were not the ones who'd rented it. She exited and began her approach.

Barnes had spent plenty of nights during her time in SAU posing as someone else to move among criminals undetected. One of the best cloaks of invisibility was the cell phone. Barnes withdrew her phone as she closed the distance between the two men. She flicked the screen open and began scrolling through her old text messages.

The door to room 612 opened when she was one room away. The two men said nothing and stepped in. Barnes felt their eyes upon her as she approached. She didn't look up.

The two disappeared inside. Barnes passed by just as a large man was shutting the door behind the two visitors. She looked up from her phone and shot a peek to the right. Coming out of the bathroom was Tabitha Porter. Barnes averted her eyes and the door closed. She wasn't sure if the doorman noticed, but she needed to regroup and call Kelly.

Barnes sprinted down the stairwell and collected her composure before returning to the lobby. The couple at the main desk were no longer there. The older man who'd been reading the paper was now huddled by the bubbler, taking advantage of the complimentary water. He smiled at her as she moved outside.

She pulled her phone as she walked in a hurried pace toward her unmarked. Kelly's phone went straight to voicemail. She hung up and hit redial. Same as before. This time she waited for the greeting message to finish, followed by the tone.

"Hey Mike, it's Kris. I got an eye on—"

Her head fell forward. The stinging blow to the back of her skull sent shockwaves down her spine. She felt the impact of her forehead as it struck the driver's side door of her Caprice. Phosphene stars fluttered across her field of vision before being swallowed by the darkness.

25

Kelly woke disoriented by his surroundings. Light seeped in through the thin lace of his mother's curtains. He sat up and rubbed his eyes, Embry's tiny frame slumped over his lap. She stirred at the jostling, but didn't wake. Kelly checked his watch, 8:21 a.m. He couldn't remember the last time he'd slept in.

His joints popped as he stood and gave a long, welcomed stretch. The position he'd conformed to on his mother's loveseat caused some soreness. Kelly rubbed at his rib cage.

He took a moment to cover Embry with the blanket his mother must've placed on them before retiring for the evening. She was so peaceful, curled up in a tiny ball. Kelly laid a gentle kiss upon the top of her head before moving into the kitchen to fetch some coffee.

Kelly's mother was already up. She took a bite of her peanut butter and jelly toast, her morning dietary staple. She gave a warm grin as he entered.

Kelly moved over to the pot. His mother made a strong batch of coffee and he looked forward to his dose of caffeine.

"Why didn't you wake me?"

"Looks like you needed the rest. Plus, Embry didn't want to separate from you and go to her room."

"I haven't slept like that in a long time."

"I wish I could say the same. Your daughter had me watch the entire movie while you snored away. That giant shark gave me nightmares."

Kelly laughed. "I didn't believe anything could scare you." He gave his mother a kiss and pulled up a nearby chair. Kelly spoke in a quieter tone. "Do you have any idea what Brayden was referring to the other night?"

"What do you mean?"

"He said, maybe it's time I knew. Knew what? Not sure what he meant by it. I've been kicking it around in my brain ever since."

His mother refused to make eye contact and picked up the last bit of her toast. "You know Brayden. He says crazy things sometimes, especially when he's hopped up on whatever kind of poison."

"That's the thing. He wasn't high. Trust me, I know these things. Brayden's a mess, no doubt about it, but the other night he was clear of mind. Clearest I've seen in a while."

She chewed slowly. He could tell there was more to this conversation than she was letting on. He'd never registered any deception from his mother in the past. She was a woman who was open and honest. But everything he saw in her now pointed in one direction. His mother was holding back almost to the point of lying. Kelly burned with the need to know why.

His daughter crept in from the living room shrouded in the blanket. She shuffled her feet without picking them up off the ground. Kelly saw his mother was glad for the interruption; she slowly got to her feet. Balancing on her cane, she ambled to the cabinet above the counter. "What can I get you for breakfast, my dear?"

"PB and J on white toast." Embry sat on the other side of her dad.

"A girl after my own heart."

"Can you put extra jelly? My mom doesn't let me have it at home. Says it's too much sugar."

"Maybe that's because you're already too sweet." Ma Kelly set about making the meal.

Embry handed her dad his cell phone. "Here you go, Dad. Sorry I made you turn it off last night. I know you got important stuff to do."

Kelly smiled at his daughter's gesture. "Nothing's more important than you."

Kelly forgot he'd turned the phone off. He realized that was also a contributing factor in sleeping through the night. He pressed the power button and sipped at his coffee while the phone booted up.

Once the startup was completed the phone repeatedly beeped and vibrated with text and voicemail alerts. He scanned the texts first and saw the majority were from Devers, with one from Barnes. Then he looked at the voicemails, one from Devers and one from Barnes.

He listened to the message from Barnes first. "Hey Mike, it's Kris. I got an eye on—" The words interrupted midsentence. There was a bang of metal and it sounded like the phone hit the ground. He could make out the garbled voices of a male. Maybe two men. Then, a loud crunching sound before the message ended. Everything about it registered as bad. Very bad.

Kelly tried calling Barnes back. It went straight to voicemail. He then checked the message from Devers.

"Hey Kelly, it's Brush. Got the skinny on that girl you be looking for. Told you I'm good like that. Yo, anyways. She at the Bayside, room 612. The spot by the old lotto joint. Hit me back. If I don't hear from you, I'll give a shout out to your fine-ass partner. Later days." The message ended. He looked at the time. Devers left his message an hour before Barnes's disconcerting voicemail. Devers's text messages said much of the same.

There was one text from Barnes. *Heading to Bayside. Checking out Devers's intel. Let you know if it's good.*

"Ma, I need you to watch Embry. I've got to go."

There was no argument from his daughter this time. She must've seen the worry in his eyes.

* * *

Kelly drove through the steady traffic like a Richard Petty on the last leg of the Daytona 500. The Saturday morning flow was nothing like the bumper-to-bumper of the weekdays, but this was Boston and traffic was never great. Barnes would've been proud of the way he rode the bumper of the car in front of him. He had his wigwags and visor strobe activated, but in the gray light of day his unmarked Impala did not catch the attention of the other commuters. Kelly chirped his siren and cleared a path.

He'd already called Sutherland and given him the situation. To say his direct supervisor was a ball of concern, and pissed to boot, would be a disservice to the definition of either word. Members of the Eleven were dispatched to assist.

The tires squealed as he entered the hotel's parking lot. Kelly recognized the familiar face of Sergeant Cooper, a man he'd served under and with during his time as a street cop in the rough C-11 District. The man was as tough as he was fair.

"Sarge, how's it looking so far?"

"Detectives Hardy and Casallas are processing the scene by the car." Cooper pointed in the direction of Barnes's vehicle. "I've got a few officers inside the hotel working on pulling the surveillance. The manager was initially less than cooperative about coming in on his day off to assist. Apparently not a fan of police, but not to worry. I told him we'd have to shut down the main lobby until we were able to figure out what's going on." Cooper gave his version of a smile. "I think he got the message. He arrived a few minutes ago."

Kelly walked over to where Barnes's Caprice was parked. He recognized one of the detectives. Hardy had been in C-11's bureau when Kelly had been a patrolman. The other face, a younger man, he did not recognize.

"Hey, Greg. Anything?"

"Not much. Her phone's smashed, but other than that we're not seeing much in the way of evidence. We'll know more once we process the car. Maybe we'll get lucky and get a usable print." Hardy shrugged. "At least there's no blood."

"Thanks. Keep me posted if something pops up."

Kelly strode away toward the main entrance to the hotel. Prints or lab work wasn't going to cut it. Barnes was in trouble and he needed something to go on, and he needed it sooner rather than later.

The doors slid apart, and Kelly entered the lobby. He veered right and walked to the clerk standing behind the desk. He flashed his credentials. "Where are they?"

The receptionist lifted a plank where the front desk connected to the wall and ushered Kelly into a short hallway to a door marked Manager. It was ajar, and Kelly entered, bumping one of the patrolmen in the back.

"Tell me we've got something, fellas." Kelly squeezed himself in. The small office was now much smaller with the two patrolmen, the manager, and Kelly.

"The person who paid for the room did it in cash and used a BS name of John Smith. They checked in at 9:17 p.m. so we're running the tape to see if we can get a visual on a car from the camera on the exterior of the lobby entrance."

"Good thinking," Kelly said.

The manager was hunched over the controls, manipulating the frames. A few minutes before the check-in time a white van pulled in. Kelly watched as Tabitha Porter stumbled out with several other girls. The frames edged forward, but the plate had a cover, and at the angle of the camera, nothing was visible.

The manager continued to slow play the footage. Then Kelly saw something. "I need you to slow it down even further."

The manager did as he was instructed, and the images on the screen jittered frame by frame. "Stop."

Frozen in black and white was a dark-colored sedan, the same vehicle he'd seen Tabitha Porter and the unknown girl drive away from the nail salon in.

"Can you zoom in?"

"I can try. Sometimes this system doesn't cooperate." The manager pressed a button on the keyboard and Kelly almost did a rendition of his mother's jig.

On the screen was a clearly discernable license plate. Kelly wrote the alphanumeric combination in his notepad. "Keep running the tape and see if you can get any clear visuals of any of the men escorting these girls. Send me anything you get."

Kelly called in the vehicle information to dispatch. The Audi A8 returned to a leasing company out of Ohio. No information came up regarding the registered owner. It would take some digging to get that. In the meantime, dispatch put out a BOLO, or Be on the Look Out broadcast, on the car to all members of the department and neighboring agencies.

He left the cramped space of the manager's office and made his way through the lobby and back outside. Kelly made a point of stopping by Sergeant Cooper before he left.

"I put the plate out on the broadcast."

Sergeant Cooper nodded. "It just came over the radio. Where are you headed?"

"I'm going hunting."

* * *

"You didn't know, or you did. Either way, it makes you one of the dumbest people on the planet! Who kidnaps a cop? And worse, you brought her to this house."

"What did you want me to do?"

"I should've taken off your damned head instead of your hand!"

"Let me make it right."

"No. You've already proven yourself worthless lately. Maybe you lost too much blood during your little surgery. Regardless, it's his turn now. Hopefully, he proves more capable."

"Please. Don't put this on him." The man's voice quavered slightly. "He's just a kid."

"I told you, he's part of our crew now. It's his rite of passage. We all had to do something similar. Now it's his turn."

Barnes heard the voices. They were close, but there was a barrier muffling the clarity. She had a splitting headache resonating from the back of her skull. It was dark. She smelled a strange combination of dank mustiness and heavy cologne. Barnes made an effort to move, but her arms were restrained behind her back by some type of cord. Her wrists were tethered to her ankles, hogtied. The more she squirmed, the tighter the bindings cinched down, cutting into her skin. Her eyes were wrapped in a cloth, sealing out the light. Barnes had no reference for time, nor could she account for how long she'd been unconscious.

She was lying on her left side in a distorted fetal position. Panic started to set in when she felt the plastic she was lying on. The cold seeped up through the ground, penetrating the plastic and entering her bones.

"It's time to earn your keep, little man," a man's voice echoed. Barnes noted an Eastern European accent, but in her haze couldn't bring forth the mental clarity to pinpoint its origin.

Barnes listened to footsteps walking away from her. The voice hollered back from a distance, "Not here. Drive her to the Lower Mills." A door slammed, followed by the roar of an engine.

"Grab an end," an accented male said.

Barnes felt the plastic curl around her. Suddenly the air around her mouth turned warm and sticky; she found it difficult to breathe. And then she felt the hard tug as her body dragged over the concrete floor. Her mind raced as she was hauled away.

26

Kelly looked at the map on his phone. His mind raced to connect the dots, knowing every second Barnes went unaccounted for meant a diminished return on the probability of finding her alive, if at all. After Danny's death, he vowed to never let anything like that happen again.

The body of Faith Wilson was found on Von Hillern. The nail salon was on Dorchester Ave. The brothel was on Millet Street. Barnes was snatched while surveying the group at the Bayside. All of those places were located within Dorchester. Kelly wagered whoever was responsible must be local to the area.

Kelly knew these streets. He also knew there were a million places to hide among the homes and businesses packed into the six square miles of Boston's most population-dense, diverse section.

He started his search at Dot Center and began spiraling out from the intersection of Dorchester Ave and Savin Hill. The one-way streets and staggered loops slowed his pace. Most of the houses in the residential areas were multi-family triple-deckers, which meant lots of cars parked in the streets and small lots behind the houses. Kelly didn't have time to get out and check the backs of each house. He hoped he'd get lucky by covering more ground and did his best to scan the vast rows of curb-parked vehicles for the Audi. He'd driven by several, but none matched the plate he was looking for. He noted the location and license plate of each in his notepad as he passed by, in the event they'd changed plates. Kelly tried not to think about that and focused on what he could control. Right now, it didn't feel like much.

As he crept down Pleasant Street the radio crackled to life. "Car forty-one, I got eyes on the suspect vehicle heading south on Treadway. Coming up on Savin Hill."

Kelly's heart skipped a beat. While experience had quelled most of his physiological reaction to police stress, the thought of stopping this car and getting a lead on finding Barnes caused his adrenaline to kick in. The dump of epinephrine coursed through his blood and his hands trembled. Kelly gripped the wheel tightly and pressed down hard on the accelerator. The Impala resisted and squeaked out its mechanical protest.

"Turning onto Savin."

"Keep a loose follow. Wait until you have another unit with you before you attempt to stop," the distinct voice of Cooper ordered.

Kelly picked up his mic. "I'm only a block away. Forty-one, you should be seeing me behind you in a sec."

"Forty-one copies. Passing Dot Ave now."

Kelly whipped the car hard taking the corner at Pleasant and Dorchester Avenue. It was the quickest way to intercept and catch up with the cruiser. He saw the light blue stripe of the rear bumper of the patrol car up ahead and maxed his Impala's RPMs, closing the distance. "I've got eyes on you. Light it up!"

The cruiser's light bar activated and the LED blue and red pulsed their strobed pattern. The siren reverberated off the neighboring houses. Kelly was tight on the bumper of the squad car. The Audi slowed and began pulling to the right side of the street. The cruiser slowed with it, keeping a distance of two car lengths.

Almost at a stop, the Audi's tires squealed wildly, and the car shot forward. It took an immediate right onto Aukland, down the wrong way of the one-way street. The cruiser kept pace and Kelly followed.

"In pursuit. Vehicle traveling south on Aukland. Speeds at 80."

Kelly heard responding units chiming in their location and possible intercepts. It was all background noise to the roar of his car's engine as he fought to keep pace.

The Audi blew the stop sign at the intersection with Bay Street. A vehicle proceeding from Bay barely missed a side-impact collision with the fleeing suspect. The car veered sideways and redirected into the path of the cruiser in pursuit. The right front corner of the civilian's bumper clipped the right rear of the squad car, sending it into a spin. Had it not been for the lag of his car, Kelly would've been next in line for a head-on impact. But the Impala's poor performance gave him enough of a gap in space and time to expertly navigate the two crashed vehicles.

Kelly zigzagged through the scattered cars. As he zipped by the disabled cruiser, he saw both patrolmen were dazed but okay.

"Collision at the intersection of Bay and Aukland. Forty-one is out of commission. I'm now lead in the pursuit. Audi approaching the T-intersection with Dewar. Speeds 70."

"Break it off. It's too dangerous," a nasally voice said over the radio.

Kelly focused on the road ahead. He wasn't sure who was calling termination of the chase.

"This is Lieutenant Duff. I said break it off!"

Kelly slid on his nearly bald tires as he braked to avoid a car pulling out from a back lot between two houses. The jerkiness of the erratic movement caused him to drop his microphone. He focused on driving.

"LT, with all due respect, that car may be the only lead we have in finding one of our own. As on-scene command, I'm telling him to continue," Sergeant Cooper barked. "Kelly, you catch that son of a bitch!"

The Audi approached the intersection with Dewar. It slowed and began to make the left, but approaching sirens and the fact that direction put him into a dead end told Kelly why the driver made a sudden decision to redirect. The erratic movement at the speed it was traveling caused it to swerve wildly. As the A8 began to lose control, Kelly slammed into the back end and sent the car over the curbing and head-on into a telephone pole.

The chase ended in a cacophony of screeching tires and twisted metal. Kelly was momentarily dazed by the collision, but quickly shook off the fog, and exited his car with gun at the ready. Sirens filled the air as members of the Eleven's patrol division rallied.

The front end of the Audi was wrapped around the thick wood pole. The hood was crinkled like an aluminum can, and steam hissed from the damaged radiator. The airbag had deployed on impact and was now beginning its automatic deflation. Kelly approached the car and kept a steady aim on the driver, who was mashed between the driver's side window and the crumpling nylon of the airbag. The driver obviously failed to buckle up. The picture of his twisted body would be a great poster for the benefits of wearing seatbelts.

Kelly barked orders over the deafening chaotic symphony of arriving units. "Hands! Show me your hands!"

The driver was slumped forward, and his head now rested between the steering wheel and the door's frame. No sign of movement from the man. Dead would be bad for a whole lot of reasons, the foremost being this man was his best chance of finding Barnes.

Kelly closed the distance, with arriving officers covering his movement, and yanked at the driver's side door. A grinding of metal on metal sounded. The crash had compressed the frame, making it difficult to open. After several hard pulls, and one well-placed kick, Kelly was able to gain access. Without the support of the door's frame, the driver flopped out toward the opening. Kelly grabbed the driver's left arm, which dangled loosely by his side.

He eyed one of the patrolmen close by to ensure he was covering him at gunpoint. Satisfied, Kelly holstered his weapon and placed his right hand on the neck of the man. Keeping the head stable, he slid his fingers around to check for a pulse. Faint, but the driver was definitely still alive. Without knowing the extent of the injuries, Kelly didn't move the man. Unconscious was better than dead, and in the world of policing, a lot less paperwork.

"Medic." Kelly turned to the closest patrolman. The uniformed officer was already relaying the information on the radio.

For the next three minutes, Kelly held the man in position, keeping his neck stabilized while maintaining control of his left hand. Medics arrived and took over. As soon as the driver was laid on the gurney, a patrolman cuffed both arms in place. Kelly looked down on the man and realized he wasn't a man at all. The person, unconscious on the backboard, was a teenager of not more than sixteen. He riffled through the boy's pocket and found a wallet. The learner's permit showed a geeky-looking Jakub Balicki, age sixteen. Baffled, Kelly stepped back.

"As soon as he wakes, I want a call. Understood?" Kelly addressed the patrolman assigned as the medical escort.

The sirens were now off, and a firefighter had detached the car battery, so the loud buzz of the airbag alarm died off. The street returned to its quiet mid-morning norm. The hum of chatting officers and the onlookers filling the nearby sidewalks were the only sounds. Kelly walked back over to the car. Shattered bits of glass crunched under his weight as he squatted down by the open driver's side door. He peered in, searching for any bit of evidence capable of pointing him in the right direction. He cocked his head to the left, dipping below the steering column. Kelly eyed the space under the driver's seat, a common stash area for weapons. Nothing.

As he was easing himself back out, he heard something. A soft thud came from the rear of the vehicle. He pushed back and stood, looking to see if one of the patrolmen securing the scene had leaned against the back of the car. Nobody was close by. And then, he heard it again. This time it was slightly louder than before and definitely coming from the trunk area.

"Trunk," Kelly called out to the two patrolmen lingering nearby. They were snapped from their conversation and went back into a tactical position, drawing their weapons and bringing them to a low ready as they approached.

Kelly pressed the release button. As the trunk latch released, he rushed around to the back of the mangled Audi.

Lying on a heavy-duty, black plastic drop cloth, and hogtied with duct tape over her mouth, was Kristen Barnes. Battered, but alive. There was an axe and a red plastic jug of gasoline near her feet.

Kelly pulled out a knife clipped on the inside of his front left pocket, and went to work cutting her free from her bonds. As soon as her hands were free, Barnes reached to her face to remove the silver-colored tape with one steady pull. She breathed deeply. "I thought I was a goner!"

"I'd never let that happen!" Kelly turned to one of the officers nearby. "We're going to need another bus for her."

Barnes shook her head. "No way I'm getting stuck in a hospital for the next few hours while the bastards who did this to me are still out there."

"I'm definitely not going to argue with you on that. But at least have the medics on scene give you a once-over before we go on the hunt."

"Where's Kelly?" a nasally voice called out from behind the cruisers blocking the intersection. One of the officers standing by pointed the way.

Kelly turned and saw Lieutenant Duff storming in his direction. He squared himself to the approaching man.

"Who the hell do you think you are? When I tell you to break off a damn pursuit you do it!"

"If he did, I'd be dead." Barnes stepped up and stood side by side with Kelly.

The lieutenant started to say something, but apparently seeing Barnes negated any semblance of a comeback.

Sergeant Cooper strolled up. "If you got a problem with the pursuit, direct it my way."

Duff turned and shot an angry glance at the veteran sergeant. "Policy states if a pursuit is deemed dangerous, then we break it off."

"If we're quoting policy, then you should also know it states the pursuit may continue if the threat of imminent death or harm to others persists." Cooper pointed at the axe in the trunk. "Looks like we can check that box. Also, policy states the pursuit is governed by the on-scene commander regardless of rank. Looks like my list trumps yours. And, let's please not forget the third and most important factor. I was your sergeant when you were a boot rookie and just because you made rank doesn't mean you know squat."

Duff's jaw went slack. His head ping-ponged between Cooper and Kelly. He walked away without further acknowledgement.

Cooper returned to orchestrating the fallout from the scene as Kelly and Barnes walked away, over to the rattling Impala. "Are you sure you don't want to get checked out?"

"You know me better than that." Barnes gave a coy smile as she brushed herself off with exaggerated bravado. "Plus, you're going to want me on this. Especially since our best prospective lead is unconscious in the back of that ambulance."

"Anything you can remember about where you were held?"

"I woke up in the back of the trunk. Never saw anything. I did hear a little bit before the drive."

"Anything we can use?"

"Not really. Except they had thick accents. Eastern Bloc. Most likely Polish."

"Well that narrows it down to about fifteen thousand of our city's residents."

The phone in Kelly's pocket vibrated. He pulled it out. Bobby McDonough was calling.

"Now's not a good time. Let me call you back later." Kelly moved to hit the button to end the call.

"I found him." Bobby's voice caught Kelly's attention before disconnecting.

"Found who?"

"The perv. Smalls. Remember you told me to put my feelers out? Well, he's been located."

Kelly perked up. "Where?"

"Same place you found that girl."

"What do you mean?" Kelly turned his back on Barnes, who was standing patiently by the passenger side door. He hushed his tone. "What the hell did you do, Bobby?"

"Whoa. I didn't do nothing. Walsh had already heard about the girl. Nothing gets by him in the neighborhood. You know that. All I did was tell him the perv might know something useful."

Kelly sighed in frustration. He knew tipping off Conner Walsh carried with it an intrinsic risk. Now Bobby was calling with the fruits of that request.

"Listen, Mikey, just go down there and check it out. I think it'll give you what you need."

"You know the position this puts me in?"

Bobby chuckled softly. "Don't worry. An anonymous tip has been called in from a bunk number."

Kelly hung up without responding.

Barnes exchanged her coyness for confusion. "What was that all about?"

"We might have a lead," Kelly said without looking up from his phone. He scrolled through his contacts to Sutherland's. As if by some cosmic connection, the sergeant called in before Kelly could hit the green call button.

"Sarge, I was just about to call you."

"Listen. I just heard from one pissed-off lieutenant about how you disregarded a direct order to break off a pursuit."

"I can explain. I—"

Sutherland cut him off. "Nicely done! I heard your ballsy move saved Barnes."

"Thanks."

"Besides, I never liked that prick much anyway." Sutherland changed tone.

"Look, I know you're working the Wilson case and Anderson is up on rotation for the next body, but I've requested you take this one as well."

"Why's that?"

"Because this body dropped in the same spot as the girl. And you know there's no such thing as coincidence. Not in life. And definitely not in Homicide."

"We're on the way."

27

The tires crackled over the hardpacked dirt road, leading to the all too familiar parking lot of Sheffield Electric. Kelly and Barnes arrived as several patrolmen taped off the area. Unlike the Wilson scene, Kelly was ahead of the crime scene unit and the M.E.'s office hadn't yet been called.

Barnes turned to him as they entered the scene. "So, this is where Faith Wilson took her last breaths?"

"Sad, isn't it? Not the place you'd want to meet your end. Not that any place is particularly a good place to be killed, but there's far better."

Kelly noted the time. His notepad was quickly filling up. He approached the officers pulling the tape and jotted down their names. Two he'd never worked with.

"You guys are fast. Normally it takes an hour or two before Homicide rolls in," the red-haired rookie said.

"We happened to be in the area."

"Yeah, we heard the chase on the radio. We were stuck on a domestic. Who the hell has a domestic at nine-thirty in the morning?" the larger, Hispanic officer said. "Sorry we missed the chase. Nice job ending it."

"And good job telling Lieutenant Asshat to go screw."

Kelly laughed to himself. Apparently, Duff was universally disliked. Maybe that was the secret behind his promotion—get him away from the troops. "I was told by my sergeant the body was dropped in the same spot as the one earlier this week?"

"I guess. We weren't here for that, but from what I heard from Russo, it sounds that way. He worked the Tuesday morning scene. Russo's my roommate."

"Did you go in?" Kelly asked.

"We peeked but didn't touch anything. Looks like a suicide to me. But, what do I know?" the redhead offered.

"Why do you say suicide?"

"He had a bullet hole in his temple and a gun still in his hand."

"Sounds like we did a little more than peek, huh guys?" Kelly cocked his head.

Both gave sheepish grins and the fair-skinned officer's cheeks brightened. That boy would be a disaster in a poker game, Kelly thought. He decided to let them off the hook. "But you sure you didn't touch anything, right?"

"Nah. We didn't even need to check for a pulse. Pretty obvious that dude was dead as they come," the Hispanic officer said.

Kelly was tempted to tell the story of the ankle-grabbing woman but decided against it. No time for espousing knowledge.

"Once you finish taping off, start up a crime scene log. Nobody in or out without signing the book. Understood?" Kelly never assumed experience. Always better to err on the side of caution and explain the rules every time.

Kelly left the two men to finish their responsibilities as he and Barnes strode toward the corpse. He could see the twisted body of the man as they passed through the open chain link gate of the equipment storage lot. He slowed to a stop and pulled out his phone, photographing the approach. Unlike Wilson's scene, Kelly did not work as slowly and methodically. He felt himself abandoning protocols in desperate hope of finding Faith's killer. The underlying fear of Bobby's level of involvement added to his heightened pressure.

"I'd normally run things a little different, but the call I received before Sutherland was from a trusted source, and he told me this body would hold the answer we're looking for."

"Devers?"

"No. Somebody much more trusted than him."

The body was slumped to the left. His legs were bent as if he was in a kneeling position before falling. Kelly saw the gun, a .22 caliber revolver, still clutched in his right hand. The gun arm was draped over his right thigh. The body wasn't in the hole dug for Faith Wilson. It lay just outside where her feet had protruded.

He moved in closer to the body and squatted low, balancing above the man's head. The small hole was just above the cheekbone in the small pad of flesh of the right temple region. There was stippling and a barrel burn around the entry point, indicating the gun was in contact with the flesh at the time the trigger was pulled. The left eyeball bulged out from the socket. There was not a large quantity of blood underneath the head, which meant the bullet had not exited the skull. The rounds from small caliber handguns lost a lot of kinetic energy once exiting the barrel and had a tendency to rattle around the inside rather than create an exit wound. However, without moving the body, there was no way to confirm, and Kelly would wait until the crime scene tech was on scene for that.

"What are you seeing?" Barnes peered over his shoulder.

"On first glance, I'd say your old friend Phillip Smalls was kneeling here when he pulled the trigger." Kelly stood and shook out his legs. "That's if Smalls did, in fact, pull the trigger."

"Why do you say that?"

Kelly didn't want to give the answer coming to mind. So, he gave his most accurate variant. "Seems a bit odd that this creeper all of a sudden had such remorse for raping our vic that he comes down here to do himself."

"It'd be nice if that were the case. I wish most of my cases ended with a bullet. These guys don't reform. They come out just as depraved as when they went in." Barnes pointed to the dead man. "Case in point is lying on the ground in front of you. He does a few years on a sex assault and as soon as he's back out, we find his DNA in the body of a dead thirteen-year-old."

"I'm just not sure what this body is supposed to tell us." Kelly heard the rumble of tires and turned to see the Crime Scene Response Unit van pull up, with Raymond Charles at the helm. Kelly's phone pulsed twice, and he examined the incoming text.

Bobby: *Check jacket pocket. Delete message after reading.*

The tech pulled out a cigarette and lit it while he waited by the van. Kelly bent back down and, using his pen, finagled the dead man's coat pocket. He could see the triangular white corner of a piece of paper. He reached into his back pocket and pulled on his latex gloves. He used his cell phone to photo the pocket and the visible end of paper before removing it.

Standing with the folded piece of paper in his hand, he looked at Barnes. He could tell the question was at the forefront of her mind, but she didn't ask it. Kelly unfolded the paper.

On it was a handwritten note. Kelly read the poorly scribbled words:

I'm so sorry. I never knew how old she was. I want you to know I didn't kill her. The people that did keep these girls at the gray house on the corner of Downer and Sawyer. I can't live with myself anymore.

P. Smalls

"That is the strangest suicide note I've ever seen." Barnes raised an eyebrow.

"Agreed. I'm guessing once Charles pulls in the evidence on this one, we'll be reclassifying it as a murder." Kelly hoped Smalls's death wouldn't come back on Bobby. He also knew Conner Walsh's crew well enough to doubt much in the way of usable evidence would be located on or around the body. You don't run one of the most notoriously violent Irish gangs without knowing how to make a clean kill. But everybody slipped up once in a while, and maybe this would be the body to bring down Walsh. Kelly had been looking for that opportunity since he was a kid.

Barnes blew out an audible exhalation, her breath visible in the cool temp.

Kelly added, "On a bright note, it looks like we've got an address that needs a little attention."

"I was thinking the same thing. Although this time, maybe we do it together. My head's a little sore from my last adventure." Barnes rubbed at the back of her head for added effect.

"It's not going to be just you and me on this one. We're bringing in the heavy hitters."

Kelly walked toward Charles with Barnes in-step. "Hey there, Ray. Having a little déjà vu?"

"I guess they could have left the old tape up." Raymond Charles eyed the paper in Kelly's hand. "Digging around before we work the scene? New protocols in play?"

"We're pushing the clock on this one." Kelly held up the paper. "And this is our best chance on finding the killer, or at least getting a few girls out before it's too late."

"Saving a life trumps scene preservation every day of the week in my book."

"I'm not going to be able to stick around with you on this scene. We've got to find ADA Watson and round up a search warrant."

"At least it's not warm enough for golf, so you shouldn't have too much trouble." Charles surveyed the scene. "I've got it. I'll call if anything pops."

"Here's your first piece of evidence. I removed it from the front right jacket pocket. Photographed it before removal."

Charles ditched his cigarette and gloved up. He retrieved a clear plastic evidence bag and held it open as Kelly slid in the document. Sealing it, the senior evidence technician placed it into an open box in the back of the van. "What are you waiting for? Looks like you got some bad guys to visit."

Kelly and Barnes headed back to the Impala. His phone was already on its third ring when he entered the car.

"Detective Kelly, to what do I owe this wonderful Saturday morning call?" Assistant District Attorney Chris Watson asked in his most sarcastic tone.

"Got another body. Same place as the girl's."

"Oh man."

"This one came bearing gifts."

"How's that?"

"Where can I meet you? We may have a lead on the killer, but equally important, the location of some girls in need of our help."

"I'm actually heading into the office now to finish up some unrelated case work. Let's say half hour."

"We'll see you soon. You might want to get a judge on the hook because we're going to be using tactical on this."

Kelly hung up. He drove out of the lot, leaving Charles on scene as he and Barnes prepared for the next phase. He saw the focused intensity in her emerald green eyes, a chance to get even obviously on her mind.

28

"All right. Gather around. Detective Kelly is going to fill us in on today's target, followed by Captain Lyons, who will brief SWAT's entry plan." Sutherland commanded the attention of the room. The tactical briefing area occupied a large conference room down the hallway from Homicide. It was designed to accommodate twenty normally dressed people comfortably, but the bulk and size of the men assigned to the BPD Tactical Unit had made the room feel small and cramped.

Kelly stood in front, with a projected screen behind him. The image was of the gray, three-family colonial. "Thank you all for being here today. This target location may house the killer of Faith Wilson. For those who don't know, her body was found earlier this week, buried in a shallow grave. Faith was thirteen. The person or people responsible for her death are believed to be housing young girls, like Faith, in this house. We've got Anderson and Collette with eyes on the house right now. There's been limited movement in or out since they've posted up."

Kelly clicked the mouse on the computer nearest him and the image on the screen changed. The projected image of a young girl. She was almost the spitting image of Faith. "This is Tabitha Porter. She's believed to be located within this residence. She's a runaway, but listed by SAU as a possible trafficking victim. You should expect to encounter several girls like Tabitha while inside.

Depending on how long these girls have been living under these conditions, they may not react as expected. In fact, they may even provide resistance to our efforts. Please keep in mind that these girls have been through months, even years, of abuse."

Barnes gave a supportive nod. Kelly took a moment to scan the group. His eyes locked on Lyons. He hadn't spoken to the tactical commander since giving his deposition the previous morning. Kelly wasn't able to read his expression then, and he couldn't do it now. "We don't really know much about this group, but we're pretty confident they're responsible for Detective Barnes's abduction. So, with that in mind, they obviously have little regard for law enforcement. If there are no questions for me, I'm going to turn it over to Captain Lyons."

Darren Lyons pushed off the back wall and walked forward. Kelly nodded to his former SWAT commander as he passed.

Lyons was a man comfortable leading others in combat situations. He'd served eight years as an infantry officer in the Army before joining the ranks of the Boston Police Department. Lyons was a man not known to brag and, unlike many of the veterans and cops who frequented Shep's Pub, he never told war stories. When Kelly had served under him as an operator on the BPD Special Weapons and Tactics team, Lyons let his actions speak for him.

"We're dealing with a lot of unknowns on this one. As of right now, we're not exactly sure who is running the house, or what type of resistance we'll face once inside. Looking at the schematics for the residence, the layout dictates the best entry point is going to be to the rear. We'll have an alternative entry team set on the front should we get bogged down or run into difficulty accessing the rear door. The records for the residence indicate a single person owns all three floors of the triple-decker. Be prepared to encounter threats on every level of the house."

Lyons turned off the projector and grabbed a dry-erase marker. He penned a crude representation of the house as if looking down from a bird's-eye view. Lyons used a green marker and made an X near the front door. He marked the rear with a red X. "Alpha Team, you're going to come in off Sawyer Ave. Stay tight to this house, use the backyard for maximum concealment on approach to the target location. Once on the west side of the house, you're going to be exposed when crossing over Downer Ave. Haul ass to the rear lot of the target house. I'm hoping they don't have security cameras, but we have to assume they will. Get on that back door as fast as possible. Radio when in position. As soon as you give the notification, Bravo is going to pull the raid van right up front. I want them to think the heavy hit's coming from the front door. Bravo is going to flashbang under these two windows. Alpha, when you hear the bang, that will be your cue to breach. Once inside, and the first floor is clear, I want Bravo to enter and assist in clearing the rest of the house."

Kelly watched the team intently follow the plan laid out by their leader. He knew most of the tactical members. The Baxter Green case had complicated his relationship with the group. The scrutiny the tactical unit had faced over the following year had driven some resentment and anger his way. Some blamed him for the situation breaking bad. Others were just frustrated with the situation being dragged out in civil court and the scrutiny the team had faced. The sniper who'd taken the shot medically retired shortly after the incident. Kelly shouldered the weight of all of it.

"The close perimeter will be held by Charlie Team. This is also where Detectives Kelly and Barnes will be staged. The intersection will be shut down by assisting members of the patrol division. The CCP will be staged with command."

Barnes leaned in and whispered in Kelly's ear. "What's a CCP?"

"Casualty Collection Point. It's a hand-me-down from the military, but it is always good to note where wounded or dead are to be brought. Reduces the chaos of the moment if it's predesignated." Kelly saw worry on Barnes's face. "I'm hoping it won't be needed for that. Most likely it will become a short-term processing station for any of the girls located inside."

Lyons continued for a brief block, ensuring each member of the unit knew their specific team assignment for the operation and their individual role. He ended with his post-briefing mantra. "Watch your muzzles and know your targets."

The group was dismissed to gear up and given fifteen minutes to be ready to go. As the room cleared out, Kelly saw Lyons approach. The tactical commander stood in front of him. He looked at Barnes. "Can you give Mike and me a minute?"

"Sure thing."

The last few members of the team ambled out of the room, and Kelly was left alone with Lyons. Again, without success, he attempted to read the face of the man standing before him.

"I never got a chance to talk to you after your deposition yesterday."

"I cut out pretty quickly. This case has been at the forefront."

"Listen, Mike, I know this past year has been brutal on you. Same for my team. What you said yesterday meant a lot to the guys. Not many people I know would've got up on that stand and stood their ground the way you did. For what it's worth, you're a hell of a cop."

Kelly was at a loss for words. All he could muster was, "Thanks."

Lyons gave Kelly a firm pat on the shoulder and stepped out of the room. Silence surrounded him, and a small piece of Baxter Green became unshouldered.

29

The cold weather kept the foot traffic to a minimum. The tactical element was a block away in a stacked column of vehicles, each ready to deploy to their designated position on command. Detectives Anderson and Collette were still posted a few houses down from the target location, where they had been for the past two hours. There hadn't been any movement in twelve minutes since a heavyset man had stepped out on the front porch. He smoked two cigarettes and then retreated inside. The sun had gone down, and a streetlight across the street provided the only source of light, minus whatever cast from neighboring windows and porches.

"So, this is what you did for the better part of two years?" Barnes asked, breaking the silence.

"Pretty much. They're a good team, with an equal amount of macho bravado and analytic stratagem."

"Must've been fun."

"I'm not going to lie; it was one hell of a time. Any job where you get to smash a drug dealer's house, or face off with a wanted murderer, is good for an insane adrenalin dump."

"But you left it?"

"I did. I hit a point where I thought I could do more good elsewhere." Kell paused for a moment. Conversations like this always brought forth the memory of Baxter Green. "And here I am now."

"I think Homicide suits you."

Kelly looked over at Barnes. "Yeah?"

"You care."

"I do. There's something about giving the dead their voice back. Helping them find justice regardless of the circumstance that put them in the hole has proven rewarding thus far." Kelly shrugged. "Check back with me in a year and see if I still feel the same way."

The radio in Barnes's car squawked and Lyons's voice filled the air. "The op is a go. I repeat. It's a go."

The brake lights of the idling vehicles released and a steady stream of vans, unmarked and marked cruisers, and an armored personnel carrier turned from Cushing Ave onto Sawyer's one-way loop. No headlights or emergency lights illuminated the approach. The progression was slow, the vehicles minimizing the roar of the engines. Each vehicle began to separate from the pack as they came to their designated stop position. Looking out the passenger side window, he could see the column of dark-uniformed members of the tactical team deploy at a quick pace on foot. They disappeared out of sight around the corner, heading to their post on the rear door of the gray house. Kelly knew the quiet of the neighborhood was about to be shattered.

There's always a strange calm in the moments before a tactical operation commences. A hushed silence seemed to fall, as if even the air stopped moving in anticipation. Kelly had felt it before, and he felt it now.

The stillness gave way to the concussive blasts of the two flashbangs deployed to the front porch windows. The explosions were followed by the loud thud of the breacher's ram's devastating impact against the rear door. Standing at the close perimeter, Kelly followed the entry team's progression through the first floor of the house by listening to the loud but muffled commands as they encountered people within.

"First floor clear. Two in custody. Moving up to the second," the team member relayed.

The front door opened, and the secondary team disappeared inside. Kelly wanted to be in there with them but knew his place in the operation. He looked over at Barnes and could tell she was feeling the same thing.

Kelly heard muffled commands but could no longer discern the words. The team had been inside the residence for less than a minute, but standing on the outside, time seemed to be moving in slow motion.

"Second and third are clear. Five. We've located five girls. Bringing them out shortly. Secondary search underway."

Kelly turned back to Lyons, who was standing by his makeshift command center—his black Explorer, the armored personnel carrier, and two ambulances. Lyons gave him a thumbs up.

"I hope one of them is Tabitha Porter," Barnes said.

"We'll know soon enough." Kelly couldn't have timed his words better.

The front door of the triple-decker house opened, and he heard one of the operators announce, "One walking." This was done to alert law enforcement on the perimeter each time somebody was escorted out. In high stress situations, like a tactical entry, it minimized the potential for friendly fire.

One by one the five rescued girls began to trickle out. Marked cruisers were assigned to transport the girls directly to headquarters so that they could be debriefed. Kelly and Barnes scanned each face as they passed. Four girls had come out but no Tabitha. They shared a worried expression.

The fifth girl came out. Her head was down, and long hair hung over her face. As she was led past Kelly, she tilted her head slightly and he saw the clearly recognizable face of Tabitha Porter. He heard Barnes give an audible sigh of relief.

The last to exit were two men who'd been located inside. These men were handcuffed and looked angry. The large man who'd been seen smoking on the porch before the raid had some bruising to the side of his face. Obviously, he hadn't immediately complied with the commands. Kelly smiled.

Kelly walked over to Lyons. "Hey Captain, we're going to head into the station to assist in identifying and debriefing the girls. Anderson and Collette are going to stay here and process the house."

"Did we find your girl?"

"You did. Thanks for the assist."

"Any time."

Kelly turned to Barnes as they walked back to her car. "Five girls. Hopefully, one of them is willing to talk."

"It's going to take a bit of effort, depending on how long they've been trapped. Tabitha might be our best hope."

Kelly looked at the time and pulled out his phone.

"Ma, it's me. I meant to call earlier, but things got a bit crazy."

"Michael, I understand your job. You don't need to explain yourself. Embry and I have been enjoying some quality time."

"Hi, Daddy!" Embry yelled happily in the background.

"Hi, Squiggles. You be good for Nana."

"When do you think you'll be home?"

Kelly watched as the girls were slowly driven away from the scene. "Not sure. It's probably going to be a late night."

"Well don't you worry about us. We'll be here when you're done."

"Thanks, Ma. Now don't keep her up too late. I've got to drop her with her mom early for the parade."

"We're fine. Go and do your job."

Kelly hung up. He dropped into the passenger seat. Barnes drove out of the neighborhood and back to Schroeder Plaza where the five girls would be waiting.

* * *

SAU had two soft interview rooms set aside for handling victims. The rooms looked more like lounges, adorned with plush couches and coffee tables. The girls had been split into groups and were each given a bag of Doritos and a Sprite while they waited. They were left alone, and a uniform officer stood posted outside the doors.

Kelly and Barnes checked in on them using the video camera positioned in the far corner of each room. Only a couple girls partook in the snacks. A few were asleep. One looked as though she was on the verge of throwing up. One thing was common in both rooms—nobody spoke.

"Tough crowd. How do you want to do this?" Kelly asked.

"Let's start by identifying the girls and then we'll decide the order of interview. Right now, I'm leaning toward starting with the only known we have, which is Tabitha Porter."

"I'll follow your lead on this."

Kelly followed as Barnes entered the first room. Two of the three girls looked up as the door opened, but the third remained slumped against the arm of the chair. "Ladies, I'm Kristen Barnes and this is my partner, Michael Kelly. We're detectives with Boston PD. We know you've been through a lot and we are here to help. To best do that, we are going to need your names. Afterward, we'll pull you out one at a time so we can speak privately. Does all this make sense?"

Nobody spoke. Only one girl gave the slightest of nods, Tabitha Porter. She shared a loveseat with an older girl, who identified herself as Veronica Ainsley. Kelly noted each name and date of birth in his notepad but let Barnes do all of the talking. Barnes had schooled him on the basics of dealing with this very unique type of victim. Girls sexually assaulted by males were less responsive to male investigators.

The third girl slept, noisily snoring, but still looked to be on the verge of vomiting. Her forehead was soaked in sweat, a sickness most likely brought about from whatever combination of drugs from which she was in withdrawal. Barnes called in a patrol officer and alerted him to the girl's condition. She was removed, and medics were called.

In the second room, Barnes gave the same speech to the two girls located inside. Each girl reluctantly provided her name. The last girl to speak said her name was Sabrina Green.

They walked out of the room and shut the door behind them. Kelly stared at the name scribbled in his pad. Sabrina Green.

"You look like you've seen a ghost. Everything all right?"

"I think that girl in there is Baxter Green's sister."

Barnes reared back. "You mean from the hostage situation?"

Kelly nodded.

"Talk about a twist of fate."

"I think we should stick to the game plan and speak to Tabitha first. Not sure Sabrina is going to be super excited to talk to the man responsible for her brother's death."

"You didn't kill two people and hold him hostage. His father set in motion something that was out of your control. And besides, there's a good chance she doesn't even know."

"What do you mean doesn't know?" Kelly asked.

"If she was snatched up by this group before the standoff, which you indicated was a possibility, then she probably wouldn't have heard about it. Groups that run girls like her isolate them from any and all connection with the outside world. This increases their psychological dependency."

"That girl is about to go from one nightmare into another."

"At least she's alive."

"Not much of a life if you ask me."

"You'd be surprised at the resilience of the human mind. I see it every day. Kids pulled from some of the worst conditions imaginable are able, with help, to go on to lead productive lives." Barnes put her hand on his arm. "Listen, Mike, it's your show to run, but I say we start with Sabrina. If nothing else, it may give you some closure."

Kelly hesitated. Never one to back down from a challenge, he conceded. "Fair enough." He opened the door and softened his demeanor. "Sabrina?"

The girl's head barely moved, but her eyes flickered upward in a weak acknowledgement.

"Would you come with us?"

Sabrina stood without speaking. Her shoulders were slack, and her posture was hunched. Defeated, the teen slinked behind as they guided her to an interview room down the hall.

"Can we get you anything else to eat or drink?" Barnes asked as they took their seats.

Sabrina shook her head.

"We're here to help you. Anything we discuss here is to ensure the people responsible for your circumstances aren't able to hurt you or anyone else again," Kelly said.

"You can't stop them." Sabrina's voice was barely above a whisper.

"We can and we will."

"Do you know how long I've been trapped in this life? A long time. Where were you?"

"Maybe you could start by telling us how you ended up with this group?" Barnes asked.

Sabrina shifted her attention to Barnes. She stared blankly and shrugged.

"How long have you been there?"

Another shrug.

"I want to go home. My family lives in Jamaica Plain. I can't imagine what my parents will say when they see."

Kelly felt his stomach knot. He sank a bit lower in his seat. Now was definitely not the time to tell the damaged teen her mother was dead and her father was serving a life sentence at Walpole for the murder.

Barnes came to his rescue. "We're working on that."

Sabrina flopped forward, resting her head on the table. She sighed loudly as her face disappeared under the sprawled tendrils of her dark wavy hair.

"I think she needs some rest," Barnes said, standing. "Why don't we get you back to the couch room?"

Sabrina grunted softly and stood up. Her hair still covering her face, she made no effort to clear her view as she walked out. They returned her to the room. The other girl wasn't ready to be interviewed. She was passed out, drool pooling on the armrest. Her story would have to wait.

The short conversation with Sabrina confirmed that she was the daughter to Trevor Green. Kelly pulled the missing person report and reviewed it. She'd gone missing a few months before the standoff. It looked very similar to the report for Faith Wilson. Tabitha was the only other underage girl in the group, but it was likely the other girls were brought in at a younger age. The oldest was twenty-two. She was also the only one with a criminal record. Minor stuff. A couple pinches for prostitution, petty larceny, and one assault charge.

"Ready to pull Tabitha?" Barnes asked.

Kelly nodded and the two returned to the room where the teenager was being held. "Tabitha, come with us."

The girl hesitated, looking to the older girl for approval. Kelly saw Ainsley reach over and give a quick squeeze of Tabitha's wrist. It was part motherly and part something else that Kelly couldn't quite place.

"How are you holding up? We've got somebody bringing pizza in a bit if you're hungry." Barnes guided the girl out of the room. Her words and mannerisms were a fine balance of compassion and professionalism.

Tabitha was escorted into a regular interview room set with three chairs and a table. Barnes directed the girl to sit and she pulled her chair alongside leaving Kelly alone on the other side of the table. Again, he quickly understood the purpose. She was to be Tabitha's ally and proximity would reduce the invisible barrier.

"First, I want you to understand what happened to you wasn't your fault. The people who do this are masters at manipulation. Right now, you may feel disoriented and confused as to who you can trust. I hope you come to see me as somebody who's got your best interests at heart."

Tabitha cast her eyes down at the floor.

"We've been looking hard to find you."

"Why? Ain't nobody cares about me." She spoke without looking up. Her words came out in a mumble, but the underlying anger was deeply rooted. "I know that skeezer of a foster mom didn't. You know she's running weed out that house? Good job DCF checking that piece of work out before sending me in."

"We weren't part of that, and I'm sorry the system failed you. I work with some amazing DCF investigators who can make sure something like that doesn't happen again."

"Talk is cheap, lady."

"Maybe I can prove my worth to you. Help me get the people responsible for putting you in that house."

Tabitha's eyes widened and she lifted her head. "Are you outta your mind? You want me to snitch on those people? I'd be dead in a day."

Kelly saw Barnes start to say something and then pause. He could see she was working to select her words carefully. It would be detrimental to claim the people couldn't hurt the girl. Barnes knew firsthand how close she'd come to finding out the extent they'd go to protect the organization. A group willing to kill a cop was not to be taken lightly.

"I know they're dangerous. I won't make any promises except that my partner and I will do everything in our power to keep you safe." Barnes scooted closer to the girl. "What's to say they won't hurt you anyway?"

Tabitha's tough exterior fell apart and her bottom lip quivered. Her eyes started to moisten, and the girl fought to keep her composure.

"Let me help you."

The tears fell freely now, and she covered her face with her hands. "I never saw who was in charge. The only time they let me out I was given something. It messed me up. I couldn't point out any of the people that are in charge," Tabitha said between choked sobs.

"Take your time. Maybe something will come back to you."

The girl shifted emotions, going from despondency to anger in a blink of an eye. "They showed me the picture of a dead girl. I'm not going to end up like her."

"What dead girl?" Kelly jumped in, acting on a guttural reflex.

Tabitha looked over at him as if it were the first time she'd seen him or realized he was even in the room. "Some girl in a ditch."

Kelly backed off and let Barnes resume. "Can you describe the man that showed you this picture?"

The girl shook her head. "They had me spinning. All I remember is he had dark hair."

"Is there anything else? Maybe some tattoos or a unique facial feature."

Tabitha said nothing and only offered a weak shrug as an answer.

"It's okay. Maybe something will come to you later."

"I want to go back." The girl pushed back in her seat, distancing herself from Barnes, and rebuilding her tough façade. "I'm tired."

Barnes stood. "Sure thing. We'll bring you some pizza when it gets here."

Tabitha made her way to the door, this time leading the detectives. She stopped before opening it and turned. "He spoke funny."

"Spoke funny?" Barnes asked. "How so? Like a lisp or speech impediment?"

"No. It was an accent. Never heard it before." She turned the handle. "But I'd remember it if I ever heard it again."

They walked Tabitha back to the room with the other girls. She stood next to Kelly as Barnes moved to open the door. It was quiet in the SAU office. Kelly heard a whisper. At first he wasn't even sure it was a voice. Then in the silence the words became clear. "She's one of them." He thought of Jimmy Smokes's wisdom about whispers from the dark. A chill ran down his spine, but reason overrode, and he quickly realized the words' origin.

Barnes opened the door. From her benign facial expression, he concluded she hadn't heard the words. He looked to Tabitha. She kept her eyes focused on the room or the person inside it.

He replayed Ainsley's grip on the girl's wrist. Now coupled with her whispered message, Kelly was able to place the look given to the scared teenager. Threat.

Barnes scanned the list of names. Kelly interceded. "Veronica, would you please come with us?"

The three proceeded to the same interview room as before, but this time Kelly led. He opened the door. "Have a seat over there." Kelly pointed to the isolated chair he'd just left. He felt Barnes give a sideways glance.

Ainsley entered and took a seat. Barnes stepped to enter, but Kelly subtly blocked her path. "We'll be back in a minute. Can we get you something to drink?"

"No thanks. I'm good."

Kelly closed the door and locked it.

"What gives?" Barnes asked.

Kelly put his finger to his lips. "You didn't hear her?" he asked, maintaining a hushed tone.

"Hear who?"

"Tabitha Porter whispered under her breath just before reentering the room."

"What?"

"I thought I was hearing things, it was so quiet. But she said, '*she's one of them.*'"

Barnes thumbed toward the locked interview room housing Veronica Ainsley.

Kelly nodded. "I saw something in the room when we first brought Tabitha out. Ainsley gave a quick grab at her wrist. It was a threat. Probably a warning about what would happen if she talked."

"Well, this just took an interesting turn."

"There's another thing that's been bothering me about the Faith Wilson death." Kelly pulled out his notepad and scrolled through his crime scene notes. Marked with an asterisk was a line denoting the depth of the grave. He picked up the phone.

"Hey Ray, it's Kelly. Are you available?"

"I'm collecting some sweet overtime thanks to our two-body gravesite. What's up?"

"I'm up in SAU. We just hit a house connected to the Faith Wilson case. Pulled out five girls."

"Get anything good?"

"Not sure. We're going to find out in a minute. Did you finish processing the shovel?"

"I did. Actually, finished fuming it an hour ago. I ran a few DNA swabs over it beforehand too. May take a while on that, but I did pull two partials."

"Do you think the partials are complete enough to make the necessary points for comparison?"

"I'd say yes."

"Well your yes is a guarantee."

"I'm going to go out on a limb and say you've got somebody you'd like me to compare them to?"

"I do. Veronica Ainsley. She's in the system."

"I'll get right on it. So, what is it about this person that makes you think it's our killer?"

"Something about the grave that's been bothering me ever since that day."

"Please, do tell."

Kelly heard the challenge in the seasoned crime scene tech's tone. "The depth was wrong."

"What do you mean wrong?"

"It was cold, but not extremely so. And definitely not typical for mid-March. It actually rained during the night and that left the ground soft. Easier to dig."

"Okay."

Kelly heard the tone change from challenge to interest. "So, why was the body exposed? Why would anybody dig a grave so shallow?"

"You tell me, Detective."

"Because our digger was weak. A person physically not capable of digging deep enough after hauling a limp body from the T tracks to the dirt lot."

"That's a good theory."

Kelly was taken aback at the compliment. "I'm about to put it to the test."

Kelly hung up the phone and saw Barnes staring at him, speechless. "Ready to interrogate a homicide suspect?"

"I'll follow your lead."

30

"Veronica, are you comfortable? Is there anything you need?" Kelly asked.

"I'm straight."

"Not to worry, we've got pizza on its way."

"Like I said, I'm good."

Kelly studied the girl's body language. Unlike Tabitha's attempt at toughness, the girl sitting across from him was not acting. She carried herself with an edge that could only be attributed to being brought up on the street. Those hard lessons forged certain telltale characteristics, and Ainsley bore them all.

"Okay then. I know we met when we brought you in, but just to reintroduce myself, I'm Michael Kelly, and this is Kristen Barnes. We're detectives."

Ainsley rolled her eyes. "And let me guess, you want to help me? You're going to get the evil men who did this to me?"

Her tone was thick with sarcasm. Kelly refrained from playing his card. "I didn't finish. I'm with Homicide."

Kelly let the word float in the air. He watched as the girl shifted. It wasn't an overt change of position, but was enough movement to catch his eye. She was nervous. The sneer was replaced with worry. The realization of his purpose in the room had been established. The girl was well aware of her situation now.

"I don't know about no dead girl." Ainsley folded her arms triumphantly.

"I never said anything about a girl."

She released her arms. But quickly tried to cover her mistake. "What else could it be? Everybody's talking about it." She sucked her teeth and broke eye contact. "You D's are always the last to know."

"I'm sure you've been through a lot over the years. I can't even begin to imagine the things you had to do to get to your position." Barnes leaned in.

"What do you think you know about me? What are you talking about position?"

Kelly didn't interrupt and trusted Barnes was exposing something he didn't understand.

"To be Bottom. No way you get there without going through hell first. I know plenty of girls in the game. And to get out of the stable is hard." There was an honesty in Barnes's eyes. She wasn't patronizing the girl.

"Like you know." Ainsley played with a loose thread on her jacket sleeve.

"Detective Kelly works with the dead. I work with the living, in particular, girls like you and the other four waiting on the couches back there. So, while I may never have personally experienced the horrors you have, I do have many years of dealing with those survivors who have."

The girl said nothing. But at least she didn't continue her verbal resistance. It was a step in the right direction.

"I think you need to consider the situation you're in. The only way we can provide you any assistance down the road is if you come clean with us."

"I don't know what it is you think I did, but you're wasting your time."

Kelly opened the case file he had brought in with him. It had expanded exponentially in size over the course of the past five days of investigation. He slid out the picture of Faith Wilson, her school photo, and slid it across the table. Kelly said nothing.

She glanced down and then smirked. A poor attempt at masking her recognition and a classic case of overacting. "Am I supposed to know who that is?"

Kelly said nothing. He just sat and waited. Silence was his weapon of choice in this round of the match. Like inside the ring, an interview yielded best results when strategy got applied.

The void created in the quiet of the room begged to be filled. Whoever spoke first lost. Kelly didn't move or fidget. He sat expressionless in his sea

Minutes ticked by. Kelly had done so many three-minute rounds over his years, he could gauge time in that increment. Two rounds had passed. Six minutes of silence. His opponent was weakening, and during the second round, Veronica Ainsley started to gaze down at Faith's picture with increased frequency.

"So what if I've seen her? Is it a crime to know somebody?"

"That depends." Kelly leveled his eyes on the girl seated across from him.

She sighed loudly in dramatic fashion. "Depends on what."

"The last time you saw her."

The girl slid the picture back toward Kelly. He noticed open blisters, red and irritated, in the web of both of her small hands. Flesh unaccustomed to physical labor bore testament to toils. Like digging.

"Those look like they hurt."

She retracted immediately as if she'd touched a hot stove. "Nah, it's nothing."

"How'd you get them?"

"You ask a lot of questions."

"It's my job."

"Well, your job sucks."

"Sometimes it does, and sometimes I get to help a young girl killed by some heartless thug." Kelly slid the next picture across to punctuate the statement. This one depicted the same girl, one year later, face-down in a shallow grave. Dead.

In boxing there's a time to commit fully to ending the fight. In an interrogation the term is called pulling the trigger. Once committed, there is no turning back. The point of no return.

"Have you ever heard the term forensics before?"

She shrugged, still hypnotized by the image captured in an 8x10 glossy print.

"CSI ring a bell?" Kelly hated using the television show as his reference, but in the years since it started airing, followed by its million spin-offs, the general population related all criminal investigations to those three little letters.

"Yeah. I know what that is."

"There's a lot of stuff television gets wrong, but they're right about a couple of them. DNA is irrefutable. Jury members eat that stuff up. The other is fingerprints. We don't even need a whole print to identify someone. Even easier if that someone has been arrested before. Do you see where I'm going with this?"

Ainsley said nothing. The tough girl was scared, and Kelly pushed harder. Pops had taught him once an opponent's legs buckled, you never let up. Swing until they're down.

"Here's what I know. You didn't wear gloves that night. Those blisters you don't want to talk about are a clear proof of that. What that also means is all the torque you used to dig rubbed billions of skin cells off on the handle and shaft of the shovel. And do you know what's in each of those tiny imperceptible skin cells?" Kelly waited a fraction of a second because he could see the girl was frozen. "DNA."

"That shovel is down in the lab and just before we came in to talk to you, one of the city's best forensic investigators told me that he lifted two prints off the shovel. Two usable prints, and while we've been in here talking, he's been doing a comparison from your print card in AFIS."

Ainsley looked as though she was going to be sick.

"That red-handled shovel that you tossed away is sitting downstairs in our evidence locker, coated in your DNA and fingerprints. You might want to think really hard about what comes out of your mouth next. Because if it's another lie, then my partner and I are walking out that door."

"You're putting her body on me? Are you outta your mind? I didn't kill that girl. Her uncoordinated ass killed herself."

"You buried her though."

"I'm not saying nothing about that." She folded her arms.

"It's probably in your best interest to talk. Otherwise we're going to be forced to draw conclusions and I don't think any jury is going to want to hear our version." Kelly didn't give her a chance to speak and continued. "My partner and I understand that you are but a piece of a much bigger problem. We are working closely with the prosecution, and as long as you cooperate, we may be able to assist in the amount of time you spend in prison."

"Prison? For what?" Ainsley looked thoroughly confused.

"Murder."

"You are some crazy ass cops. Murder?" The twenty-two-year-old girl from the streets tossed the paper back in the direction of Kelly. She threw her hands up. "Fine. I buried her, but that's it. She was already dead. And like I said, that girl was a clumsy fool."

"It's obvious you don't have all the facts."

"What facts?"

"Faith Wilson, that was the girl's name if you ever cared to ask, fell on the T tracks heading into JFK/UMass station. We actually found the spot where her head struck the first rail."

"Like I told you. It was an accident."

"No, actually you said she was a klutz. Sounds like there's a little more to the story. What was an accident?"

Ainsley pushed her chair back, distancing herself from the table and the question. Kelly didn't press. He waited. Overt physical reactions were an indicator of a person's subconscious release.

"I was just trying to get her to come back with me."

"Come back where? The Bayside?"

The girl gave a barely noticeable bob of her head.

"Then what?"

"She shoved me and fell back. Tripped on the damn train tracks." Veronica eyed Kelly and Barnes with a bit more confidence now. "So, tell me, how is that murder?"

"Because she wasn't killed by the fall. Unconscious and paralyzed, but not dead."

Veronica Ainsley's face was the definition of disbelief. "What?"

"Faith Wilson died from asphyxiation. In layman's terms, she was buried alive." Kelly paused to let the words sink in. "Buried alive by you."

"I never—I mean it was an acc—" The rigid toughness dissipated as her shoulders went slack.

"I can see from your reaction this is news to you. As horrible as her death was, there were other things in play. Help us go after the people running the girls, and we'll work with you on your case."

"If I talk, I'm as good as dead."

"You're willing to take a murder rap for somebody who wouldn't do the same? I haven't seen a lawyer show up to defend you. The hired muscle already had an attorney come through and set bond."

"You know you aren't going to stay the Bottom Bitch forever. You're twenty-two. That's an old hag by their standards, judging by the girls in the other room. They're probably looking to replace you, if they haven't already." Barnes weighed in with her knowledge of the trade. "What's a retirement plan look like in your line of work? I'll tell you. You'll be working a corner, fighting for scraps. And let me tell you, the end result is not pretty."

"What do you want from me?"

"Everything."

31

The interview with Veronica Ainsley had gone late into the night. Kelly pulled into the driveway and got out of his busted car. The floorboard of the porch creaked its familiar greeting. Exhausted, he entered through the unlocked door. Kelly went straight upstairs and to the guest bedroom. The glow of the nightlight ebbed out from under the door and danced on the hardwood.

Embry was in a deep sleep. For a kid who didn't like to go to bed, once down, she was impossible to wake. Kelly sat on the bed next to his daughter. He moved an opened book off her covers and placed it on a doily on her nightstand. He leaned in and gave her a gentle kiss on her cheek.

He watched as his eight-year-old took deep, contented breaths. Kelly couldn't imagine his world without her. He thought of Faith and how she disappeared from a good neighborhood. He shuddered at her demise and wondered how Faith's father had survived. He had left a message for Mr. Wilson and planned to pay him a visit on Monday after he tied up a few loose ends.

It was late and he needed to be up early. The parade goers took to the streets early, and Kelly needed to get Embry to her mother before he went on his annual pilgrimage to visit Rourke's grave.

Kelly absorbed one more round of his daughter's angelic face before heading off to his bed.

* * *

It felt as though he'd just closed his eyes when he felt the pounce of his daughter as she climbed into his bed.

"Daddy, get up! It's parade day!"

She was already dressed and ready. Embry climbed onto his chest and began shaking him at the shoulders. Kelly double-checked the clock on the wall, still a couple of minutes behind. He sat up and his daughter flopped over onto the bed. Kelly tickled her ribs and she giggled wildly.

Downstairs his mother was already cleaning up the dishes. The peanut butter and jelly toast breakfast routine was complete.

"Good morning. There's some fresh coffee in the pot."

Kelly poured himself a cup and took a sip.

"I didn't hear you come in last night. Must've been a late one?"

"It was."

"Would you like me to make you something to eat?"

"I'll grab something later. We are running late. I've got to get Embry to her mother. Parade day."

His mother stopped washing the dishes and limped over to where Kelly was standing. She swallowed him in a silent hug and kissed his cheek.

Kelly downed the hot, black, liquid energizer and scooped up Embry as if she were a sack of potatoes, hoisting her high onto his shoulder. Her head bobbed near his ear, filling it with her infectious giggle.

* * *

Kelly took the back streets, navigating his way to the closest spot before parking. He'd made one quick pit stop at the family liquor store. He always shared Danny's drink of choice on this most somber of days. He tucked away his pain and forced a smile. No need to burden his daughter with such things. It was her brightness that pulled him from his darkest times, and he didn't want his pain to dampen her glow.

She bounced along the crowded sidewalk as if the concrete were the inflated rubber of a bounce house. Embry's small hand tugged at his, pulling him forward.

Ahead he saw Samantha wearing the green Red Sox cap he'd given her two years earlier. She looked good in it. Seeing her standing shoulder to shoulder with Marty lessened its charm. Ten years ago, before Embry was born, he and Sam had found this spot along the parade route, the perfect vantage from which to see the throngs of bands and dancers round the bend on Telegraph Hill before making the half loop through Thomas Park. It soured his mouth seeing the spot shared with another man.

Kelly sucked it up and approached, focusing his energy on Embry.

"I didn't think you were going to make it." Sam bent and kissed their daughter, but Kelly knew the comment was directed at him.

"Mike." Martin Cappelli held up a plastic cup of beer in a symbolic cheers.

"Marty."

Kelly crouched to his daughter's level and scooped her in close. "I love you, my squiggles. Enjoy the parade, and I'll see you in a couple days."

"Stay." Her voice tickled his ear.

He kissed her on the forehead. "I've got to go see Danny."

She knew what that meant and put up no further protest. Kelly turned and walked back in the direction he'd just come, separating before his daughter's charms derailed him.

Kelly no longer wore a smile as he moved against the pedestrian flow like a trout swimming upstream.

* * *

The drive to Saint Mary's Cemetery was relatively quick compared to his trip into the heart of the city. Not too many people spent Saint Patty's Day at a graveyard, but if Michael Kelly was anything, he was unique.

He navigated the familiar path. The cemetery had been founded in 1851. Over one hundred and fifty years of personal loss covered the grounds. Danny's marker was in a newer section. In the eight years since his body had been interred, the granite still looked brand new in comparison to neighboring plots.

Kelly took a seat next to the headstone. He took a moment to wipe away the winter's grime with the sleeve of his sweatshirt, making the lettering more visible. He read the inscription at the bottom. *Loving son. Devoted husband. Guardian angel of the city. One of its finest.*

He pulled the small bottle of Tullamore Dew whiskey from his back pocket and wrenched open the cap. Kelly poured out a small amount on the browned grass at the base of the stone. He then raised it up to his lips and took a swig. The smooth heat worked down his throat, into his empty stomach.

The conversation that would take place between Kelly and his former partner and best friend would last the next hour or so. No words would be spoken aloud. It was an internal dialogue. Kelly would catch his friend up on the events of the past year. This year's tumultuous passing left much to be discussed.

The warmth provided from the whiskey negated the cold of the ground and the gusty March winds. Kelly settled in.

32

Kelly woke with a splitting headache matched only by the knot in his stomach. Most residents of the city were waking to a similar malaise. His day of remembrance always started at the hallowed grounds of Saint Mary's but ended at Shep's. The pub was a favorite of the duo when they worked the streets of the Eleven together.

Out of tradition, Kelly always ordered the shepherd's pie. Ironically, for a place named Shep's, the menu item was the worst food the kitchen offered. But it was a miracle cure for absorbing alcohol and reducing the next day's fallout. He'd be in a much worse state had his stomach not been lined with the layers of beef, corn, and mashed potatoes.

The doorbell rang. He looked at the clock, vowing to fix it, and saw it was already close to nine. Late start. He checked his phone and saw he'd missed a call from Barnes. Downstairs, he heard his mother's voice. It was more pitchy than normal, and she sounded excited in speaking with whoever had come to the door this morning.

After taking a minute to get himself ready for the day, Kelly went downstairs. He heard his mother laugh from the kitchen as he made his entrance.

Seated next to his mom was Kristen Barnes. The two were sharing a cup of coffee and catching up like old friends.

"Well, look at this sleepyhead finally deciding to join the land of the living."

His mother laughed.

Kelly rubbed his head. "I just saw I missed your call. As you can see, I'm running a bit behind this morning."

"I can see that." Barnes winked. "I was just calling to tell you I was going to stop by and pick you up. No riding in your death trap of a car today."

Kelly poured himself the dregs of what was left in the pot. He drank it black, needing to get the caffeine in his system as quick as possible.

"I did a little digging this morning." Barnes was almost giddy with excitement.

"Early start?"

"You know me. The kid from the car crash lawyered up the minute he woke up in the hospital. So, I made some calls and finally got hold of the Audi's leasing company. After faxing over an official request, they gave me the registered owner's information. Aleksander Rakowski. Does the name ring a bell?"

"The last name does. Not sure why."

"It didn't for me, but I sent an email out to the other units and Jim Sharp in OC got back to me. Apparently the Rakowski family have been on their radar for a while."

"I assume you've got a plan?"

"I did, but it fell apart on my way here. I had hoped to pay Mr. Rakowski a visit, but shortly after my email went out, I received a call from an attorney telling me he'd been retained as counsel."

"That's not good. Means whoever this guy is, he's got ties to the department."

"I know." Barnes had a disconsolate look. "There is a silver lining."

"Yeah? What's that?"

"His attorney said Mr. Rakowski is willing to make a statement."

Kelly raised an eyebrow. "Well, that's a first."

"It gets better. You're not going to believe who the attorney is."

"Who?"

"Lawrence Shapiro."

* * *

Kelly and Barnes consulted with ADA Chris Watson while they waited fo

Shapiro to arrive with his client. Watson was generally willing to take things to trial rather than bowing to a weaker plea deal, but he was taking a wait-and-see approach with Rakowski. An officer escorted the attorney and Rakowski up to the second floor. Both were dressed in expensive suits, and they walked purposefully behind the officer. Rakowski had a scowl on his face and appeared to be peeved about this meeting.

Kelly guided them into the same room where Lawrence Shapiro had represented Clive Branson. This time no games. There were four chairs, two on each side of the table.

"Before we get started, can I get either of you something to drink?" Kelly knew the offering would be rejected but wanted to keep things cordial and non-confrontational until he knew the savvy defense attorney's goal.

"No thank you. We'd like to get right down to it. My client is a very busy man and needs to get back to running his business."

Kelly refrained from taking a jab at the man's definition of business. "Okay. What is it you'd like to discuss? Because we've got a few questions for Mr. Rakowski."

"My client isn't here to answer questions. He is here to make a statement and then leave."

"A statement."

"The other day his car was stolen. It's our understanding you located the vehicle."

"Whoa. You're seriously not here trying to convince me that your client is here to file a stolen vehicle report?"

"It's exactly that. He didn't realize his vehicle was missing until this morning. Rest assured, he wants to ensure the person responsible for the theft of his motor vehicle is prosecuted to the fullest extent of the law."

"You're trying to tell me that the Balicki kid has no affiliation to the Rakowski crime family?"

"Detective Kelly, if you're insinuating my client's family-run deli is in some way related to a criminal enterprise then you've been poorly informed. Or, if you're implying simply that because the car thief happened to be Polish that in some way links Mr. Rakowski to the crime, that is absurd. Every time an Irish kid commits a crime is he somehow related to you?"

Kelly fumed.

"When you write down whatever load of crap you've concocted, make sure your client signs it so I can go after him later for lying on an official police report, and you can be disbarred for the shady practice you run!"

Kelly stood abruptly, knocking over his chair. He rarely lost his cool in an interview, but the events leading up to this moment left him without the faculties to control himself.

Barnes stood too, not as dramatically. She leaned across the table and met Rakowski's arrogant stare. "Your biggest mistake was not killing me. I'm still here, you snide son of a bitch. By the time we're done, you're going to wish you had."

"Is that a threat, Detective?" Shapiro asked.

"It's a promise. Big difference in my world."

Kelly and Barnes stormed out of the interview room. Sutherland was standing nearby with a quizzical expression.

"Have somebody else take that piece of crap's statement." Kelly walked away without waiting for an acknowledgement from his supervisor.

"That appears to have gone well," Sutherland said, more to himself, as the duo were already making a beeline for the exit.

Kelly walked out of Homicide and into the hallway with Barnes close behind.

"Wait." Barnes jogged up.

"Sorry, I lost it in there. Seeing that smug bastard sitting there with his shady attorney mocking us sent me over the edge."

"Trust me, I know." Barnes put a hand on his shoulder. "We've still got Veronica Ainsley's statement. Watson's going to try to make it stick."

"We've got the statement of a murderer looking to shed some of the blame onto a man with no direct ties to the case, except for the car that he's now claiming was stolen."

"Let's go back to the beginning. Maybe now that we know who we're looking at, we'll see the link."

Kelly was about to sputter an underwhelming platitude but stopped himself. And then it hit him. "I think you might be onto something. If nothing else, I think you've just filled a nagging gap in the disappearance of Fait Wilson." Kelly was suddenly energized again and turned back to his desk, ignoring the looks from his boss as he retrieved Faith's file.

33

Kelly sat in the same lot he'd been in six days earlier. At that time, he'd approached with more questions than answers. Today was different. He wasn't alone, and the majority of the questions had been answered, some he hadn't even thought to ask until earlier this morning.

The two exited Barnes's Caprice and walked toward the door. The same nasty welcome mat greeted them. Kelly banged loudly on the door and waited. As before, the man inside moved with the speed of a sloth. Kelly heard the creak of the floor from the other side and knew Gary Wilson was peering out through the peephole, then came the sound of a deadbolt unlatching.

"Detective," Gary Wilson slurred. The day's eventful drinking had taken hold of the man.

"Mr. Wilson, may we come in?" Kelly asked.

"Free country." The man staggered back. He was wearing a robe loosely tethered around his bulging gut. It did little to cover the striped boxers and stained tank top serving as his only clothing for the day. From the looks of it, he'd been in this hobo's ensemble since the last visit. The funk surrounding him only added to the man's overall presence.

Kelly entered and Barnes followed, closing the door behind them. Once inside, Kelly decided to keep the conversation to the confines of the hallway stairs. The interior was littered with trash as if the quaint town of North Andover had begun using his condo as a secondary landfill.

"Did you get my message?" Kelly asked.

Wilson plopped heavily onto the stairs, missing the one he'd aimed for and sliding down to the next. "I did. Meant to get back to you, but forgot."

"That's a shame. Maybe you don't recall, but I'm the guy who's been hunting your daughter's killer."

"Of course I remember!" Wilson tried to stand in an effort to show his outrage at the insinuation, but failed miserably. His hand slid off the railing, and he only managed to get an inch rise before flopping down.

"You can save the theatrics." Kelly closed the distance, ignoring the man's stink and leaning down toward him. "Your daughter's killer's been arrested."

"What? You found him?" Wilson looked genuinely pleased. His eyes watered.

"Not him. Her."

"A girl killed my Faith?" Wilson rubbed at his greasy scalp.

"Looks that way." Kelly paused and evaluated the grieving father. "But there were a lot of people responsible for her death."

Wilson put his face in his hands and wept loudly.

"I won't be able to bring them all to justice. At least not just yet. But some are already facing their own punishment."

Wilson wiped his nose on his sleeve and met Kelly's gaze.

"I never saw it. Couldn't make the mental jump. But today, one of the people I believe had a hand in your daughter's death walked into my office with his attorney. The same lawyer who represented Clive Branson."

Wilson's tears still fell, but his sobbing stopped.

"When you told me you were a manager at a grocery store, I didn't realize it was the same one Clive Branson's father owned. You worked for the man whose son was responsible for the disappearance of your daughter." Kelly gritted his teeth and felt the disgust rise up. "You didn't get a mental health disability from the store. I did some digging into your compensation package. Seemed strange to me that in the interim, since you left work, you managed to keep your condo here in North Andover. But your accounts didn't add up. You've got a pretty healthy bank account. Although, I've noticed, since the initial deposit made eight months ago, you've drank your way through a bit of that quarter million."

Kelly kicked a nearby empty can of beer on the floor. "I don't know many grocery store managers that get a two hundred fifty thousand dollar payout when they take an early retirement. But you and I both know it wasn't a retirement payout. It was a payoff to keep your mouth shut."

Wilson opened his mouth to speak, but no words came out.

"Your daughter may have died cold and alone in a shallow grave, but your hand might as well have been on the shovel that filled it."

Wilson slumped back. "Do you know what I gave up because of that girl? I had scholarships to the big name schools. I was on my way. Then she came along and everything fell apart. After her mother left us, it all went downhill from there. It was all on me to raise her."

"That's your job. You signed up for it when you became a parent. And nobody ever said it was supposed to be easy."

"I was buried in debt."

"Please don't try to rationalize what you did. There's nothing you can say that'll ever come close to making sense to either of us."

"Are you going to arrest me?"

"I would if I could, but seems to me you're already a prisoner."

"What about the money?"

"What about it?"

"Are you going to take it?"

"No. Branson made sure it was properly accounted for. So, your blood money is safe."

Wilson belched and rubbed his ruddy face.

"Doesn't look like that money was worth it."

Kelly didn't wait for a reaction and turned to leave. Barnes opened the door and the two detectives walked away, leaving the man to his own version of hell.

"What father would turn a blind eye to his daughter's abduction?"

"I'm pretty sure karma's kicking the proverbial crap out of him. There's no light at the end of his tunnel."

"Where to now?" Barnes asked.

"I've got to make another stop, but this is one I've got to do alone."

34

The phone rang. He saw the incoming caller ID and was tempted to let it go to voicemail, but after the third combination of vibration and chime Kelly answered.

"What's up, Marty?"

"Hey Mike. Bad time?"

Kelly had several preloaded retorts but refrained. "What do you got?"

"Judge Coleman rendered his verdict in the Baxter Green case."

"And?"

"The death resultant of the shooting was deemed accidental. He saw no cause to fault the actions of the tactical team."

There was a pause and Kelly remained silent, assuming there was more.

"Judge Coleman said you acted in accordance with policy and procedure. Your decisions to try and effectively resolve the situation were sound. He further went on to commend you for your efforts."

"Doesn't put the bullet back in the gun. Doesn't bring back the boy."

"No, it doesn't. But hopefully this gives you some peace. As for the Green family, the judge awarded a two million dollar settlement."

"Is that the going cost for a dead child?" Kelly thought about the value Wilson placed on his daughter. Comparatively better, but in no way would ever compensate for the loss.

"For what it's worth, I respect the way you handled yourself during the trial even if you went against everything I advised you to say."

"Thanks. Just trying to do the right thing."

Kelly swiped the red digital button, ending the call.

* * *

The room was private. A secluded space set aside for attorney-client meetings and, on occasion, a law enforcement interview. This meeting could be clearly defined by either category. Although he was a detective and the man he was scheduled to speak with was a convict. Aside from those parallels, this meeting was designed with one thing in mind. Atonement.

A buzz and the door unlatched. A mechanical clanking retracted the heavy steel. Behind it stood a thin man in the correctional garb of MCI Cedar Junction's correctional facility. Even though the name had changed, inmates and cops alike still referred to the prison as Walpole, home to the commonwealth's most violent prisoners. A thick-necked guard with a fresh crewcut escorted the man in.

Kelly sat patiently while the prisoner's shackles were linked to the table's steel.

"Never thought in a million years I'd see you here."

"To be honest, I never thought I'd be here, either," Kelly said. "I found your daughter."

The man stammered and started to shake. "How? When?"

"She was in a house we raided. I'm not going to lie, she's going to need a lot of assistance getting past what she's been through. But, at least she's safe."

"A house? Where?"

"She was found with a group of girls. I'm not sure how long she was there, but hopefully in time Sabrina will open up and clarify. I've got some good people helping her through this. But it's going to take some time."

Trevor Green wept.

"Listen, I can never undo what happened to your son. His death haunts me to this day." Kelly cleared his throat. "But you have one child that's going to need you. You're about to receive a fat check from the city. Although it doesn't begin to make amends for your son's death, you can put it toward giving your daughter a fighting chance at a better life."

"How could she bear to look at me after what I've done?"

"Family first. Family always. It's something we say in mine. Basically, no matter how bad things get, they are always there."

"Maybe we come from different stock?"

"I've got a girl waiting on the other side of that door who proves otherwise."

Trevor Green's jaw dropped as Kelly stood and walked to the closed door. He knocked twice and another guard opened it.

Sabrina Green entered as Kelly exited. The door closed behind him as the two were given a chance to reconnect and he was given a fraction of redemption.

35

Kelly had spent the majority of the day organizing the details of his case. Veronica Ainsley, who Sabrina Green knew as Slice, didn't receive the red-carpet treatment from the Rakowski family. She was being represented by a public defender and had a bond set well beyond her means. Her sworn statement was still under review at the District Attorney's office as to its ability to bring charges against Aleksander Rakowski, who she identified from a photo lineup as the handler running the girls. Kelly desperately sought to find a shred of evidence connecting Rakowski to the organization, but whoever kept their books did an excellent job of hiding any breadcrumbs. Even the teenager, Jakub Balicki, managed to duck the justice system, and didn't end up spending a night in juvenile detention. He was out free, awaiting a hearing on watered-down motor vehicle charges. Furthermore, he refused to speak to police.

With Ainsley in custody for the murder of Faith Wilson, his regular case-load began to resume precedence. Kelly stared at his Murder Board and took down Faith's red card, replacing it with a blue one.

His newest red card, Phillip Smalls, taunted him. Bobby's potential connection with the death bothered him, and he wasn't sure where it would lead. His homicide partner, Jimmy Mainelli, would be back from vacation tomorrow. He listened to Cliff Anderson in the cubicle across from him talk up his amazing week with one of his many mistresses and longed to have Barnes back at his side. She was back working her own cases, and although only down the hall, it felt like miles apart.

Kelly picked up the phone. "Hey Ray. Any luck with the Phillip Smalls scene?"

Charles chuckled a throaty laugh. "On the initial pass everything seemed to point to a suicide."

"I know." Kelly rubbed his temple.

"There are a few oddities that need exploring."

"Like what?"

"Well, for one there was no GSR on the gun hand."

"A guy fires a gun and there's no gunshot residue?" Kelly did not like that.

"And then there's the strange wound on the left hand."

"What wound?" Kelly tried to recall it but wasn't able to visualize anything specific.

"In the meat of the hand between the thumb and pointer finger is a small X."

"An X?"

"It looks like an X. Had it been on the right hand I might've written it off as the shooter riding too high up on the tang of the weapon and maybe catching a piece of his skin. You'll have to wait for the official report from the autopsy, but in my humble opinion, the injury appears to be done postmortem."

Kelly said nothing. His mind raced to the details of another case file, one he'd committed to memory and one that, in his world, trumped all others. "Ray, I gotta go. I'll check back with you later."

He hung up the phone and unlocked his file cabinet. His hand ran along the files, finding the thick bulk of the tab he was looking for. Kelly withdrew the hefty beast and set it down on his desk. Removing the thick rubber band holding it together, he thumbed through its contents in search of a particular photograph.

After a few minutes of scouring the several hundred photos contained therein, Kelly freed the one he'd been searching for. He sat back in his chair and peered at the image, focusing on one particular section—the zoomed view of the left hand with two same size cuts forming a clearly identifiable X. The hand belonged to his best friend and former patrol partner, Danny Rourke.

Kelly stuck the picture back inside and returned the case file to its rightful place. Getting up from his desk he checked the clock. For once he'd be on time.

* * *

He walked in and saw his friends already gearing up for their match. Edmund and Donny were stretching and idling near a heavy bag. Bobby was lacing up his gloves.

Kelly crossed the floor with a focused intensity. He grabbed Bobby and spun him by the shoulder. "Tell me you didn't do it!" Kelly yanked his friend's tank top, lifting him up off the stool he was using.

"What gives? Have you lost your ever-lovin' mind?" Bobby shoved hard at Kelly, knocking him backwards, breaking free of his grip.

"Say it! Say you didn't have nothing to do with it!"

"You need to lower your damn voice in here." Bobby set about adjusting his now stretched-out tank top.

Kelly saw the others in the gym had stopped their drills and were intently watching him. Pops made his way over to intervene.

"You boys know where to take this if there's a problem," Pops said.

There were two places arguments were handled, the ring or the parking lot. In the ring, all were free to watch. But Pops's rules were that if the issue needed to be addressed in the parking lot then it was to be done in private. Either way, the etched wood hanging above his office said it all—*Fighting Solves Everything.*

Kelly eyed his friend. "Parking lot."

Bobby didn't answer. He pulled off his gloves and stormed out. Kelly loosened his shoulders as he walked behind.

As soon as the door closed behind him, Bobby McDonough took a swing. Kelly, caught off-guard, wasn't able to completely avoid the haymaker. But he did move enough to deflect the full force of the heavy blow.

Kelly popped Bobby with a quick jab to the head, creating distance. In the separation, Kelly found his range and began his attack.

Bobby was tough. Probably could've been better than Kelly, but he'd fallen in early with Conner Walsh's crew and the two lifestyles didn't mesh.

Kelly saw red. He was bathed in a rare anger. The flurry of blows he unleashed on his friend was devastating. Bobby desperately tried to counter, but his defense proved useless. Within seconds he was down on one knee with his left fist raised in defeat.

Kelly reared back to deliver one final crushing punch, but stopped himself. Bobby looked up, his eyes showing something not found in the man's normal demeanor. Fear.

Kelly looked around, ensuring nobody was within earshot. "Did you kill Smalls?"

"No." Bobby spit blood onto the blacktop of the parking lot, then sat back, rubbing at his jaw.

"Then who did?"

"Mikey, you know there's things I can and can't tell you. This is one of those I can't."

Kelly seethed.

"Look. I went out on a limb to get you that information. Didn't it help? I heard you saved a bunch of girls."

"It did. I'm not talking about that. I'm talking about who killed Smalls."

"Who cares about that perv anyway?"

"I don't care about Smalls. The world's a better place without savages like him walking the street."

"Then what gives?"

"Because whoever did Smalls was the same guy who killed Danny."

Bobby said nothing, but from the expression on his face Kelly realized his friend was definitely not the killer.

Without a doubt, his lifelong friend knew who killed Danny Rourke.

"Are you going to tell me who the shooter is?"

"You know I can't do that. You better than most know why."

Kelly walked over to the atonement cooler Donny had left outside the back door. He pulled two cold beers out from the ice chest and returned. He handed one to Bobby, who immediately placed the cold can on his swollen left eye.

"Tell Conner Walsh I'm coming for him. One by one, I'm going to tear down his crew until I find who I'm looking for."

"You're asking for a death sentence."

"Maybe. Maybe not. This is my neighborhood too. Don't forget that. Only difference is I bleed blue."

36

His mother sat across from him. Their knees touched ever so slightly. "I've tried to give you every opportunity. You've brought the police to our door. All that we have worked toward is vulnerable to exposure."

"It's not my fault," Aleksander Rakowski pleaded.

"That is the problem with you, my son. You don't accept responsibility. You never have. Your brothers have never failed me, and their responsibilities to the family business are far more volatile and exposed than yours. They do not bring detectives to my home."

"The lawyer said we're in the clear. He said there is nothing linking us directly to any of it. The house the girls were found in isn't traceable to us. You made sure of that when you bought it."

"Do you think the detectives will stop there? If you are that naive then it further proves my point."

"There must be something I can do."

"There is."

Nadia Rakowski pushed her chair back and stood. She leaned in, cupping his face in her strong hands. She pressed her lips hard against his forehead. Aleksander longed for this affection every day of his life and resented it now for coming to him at this time. He wanted to reach out and hold his mother in a tight embrace, but the restraints locking his arms to the chair prevented him from acting on his desire. A well of repressed emotion rose up. A man unaccustomed to such feelings, he wasn't sure if he was on the verge of tears or bursting into a fit of rage.

"My regret is I failed to raise you to handle this life. It's my burden, and I will carry it forward."

"*Matka*, please don't do this. I'm family."

"Our family business will outlive all of us."

A tear fell. His mother wiped it from his cheek. Her eyes softened but she didn't weep for him.

She abruptly turned and walked away. The door opened and his mother disappeared from view as she shut it behind her without ever looking back.

Aleksander was swallowed in the dim light of the room, a room he'd used many times before. Too many, in fact, to count. He knew he was not alone. Making a fruitless effort to shift his position to catch sight of his executioner, he did nothing more than scrape the chair leg along the plastic drop cloth.

Radek Balicki stepped into view. He pulled the cart with him. On it was a single tool, a silenced .22 caliber pistol resting on the metallic tray. Alex sighed at the sight of it, taking solace in the knowledge his death would be quick.

"You don't have to do this, Radek. We can figure something out."

Radek held up his left arm, now minus the hand, and put the bandaged stump to his lips. "Shh."

"Your hand was just business. Nothing personal."

"I know," Balicki said. "Neither is this."

Aleksander Rakowski clenched his jaw. "Then get it over with."

"Not my job. I'm just here to supervise."

"Supervise?"

The geeky face of sixteen-year-old Jakub Balicki appeared out of the dark. The shadows cast on his acne-covered face and deep dark circles under his eyes gave him a menacing look. His nose, broken from the impact with the airbag, had medical tape across the bridge. He was deep breathing, nervous about his assignment.

"Why him?"

"Like you said. It's his rite of passage into the family." Radek picked up the gun and handed it to the boy. Then Radek stepped closer and whispered in Aleksander's ear. "You brought him in against my wishes. Now here he is."

Radek stepped back and let his youngest brother step forward. Alex looked into the boy's eyes. He recognized the commitment. The first was always the hardest. The cold metal pressed against his forehead in the same spot his mother had kissed.

Aleksander leaned in, pushing against it, accepting his fate.

BLEEDING BLUE
A BOSTON CRIME THRILLER NOVEL

With two street gangs on the brink of war, Detective Michael Kelly must solve a murder before the entire town goes up in flames.

Boston Homicide Detective Michael Kelly just took his latest case.

It seemed simple enough: a convenience store clerk gunned down in cold blood.

There's just one catch...the store was under the protection of the Irish mob.

When all evidence points to an up-and-coming street gang, the mob closes in. But after a second shooting occurs, the city is set on a course for all-out war—unless the shooter can be brought to justice.

Kelly is in a race against time to solve the murders and prevent further bloodshed. But his investigation leads him down a dark path...and exposes a greater level of corruption than he ever thought possible.

Get your copy today at BrianChristopherShea.com

JOIN THE READER LIST

Never miss a new release! Sign up to receive exclusive updates from author Brian Shea.

Join today at
BrianChristopherShea.com/Boston

Sign up and receive a free copy of
Unkillable: A Nick Lawrence Short Story.

YOU MIGHT ALSO ENJOY...

The Nick Lawrence Series

Kill List

Pursuit of Justice

Burning Truth

Targeted Violence

Murder 8

The Boston Crime Thriller Series

Murder Board

Bleeding Blue

The Penitent One

Never miss a new release! Sign up to receive exclusive updates from author Brian Shea.

BrianChristopherShea.com/Boston

Sign up and receive a free copy of

Unkillable: A Nick Lawrence Short Story

ACKNOWLEDGMENTS

The relationship between writer and editor is the single most important piece in the successful development of a story. And not all editors are equal. I've been blessed to have found Randall Klein. He challenges my vision for plot and character, making this story shine. I look forward to our future collaboration as this series builds. Randall, thank you for your patience and insight.

I'm grateful to the team at Severn River Publishing. Your backing of my work has been second to none. And your treatment of me as a writer has been first class. Finding a home within your publishing house has been a turning point in my career as a writer. Andrew, Amber, and Jason, thank you for taking a chance on me and helping me achieve so much.

K.F. Breene, thank you for bopping me over the head and waking me up as to the type of story I needed to tell. Our candid conversations became the blueprint for what has become this book and the series concept. I'm forever indebted to you. The world needs more people like you, who speak their mind and pull no punches. I'm better for it.

To the men and women in law enforcement past, present, and future, your service often goes unpraised. Serving alongside you has been one of the great pleasures of my life. Although my watch has come to an end, I know I've left it in good hands. I hope this book does honor the good, bad, and ugly of the world we've faced.

Mom, thank you for being a cheerleader for my work. I'm pretty sure you've flagged down or darn near tackled every neighbor in your community and forced them to read my books. Your love and support have been amazing in this new chapter of my life and I'm glad you've been able to be a part of it.

I'm grateful to the collective of authors who've encircled me, guiding and coaching my growth as a writer.

ABOUT THE AUTHOR

Brian Shea has spent most of his adult life in service to his country and local community. He honorably served as an officer in the U.S. Navy. In his civilian life, he reached the rank of Detective and accrued over eleven years of law enforcement experience between Texas and Connecticut. Somewhere in the mix he spent five years as a fifth-grade school teacher. Brian's myriad of life experience is woven into the tapestry of each character's design. He resides in New England and is blessed with an amazing wife and three beautiful daughters.

 facebook.com/BrianChristopherShea

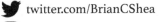 twitter.com/BrianCShea

instagram.com/BrianChristopherShea

CPSIA information can be obtained
at www.ICGtesting.com
Printed in the USA
BVHW041952230822
645296BV00008B/32/J

9 781951 249045